Dinuka McKenzie is an Australian writer. She is the winner of the 2020 Banjo Prize, and her writing has been longlisted for the Richell Prize and highly commended in the Australian Crime Writers Association Louie Award. Her short fiction has appeared in the *Dark Deeds Down Under Crime and Thriller Anthology*. Before turning to writing full time, Dinuka worked in the environmental sector. She now volunteers as part of the team behind the Writers Unleashed Festival and lives in Southern Sydney on Dharawal country with her husband, two kids and their pet chicken.

Also by Dinuka McKenzie

Detective Kate Miles

The Torrent
Taken

TAKEN

DINUKA McKENZIE

CANELO CRIME

First published in Australia in 2023 by HarperCollins Publishers Australia
Pty Limited

This edition published in the United Kingdom in 2024 by

Canelo
Unit 9, 5th Floor
Cargo Works, 1-2 Hatfields
London SE1 9PG
United Kingdom

A CIP catalogue record for this book is available from the British Library.

Print ISBN 978 1 80436 640 0
Ebook ISBN 978 1 80436 641 7

Look for more great books at www.canelo.co

Printed and bound in Great Britain by Clays Ltd, Elcograf S.p.A.

1

To my fam, Scott, Harvey and Edie, always.

The need to touch the child is overwhelming. Just to graze my finger across her cherub cheek and her soft, downy hair. She is asleep in a bassinet pram. Her little fist has wriggled itself out of the wrap and lies beside her face, a hair's breadth from her tiny wrinkled ear.

The pram sits by a park bench, alone and vulnerable, the ragged branches of a gum tree creating dappled shadows across its stroller cover. The park is deserted in the afternoon. An empty swathe of grass, green and blunted, recently shorn. Where is her mother?

Anyone who wants to can take the child. Whisk her away and no one would be the wiser. Her mother would be blamed. As she should be. Who leaves a newborn out in the open like this, without protection? A woman like that deserves everything she gets. That's what people would say.

Just one more peek. A light hand on the bub's tightly wrapped form. Not enough to wake her, but enough to feel the soft rise and fall of her chest. Up and down. Up and down.

The sound of voices. They are returning. The woman and her boy.

I whip my hand away as if burned. The baby starts to wail, my jerking movement having woken her. Too late now. I have to get away. Don't be seen. Don't get caught.

Phone out. Pretend to be scrolling. Cap down over my eyes. An innocent passer-by on their phone. Move away but not too fast. Slow and steady.

Breathe. In and out. In and out.

1

Thursday

Detective Sergeant Kathryn Aneesha Miles slammed her foot on the brakes and felt her body recoil, the seatbelt digging taut and tight into her chest. The car came to a shuddering halt, inches away from a zebra crossing.

She had not seen the walker. Her body had reacted unconsciously to something her eyes had not yet fully registered. He had been right in her dead spot directly behind the pillar dividing the windscreen from her driver-side window. A car horn beeped and onlookers stared. Sickening heat rose through her body and she felt light-headed at the thought of what could have been.

The pedestrian, a young man in a worn and paint-splattered hoodie and work pants that marked him as a tradie, death-stared her before continuing along the crossing. She could feel the outrage of the bystanders. A mother in immaculate office clothes herded her rugged-up offspring away from the road and waited pointedly for the car to pass. Kate drove on, rigid at the wheel, her eyes fixed ahead, not meeting the stares of the passers-by.

Stopping the car at the first opportunity, she fought a wave of nausea. Her hands shook as she gripped the wheel, fighting to regain control, goosepimples prickling her skin. Outside along the verge, silvery-grey eucalyptus trees thrashed against a brisk late-August wind; a cold spell bearing uncharacteristically bleak winter conditions to the north coast. A political candidate on a poster for the upcoming council election grinned inanely down at her from an electricity pylon.

You're not ready, Kate. It's too soon. Her husband's words rang in her ear as she breathed through the flood of anxiety pressing against her ribs – *inhale for two counts, exhale for four, in and out, until it passes.*

Geoff had expressed his concern when she had first spelled out her intention of going back to work once Amy, their baby daughter, had turned three months. His worry still lingered, screaming its misgivings in every meaningful look, sigh and unhappy glance he threw her way. Yes, the financial imperative was real, but he hadn't thought her serious, that she would actually go through with it. No one had. Geoff had been adamant that his work would pick up. Her father had offered to lend them money.

They had all been watching: her husband, her father, her partner, Josh Ellis, and her chief inspector, Andrew Skinner. Observing and assessing. Waiting for her to break. But she had pushed through anyway.

It had been six weeks since she had pressed the point, juggling child care, overfull breasts and the rest. Six weeks with Skinner relegating her to desk duty, judging her incapable. Tasked with checking the paperwork for local court, traffic and minor offences like she was some newbie constable fresh out of Goulburn. Her years of experience counting for nothing; her position in the team supplanted by Detective Ellis, the rising star.

'I think this'll be good for you, Miles. Take things slowly until you get into the swing of things again. You'll get home at a reasonable hour. See the kids. Just until you're settled, and then we can see how you're travelling.'

Her first day, sitting in Skinner's office in the late afternoon, weak sunshine pooling through the dusty fingers of the venetian blinds behind Skinner's head. On the desk between them lay her psychologist-endorsed return-to-work plan, prominent and inescapable in all its carefully crafted wording. The detailed assessment of her state of mind that was now part of her permanent record.

Unconsciously, her fingers dug into her left shoulder, the site of her gunshot wound. A mere graze, really, now entirely healed. She could hardly feel it through her shirt. Only the ruptures in her mind remained, gaping and sore to the touch.

She recalled Skinner's final words, spoken almost as an afterthought: 'Prove me wrong.'

Gritting her teeth at the memory, she waited for her breathing exercises to work, for the shaking in her hands to stop.

A call crackled through the radio: ... *Esserton dispatch to any car in the vicinity. Domestic disturbance at thirty-three Denman Drive...*

Kate heard Constable Darnley's voice, partially obscured by static, responding: *Esserton Two. Copy that. We're nearby. About ten minutes out...*

Digesting the address spat out by dispatch, she realised it was less than a block away. She had passed the turnoff not two minutes ago. She could get there before Darnley.

The past few weeks of forced inactivity nagged at her, her instinct wrestling with her better judgement. *Fuck it!* She waited for the traffic to pass and made a U-turn.

2

Even as Kate pulled up outside the two-storey brick veneer, she could hear the screams issuing from inside. An elderly man in a shapeless woollen sweater and saggy sweatpants stood waiting near the letterbox, clearly the neighbour who had called it in. The rest of the street remained empty and shuttered, the occupants at school or work. As Kate stepped out of the car, the man, stooped and shrunken yet with eyes that were sharp and alert, regarded her doubtfully.

'You the police, are you?'

She didn't miss his clear derision as he took in her appearance, obviously neither the sex nor the skin colour he had expected. She ignored his question and concentrated on the house. Another wail rose and fell within the house. It sounded like an infant crying.

'They've been at it all morning. I've never heard it this bad before. Veliu's his name. He's a bastard when he's had a skinful.' He hocked a globule of phlegm on the ground for emphasis.

'Are there any kids in there, do you know?'

'A couple of little tackers. Boys.'

She nodded and started for the door.

'You're not going in there alone, are you?'

'Stay here,' she instructed. 'There's another car on its way.'

She stepped carefully around the perimeter of the house. Despite the mid-morning sun, a raw, blustery wind whipped through her and she shivered, unsure if it was a reaction to the weather or something else. Out of sight from the neighbour, she drew her weapon, its weight sturdy and reassuring in her hands.

Along the exterior wall, an overflowing bin ripe with the smell of used nappies made her blanch. She held her breath as she edged past to the back doorstep. The door was flung open. Through the half-ajar screen door, she spied an aging but serviceable kitchen: spotless apart from a bowl of something thick and red smashed across the cabinets. Bits of porcelain mixed with gloopy trails of red sauce dripped from the counter, staining the floor tiles and pooling in the grout lines.

She knocked sharply on the open door. 'Police. Anyone home?' Her voice rang through the house without a response.

A baby wailed again somewhere inside, a pitiful mewling that caught at her heart. Entering, she followed the noise into a darkened hallway, stepping cautiously along threadbare carpet. She stopped at a door marked 'Brayden' in bright-purple stick-on letters. The baby's cries seemed to have subsided into muffled whimpers.

Her Glock at the ready, she gingerly pressed down the handle and pushed open the door into a darkened room to find a gun barrel pointing directly at her face.

Adrenaline screamed through her body as she stopped herself just in time from pulling the trigger. Her assailant was a young boy, no more than four or five, and she could see that his weapon was only a toy, a dinky plastic thing. Relief flooded her, sharp and keen, the thudding of her heart loud in her ears. The boy's thin arms trembled as they held the play gun aloft, his expression a concentrated fold of worry and determination.

'It's okay. I'm a police officer. I'm just here to make sure you're okay.'

The baby had started crying again and the boy's eyes darted between Kate and the infant.

'You can put that down, buddy. Everything's going to be all right. Can you tell me where your mum is? It sounds like the bub might need her.'

The boy motioned his head in the direction of the ceiling. 'She's upstairs with Dad. He won't let her come out,' he added, his voice catching.

'Okay, matey. I'm glad you stayed with your baby brother. That's really brave of you. Is his name Brayden? Do you mind if I see if he's okay?'

The boy nodded, finally lowering his makeshift weapon.

Holstering her gun, Kate made for the cot. The baby was red-faced and exhausted with crying, his nappy full and sour with urine. She lifted the infant to her, resting his hot brow to her chest and shushing his cries. The baby whimpered but seemed to settle into her almost immediately, his tiny mouth searching frantically across the surface of her shirt, sensing her milk supply.

She heard scuffling outside and the sound of voices. Darnley and a female probationary officer, a fresh face she didn't recognise, stood at the entrance to the room. She caught the flicker of doubt on Darnley's face, but ignored it. He shouldn't be surprised to see her here. She had radioed in on arriving at the scene.

She locked eyes with the new officer and gestured to the baby. 'Can you take the kids outside and make up a bottle for the little one? I saw some formula in the kitchen.

He's starving.' She placed the now-quiet baby into the officer's rigid arms. At the look of panic in her eyes, Kate added, 'The instructions are on the tin, Constable.'

She waited until the officer had left with the children before joining Darnley in the hallway. 'C'mon. They're upstairs. He's holding her in one of the rooms.'

Darnley looked like he was about to say something but thought better of it. They rounded the corner to a flight of stairs leading up to a landing and two doors. One lay open, showing a small bathroom – powder-blue tiles with white trim. The other door was closed. Muffled grunting and the sounds of exaggerated moaning could be heard from within. Kate met Darnley's eyes as she felt for the door handle. It swung open easily.

–

The concrete carpark lay in shadow. A discarded burger wrapper trapped in the gutter moved sluggishly in the breeze. Kate gazed out of the station window at the wiry frame of Jason Veliu, swaggering for her benefit, a sneer on his face, for all the world like some big-time gangster. Making an exaggerated show of kissing the forehead of his pasty-faced lawyer, who she knew was actually some sort of relative – a distant cousin pulled into service by the bonds of family, or possibly a different kind of hold. Something closer to home like debts or drugs. The man was clearly uncomfortable with Veliu's public demonstration but unable to prevent it.

Veliu had made bail, despite everything they had witnessed inside that house, inside that room. She stared at the intricate tattoo vines that stretched their cobalt tendrils from under his shirt, up the nape of his neck and into the coarse undergrowth of his dirty-blond scalp. She had stared at that tattoo all afternoon in the interview room. It was a statement piece. Another none-too-subtle sign that established his power, his inviolability. He smirked in her direction. Knowing she was watching, he poked his tongue through his forefingers and wriggled it suggestively. She turned away. He'd keep.

Inside, the squad room was mostly empty, the afternoon fast leaching into dusk. Kate caught Skinner's silhouette framed behind the glass walls of his office, pacing the floor, mobile in hand. At least she had achieved her aim there. In Skinner's mind, she had proved herself capable of handling a stressful incident without falling apart. He had taken her aside after the Veliu interview and had a quiet word. He would be approaching HR about reinstating her to full duties, subject to the psychologist's endorsement. She was back in the fold.

The only snag was Darnley. He had been within earshot when Skinner had cornered her and had no doubt heard everything. Her mind flew to the aftermath of Veliu's arrest: her dry-retching in a cold sweat in the rear garden, racked with shivers. She had thought that she was alone. She had only spotted Darnley, wordlessly regarding her from the porch, when she had made her way inside.

'Sarge. Could I speak to you for a second?'

Jolted back to the present, Kate turned to find a uniformed constable standing at her desk. She hadn't noticed him stealing up beside her like a shadow.

'Sure, Constable. What's up?'

She recognised the young officer. Somewhere in his mid-twenties, quiet and diffident and with skin that appeared to have only recently recovered from adolescent acne, Constable Anthony Roby was a relatively new recruit to the station. He had helped out peripherally in her last case before maternity leave, but Kate realised that she didn't know much about him.

'It's just about a call-out we got this afternoon. A suspected prowler at a property off Elliot Pass.'

Kate knew the area. Elliot Pass was an isolated road on the southern edge of town that wound its way around dairy paddocks and thick bushland.

'A Mrs Elissa Ricci – she's alone at home with two kids, with the husband away on business – thought she heard noises around five o'clock this morning. Someone moving around in the yard. She didn't do anything about it. She wasn't sure if it was real or whether she'd imagined it. It was her mother...' Roby paused to check his notes, '...a Mrs Rayna Gardiner who called it in. She got the story out of Mrs Ricci this afternoon and insisted on calling the station.'

Kate listened patiently, guessing there was more to come.

'Mrs Ricci's story is that she thought she heard the back door rattling like someone was trying to get in. But it's been blowy all day and last night, and she reckons she's not sure if it was just the wind. She was sitting up in bed feeding the bub at the time and didn't get up to check. There was no sign of forced entry when we checked this afternoon. The doors and windows looked secure. Nothing was broken or seemed out of place.'

'Do we know why the mother was so insistent on reporting it? Do they suspect it was someone in particular?' She watched Roby's face closely. 'Did you get the impression that Mrs Ricci is afraid of someone?'

'She insists there's no one she can think of who would want to hurt the family.'

'Okay, so we have a false alarm and an over-protective mother.'

From his expression, it was clear to Kate that Roby held a different opinion.

'What exactly is worrying you, Constable?'

'I think she's lying, Sarge. Her story just doesn't feel right. She was nervous, you know? Like jumpy. I reckon whoever came around this morning, she knew who it was and she's afraid.'

Kate assessed the constable. She wondered what it was in his past that fed into his certainty, that made him want to rescue this woman. Had he suffered through an abusive father? Perhaps watching his mother cower and flinch, lie and embellish, learning as a young child to recognise the signs of fear and pain concealed in a woman's face. Or had it been someone else that he had been unable to protect? A younger sister, maybe?

'You're probably right, Constable. There is likely more to the story than she's telling us. Probably more than she's telling her mother, too. But without an offence being committed or something definite to go on...' She shrugged her shoulders, leaving the rest unsaid.

Roby nodded, turning away, his disappointment obvious. Kate watched his receding figure, unable to escape a vague unease that she had let the young man down.

3

Friday

'This is bullshit!'

Geoff didn't reply but wordlessly observed his wife as she stared transfixed at his mobile screen. Kate was viewing a news article that Geoff had come across while browsing the morning news on his phone at the breakfast table, a habit that Kate detested. She had been in the middle of organising their four-year-old son, Archie's breakfast – toast with jam, no crusts, cut into squares – when Geoff had stuck the phone in front of her and insisted that she take a look.

THE MINISTER AND HIS LOVER screamed the headline. Kate scrolled down what seemed like an endless stream of words, lurid and sensational, that would no doubt splatter the front pages of all of the day's newspapers. Her eyes rapidly scanned the article, trying to contain a rising panic with each new sickening sentence.

> *The secret life of former Attorney-General Martin Jackson, the darling of the NSW Conservatives, has been exposed in a series of exclusive interviews granted to* The Tribune Online *by former staffer and alleged lover of the minister, Mr Simon Lahey. The Hon Martin Jackson MP, who served*

as the NSW Planning Minister and subsequently as Attorney-General before his untimely death three years ago following a heart attack, was widely tipped to take over the leadership from Premier Coulson and head up the party's charge to seek a third term of government.

Mr Lahey alleges that he commenced an affair with Mr Jackson soon after joining his office in 2008 as a young political science graduate in his early twenties. At the time, Mr Jackson was the newly elected Planning Minister, married and with two grown children, Maya, twenty-two, and Lesley, thirty. While never 'exclusive', Mr Lahey alleges that the couple continued their affair off and on up until Mr Jackson's death, and that they shared a unit together in Surry Hills. The property in question is now the subject of legal wrangling between Mr Lahey and the Jackson Estate.

As his executive assistant, Mr Lahey had access to both Mr Jackson's personal and official diaries, and claims to have knowledge of at least two other high-profile relationships sustained by Mr Jackson: a senior police officer in the Northern Region Command who was a childhood friend of Mr Jackson, as well as a well-known developer with property interests along the north coast. In his most explosive revelations, Mr Lahey alleges that Mr Jackson's affair with the said developer coincided with a period when a number of the developer's subdivision proposals were under consideration by the State Planning Department, placing a shadow over approvals granted by Mr Jackson during his tenure as Planning Minister.

Mr Jackson's estate includes significant business and property interests in Sydney and the north coast of New South Wales. 'Martin always knew how to spin a deal to his best advantage,' says Mr Lahey.

The revelations could not have come at a worse time for Premier Coulson and the NSW Government, already reeling from multiple MP travel-expenditure scandals and growing calls for an independent enquiry. Mr Lahey refused to be drawn on why he was choosing the present time to make his sensational allegations public, stating only that these questions should be put to the Coulson Government, leading to speculation on how much of Mr Jackson's conduct was known to his Cabinet colleagues at the time, and what, if any, influence had been brought to bear on Mr Lahey to maintain his silence.

In a statement, the premier's office strongly denied any knowledge of wrongdoing by Mr Jackson during his time as the Minister for Planning and denounced in the strongest terms 'the muckraking by a disgruntled staffer of a well-respected, long-serving politician and much-loved family member. In besmirching the good name of Mr Jackson—' the statement reads, '—Mr Lahey is engaging in the lowest form of slander by attacking the personal life of a man who is no longer able to defend himself, and hurting innocent family members in the process, all for the sake of self-publicity and notoriety.'

Mr Lahey has promised to stand by his allegations, which he claims are supported by personal

> *documents in his possession. Mr Jackson's family*
> *was unavailable for comment.*

Kate felt nauseous. The porridge she had consumed just minutes before congealing in her belly.

A senior police officer in the Northern Region Command. Arthur Grayling, the ex-chief inspector of Esserton Police Station, now retired. Kate's father. *A childhood friend of Mr Jackson.* Her dad, who had been in love with Martin Jackson his whole life, their relationship carried out in the shadows, brief moments snatched together while they had each supported a wife and family. With the death of Kate's mother to pancreatic cancer, there had been a cementing of sorts. A semi-permanent relationship whenever Martin could escape from Sydney, tucked away at her dad's cottage out of town, where he had moved after selling up the family home. In the end, after a lifetime of false starts, they had only managed a couple of years together before Martin had died without warning, leaving her dad with nothing but the house and garden that Martin had loved, to care for in his memory.

Kate met Geoff's eyes and they shared an unspoken moment of understanding.

Her father's past had come home to roost.

This had been their family's private affair. A schism that Kate carried with her, her loyalties forever torn between her father's happiness and its effect on her mother. It was a subject she rarely broached with Gray. Her parents' relationship was as complicated as it had been fraught. There had been knowledge, hurt and compromise on both sides, but there had also been love, entangled in the thorny briar that had been their life together.

There had been consequences, too. Kate's mother had battled depression and succumbed to her diagnosis of cancer, refusing to fight and yielding to the solution that the universe had presented her with. Kate's younger brother, Luke, was holed away in Sydney and permanently estranged from their father. The Jackson family – Martin's wife, Lindsay, and their two daughters, childhood friends of Kate's family – no longer on speaking terms.

Now this article had cracked open the door, exposing their past. Esserton in the Northern Rivers hinterland south of Murwillumbah was still a relatively small community. It had expanded rapidly with the influx of tree-changers seeking a regional lifestyle within driving distance of the Queensland border, but old connections still ran deep. It wouldn't take much for people to put two and two together. Martin Jackson was a local boy. His family still owned property in the area, although none of the Jacksons had lived in Esserton for years. Everyone knew of her father's friendship with Martin. The article had just about painted a red arrow to Gray's door.

'Are you going to give him a call?' Geoff asked.

Kate nodded and reached for her mobile. The call rang out and went to voicemail. She heard her father's measured tone asking the caller to leave a message, and wondered if he was already being inundated by phone calls. Journalists who had tracked him down, seeking comment.

'Dad, it's only me. Call me when you get this.'

'I'm not surprised he's not picking up. Are you going to try Luke?'

Kate made a face. 'Later, maybe.'

Geoff nodded, letting the matter drop.

'C'mon, little man. Let's get you organised.' Leaving Geoff to clear away the breakfast things, Kate followed

Archie into his room, tiptoeing past the closed door of her sleeping infant daughter.

She helped Archie out of his pyjamas.

'Mummy, the fire trucks are coming to preschool today.'

'Really? That sounds exciting.'

'Yeah, I told you yesterday.'

'You did too, matey. Mummy's so silly. I remember now. Will you get to climb in the front, do you think?'

'Miss Le-noni said maybe, only if we're good.'

Kate smiled. Archie had yet to work out the pronunciation of his preschool teacher's name, Leoni. She resisted correcting him because he had grown out of so many of his cute little-boy mannerisms that she wanted to hold onto the ones that still persisted.

'Well, I guess you'll have to be extra good today.' She pecked him lightly on his nose and he responded by scrunching up his face and blowing a raspberry onto her cheek.

She tickled his tummy as he giggled. 'Quick, let's get you dressed so you're not late. Daddy's going to walk you to preschool with Amy in the pram.'

As she helped her son into his clothes, listening to his prattle with half an ear, she found her mind sliding back to what she had just read, unable to stop her thoughts from picking through the implications.

This was the situation she had always feared. Martin's public standing meant his relationship with Gray, if discovered, was always at risk of scandal. Her father had always ceded to Martin's requests for privacy, understanding his fears for his political career and the consequences for both of their families. And now it had all caught up with them. Except it was her dad who would have to bear the brunt of the whispers and rumours. Kate had no illusions about the reaction her father's life would elicit from some quarters of their semi-rural community. Gray could look after himself, but worrying about his safety had become a habit. The one thing that this job had taught her was that you didn't need to scratch too hard to find the toxicity that lurked below.

And what about her own career? She wasn't naïve enough to think she could escape unscathed from the gossip and speculation that would consume her family. Her thoughts skittered like a pinball machine. There was also the small issue of the money.

'Owwwww.'

'Sorry, mate. Mummy wasn't concentrating. Sorry!' Kate rubbed her son's throat where she had accidentally snagged his skin on the zipper of his jumper. She kissed him and did his jacket up properly.

Kate's mobile rang just as she had helped Archie into his shoes. For a brief moment she froze, wondering who was at the other end and if she should answer.

She picked up the call and recognised Skinner's voice. He sounded tense and agitated.

'Miles, there's been an incident. I need all hands on deck. Can you come in?'

'On my way, sir.'

4

Kate pulled into the dirt track off Elliot Pass, which was already packed with police and forensic vehicles, and crossed the police perimeter set up to keep the gawkers and neighbours at bay. She noticed a couple of local TV reporters already circling with microphones securing first reactions from neighbours. She felt her stomach drop, instinctively turning away from the journalists before they noticed her.

She glanced at the ageing fibro cottage ahead of her: a tiny square of domesticity backing onto dense bush, set apart from its neighbours. Spotted gums creaked in the wind and she zipped up her jacket, glad of the extra layer of warmth against the chill. She took in the neat front garden: a trampoline set amongst flowerbeds and smiling gnomes. She heard barking in the distance and caught a glimpse of a dog handler making his way along the side of the house, the quivering rump of an excited labrador at his heel. The scent dogs were on the scene.

A momentary light-headedness as she contemplated the weight of responsibility. *I can do this*, she whispered to herself, the words repeated like a talisman on the drive over. She swallowed the jangle of nerves spiking her throat. Skinner's words returned to her, his meaning plain. He had cleared the way for her with the higher-ups and was giving her a chance. *Do not fuck it up.*

Signing in with the constable stationed at the entrance, she followed the designated path set up for police access to avoid contamination of the scene. Josh was waiting for her at the door. He silently handed her a pair of plastic booties to cover her shoes. She glanced at his face. If he had any reservations about Kate being called in, he wasn't showing it.

'The family is inside.' Josh gestured over his shoulder. 'It's just the mother and grandmother at home. The son, seven years, is at school. The grandmother doesn't live here but stayed over last night. No husband at present. He's apparently at a trade conference in Broadbeach. Been away for the last two nights and due home this evening. We're still trying to get a hold of him.'

At her questioning glance, Josh shrugged. 'He's not answering his mobile. We're following up with his firm.'

Kate nodded and followed Josh along carpeted floors that had been laid with access sheets by forensic officers, through a gloomy, timber-panelled hallway. They passed a couple of bedrooms that were yet to be processed.

The corridor opened up and they stepped into a dank kitchen and sitting room, where Constable Roby was keeping two women company at a tiny dining table piled high with folded baby clothes, toys and other paraphernalia. A line of bright-pink onesies and a single blue shirt, one half of a boy's school uniform, hung drying on a rack in the corner. A row of framed and mounted photos tracked the family's life across the wall. Kate zeroed in on the stills of a baby relaxed in sleep ensconced in pink wool and carefully cradled in the arms of a solemn-looking young boy. In another, the infant was awake and captured in mid-giggle, her eyes crinkled with delight, short tufts of hair escaping from a cloth bow. She had the sweet anonymity of all babies, plump, tiny and snuggled. Her individual expressions and developing personality only apparent to those who knew her best.

Roby stood up at their entrance, catching Kate's eye and looking away. She felt his judgement. He had feared something would happen and she hadn't backed him. A pinprick of guilt flared and she shrugged it away, concentrating instead on the two women seated together at the table, two untouched cups of tea cooling in front of them.

The older woman, the grandmother, sat stiff and ramrod straight in plain black pants and a dark-maroon turtleneck. Her dark hair, streaked with grey, was pulled into a tight bun, held in place by a delicate hair clip shaped like a dragonfly. A proud and determined face, untouched by make-up and with only the barest hint of fine lines, turned to meet Kate as she approached. Beside her, a younger woman sat slumped and huddled in old tracksuit pants and a frayed grey cardigan. Her blonde hair, obviously still wet from a shower, hung in damp rat's tails and she sniffed into a handful of disintegrating tissues.

Kate pulled up a chair at the table and sat down. 'Mrs Ricci. I'm Detective Kate Miles. Detective Ellis, I think you've already met,' she said, motioning to Josh. 'I'm so sorry we have to meet in these circumstances. Do you feel up to answering a few questions?'

The young mother's face was swollen with crying and appeared already aged by grief. Her eyes, large and uncomprehending, filled instantly with tears. She made a small sound like an animal in pain and crumpled into her mother. The older woman pinned Kate with a stare as she held her daughter close.

'This is why we called you lot yesterday. Too bloody late now.'

Kate accepted the rebuke. 'Mrs Gardiner, I'm very sorry about your granddaughter. We saw no indication yesterday that the baby was under any particular threat and I don't believe either of you mentioned any risk of that nature to the officers in attendance?'

The woman pursed her lips and looked away, concentrating on comforting her daughter.

'Mrs Ricci.' Kate once more turned to the grief-stricken woman. 'I know it's difficult, but it's really important that we understand exactly what occurred. Can you please take us through what happened this morning?'

Mrs Ricci slowly straightened from her mother's embrace, visibly pulling herself together. 'I was in the shower. I left Sienna in her bassinet. I didn't leave her for long, maybe five, ten minutes at the most.' There was a trace of defensiveness in her voice, but Kate was not one to judge, knowing that she had done much the same on countless occasions, leaving Amy safe in the cot while she ducked into the bathroom or put on a quick load of washing.

Mrs Ricci continued to speak, her voice breaking. 'I… When I got out, I couldn't see her. Her bassinet was empty. She was gone. How could she be gone?' Tears once more threatened to overwhelm her, and she squeezed her eyes shut, hugging herself tight.

'Can you remember what time this was, Mrs Ricci?' asked Josh, his voice probing but kind.

'Just after nine. Ten past, maybe. I'm not sure. I thought at first Mum was back home and had got her up, but when I checked there was nobody in the house, just the sliding door was open and she was gone.' Her final words were muffled by a sob.

Without being asked, Mrs Gardiner took up the story. 'I got Daniel breakfast this morning and we left the house around eight-fifty to get him to school. We were running late. His school starts at nine. I thought I'd locked the sliding door after me, but I can't remember. Maybe I didn't.' She paused, squeezing her hands together as if in prayer.

'It was twenty past nine when I got back here and found Elissa hysterical. We looked everywhere. Ran up and down the street, asked the neighbours if they had seen anything. But nothing. In the end we called triple-o.'

'Have you noticed anything else missing from the house?' Kate asked, addressing both women. 'Any of Sienna's clothes or toys. Her bottles, maybe, or even her nappies?'

Mrs Ricci stared at her in shock. 'I don't know. I don't think so. I didn't think to look.'

'Okay, that's fine. We can check afterwards. Go through her things to make sure.' The younger woman nodded numbly.

Kate glanced at Josh and continued. 'Mrs Ricci, you mentioned to officers that your husband, Aaron, is at a conference. Is that right?'

'Yes. On the Gold Coast.'

'I understand you've been trying to contact him but he's not answering his mobile?'

'He turns his mobile off when he's attending the seminars. He hates it when people's phones go off during the sessions. I left a message on his voicemail.' Her hands fiddled with her wedding ring as she spoke.

Kate regarded Mrs Ricci, allowing the quiet to lengthen, 'Could Sienna be with your husband, Mrs Ricci? Could he have come home early and taken Sienna without telling you? Are you going through any relationship difficulties that we should know about? Maybe over the custody of Sienna?'

'No!' The vehement retort was from Mrs Gardiner. 'There was nothing like that. Aaron's a good man and a good father. He looks after this family. There are no custody issues.'

Kate noticed that Elissa Ricci had not answered her. She let the matter drop for the moment. It was something they could easily check, anyway. Josh was already onto it. She changed tack, turning to Elissa's mother.

'Mrs Gardiner, you said you left the house with Daniel at eight-fifty. Did you notice anything unusual when you left? Anyone hanging around near the house or any cars parked close by?'

Mrs Gardiner hesitated then shook her head. 'I'm not sure. I passed some cars on the way, but I didn't notice anyone in particular.' She sounded more irritated than upset that she was unable to provide anything more concrete.

'And do you normally take Daniel to school, Mrs Gardiner?' Josh chimed in.

'No, I've just been helping Elissa out while Aaron's been away. I stayed over last night, to keep her and the kids company.'

'Is that something you do often, stay over?'

'Not regularly, but sometimes.' She bristled, sensing a rebuke. 'What's that got to do with Sienna?'

'We're just trying to establish the normal routine of the house, Mrs Gardiner,' Kate soothed. 'In cases like this, we often find the person responsible is someone known to the family. Someone who's likely to know the movements of the household – when people are likely to be at home or away.'

Mrs Gardiner accepted her explanation without comment. That this description could apply to Aaron Ricci wasn't lost on any of them.

Kate nodded for Josh to continue.

'Mrs Ricci, you called the police yesterday to report a suspected prowler. You indicated that you didn't know who it could be. Given what's happened, is there anything you want to add to your previous report? Is there anyone you can think of who may want to harm Sienna or get to you by targeting your daughter?'

Kate watched as mother and daughter exchanged glances, something passing between them before Elissa looked away. Her answer when it came was resolute. 'There's no one. I don't know anyone who'd want to hurt her.'

Josh persisted, 'Mrs Ricci, this is important. We wouldn't ask you if it wasn't. We need this information to help Sienna. To bring her home safely—'

He didn't get to finish. She was up on her feet, suddenly frenzied, spittle spraying the air. 'Don't you think I'd do anything, anything to get my daughter back? I don't know who took her, all right? I don't know.' She collapsed just as quickly as she had risen, her head buried in her hands. This time, her mother made no move to comfort her, a sudden distance seeming to bloom between them.

Kate regarded the two women. Based on Josh's notes, the triple-o call had come through at 9.33 am and the police had arrived on the scene by 9.50 am. An AMBER alert had been issued by police shortly afterwards – the standardised national broadcast system that was activated in the instance of high-risk child abductions. It was after 10 am and an hour and twenty minutes had now passed since four-month-old Sienna had disappeared.

Based on the women's story, they had a timeline of approximately ten minutes – when Mrs Ricci was in the shower – during which baby Sienna had been abducted.

Alternatively, it could be a timeframe of approximately one hour, from the time Mrs Gardiner had left with Daniel for school, to the time when the police had arrived, where something else entirely could have occurred in which one or both women were complicit.

From the corner of her eye, Kate saw an officer enter the room and speak in a whispered conference with Constable Roby. She rose with Josh and joined the officers, out of earshot of the women.

'Detective, this was just found by one of the search teams on the side of the road on Elliot Pass, heading north.' The officer handed over a plastic evidence bag to Kate. It encased a soft toy comforter – a small pink-and-grey koala that looked pristine.

'What is it? What have you found?'

Kate turned and faced Mrs Ricci, who was on her feet once more and straining to see what Kate held in her hand.

Placing the evidence bag on the table in front of the women, Kate watched as Mrs Ricci drained of colour, and her mother looked away.

5

Kate surveyed Mrs Ricci's bedroom, taking in the unmade queen bed, crumpled tissues on the carpet and discarded clothes. The forensic teams had taken over, each space being carefully videoed and photographed, and likely surfaces dusted for prints.

Her phone screen marked the time: 10.47 am. She felt the weight of each leaching minute, like a new grain of sand adding to the pressure building inside her chest. The AMBER alert with details of four-month-old Sienna issued to media outlets and social media had yet to elicit anything concrete. Josh was outside coordinating the search teams. Already she could feel the press of urgency like a rising tide.

She stepped inside. Careful to remain within the areas cleared by forensics, she examined a half-empty packet of antidepressants on the bedside table. For a second, she imagined how her own house would appear to Scenes of Crime Officers, if it was her rather than Elissa going through this hell. She glanced at the bassinet standing empty next to the bed, a faint impression of a tiny body still visible in the folds of the swaddle blanket left behind. Something coiled inside her, sourness rising and bucking like a wave. The comforter was so much like the snug fold she used each night to envelop her own daughter.

Amy, sweet Amy. Her own daughter was just a couple of weeks older than Sienna. Getting off the phone to Skinner that morning, Kate had felt compelled to sneak into her infant's room before leaving the house. To make sure she was all right. That her tiny body remained safe and warm in her cot. She shivered. A child going missing: the worst case scenario.

In the adjacent room, she could hear the low voice of Constable Roby speaking gently to Mrs Ricci and her mother. Kate had left Roby with the painstaking task of helping the family go through Sienna's things. So far, apart from the clothes she had been wearing – a long-sleeved zip-up onesie – and the comforter they had found on the side of the road, nothing else of her belongings appeared to be missing. Her change bag and spare bottles remained untouched. It was possible that a couple of spare nappies had been swiped from the change table, but Mrs Ricci could not be certain. After all, who kept an exact tally of disposable nappies?

Whoever had taken baby Sienna had left behind her blanket despite it being blustery outside. Were they just in a hurry, or had they no experience with children? Or did they already own everything you would need for a baby?

Taking one last look at the room, Kate made her way back up the corridor and out of the house. She joined Josh, who was on the front landing speaking to officers called in to assist from surrounding stations.

Her eyes met those of an older constable from Tweed Heads Station standing slightly to the outer of the group; orderly crew cut and a tall, powerful build, despite his age. Leading Senior Constable Darryl Murchison. She controlled an involuntary shudder, her mind automatically reverting to that night of blood and pain. She was inseparably linked to this man by a gunshot and the flash of a bullet. He had been the one who had helped stem the bleeding and had accompanied her to hospital. In the eyes of the world and to her colleagues, he was her saviour, and she was forever in his debt. But there had been other things that had come before: his hot breath and musk on her neck, his weight pressed against her back, thick with threat. She felt the familiar frisson of being in close proximity to him, watchfulness laced with fear.

She forced her mind to the present, to Constables Harris and Grant, who had been tasked with canvassing the surrounding neighbours. 'Anything?' she asked.

'Nothing so far, Sarge,' Vickie Harris replied, taking the lead. 'A neighbour two doors down noticed Mrs Gardiner driving off about ten to nine. Apart from that, no one's noticed anything. No unfamiliar cars parked nearby or strangers hanging around. We still need to recheck a few houses where no one was in when we called.'

Kate nodded. At least they had corroboration of Mrs Gardiner driving her grandson to school. The fact that nothing else useful had been gleaned so far was unsurprising. At that time of the morning, most people would have been on their way to work or to school drop-off, their minds busy on other things. The chances that anyone had taken especial notice of one extra car on the road were next to nil.

Still, the abductor had been lucky. Presumably, he or she had to have walked at least some of the way with Sienna, not taking the chance of parking an unfamiliar car too close to the Riccis' house. That meant the risk of the baby crying and drawing attention. Unless, of course, he or she had hidden the child in plain sight.

'Check with the neighbours again. See if they remember someone pushing a pram around that time or maybe carrying a large bag. A picnic basket or something along those lines, anything big enough to stash an infant in. We have to check all possibilities,' she added, seeing Harris's eyes widen in distaste.

Turning to Josh she asked, 'What about the father? What does he drive? And have we got onto him yet?'

'Still chasing the conference venue. But I've got his car details,' he replied, checking his notes. 'A blue Mazda 6 sedan. Licence plate Oscar Echo five three Charlie Golf.'

'Right. Let's check if any of the neighbours spotted Aaron Ricci's car, anytime this morning. Widen the timeframe. He could have driven here early and bided his time.'

The group dissipated and she was left alone with Josh.

'What do you reckon?' she asked him.

'Custody gone bad,' Josh replied without hesitation. 'She's definitely not telling us everything and the grandmother's doing all she can to make us look away from the marriage. I reckon we find Aaron Ricci, we find the baby.'

Kate nodded. She didn't disagree. There was something off about the women. Something more than the usual nervousness when speaking to the police.

'Do you reckon the prowler incident's connected?'

'Don't know. Could be. Assuming it actually happened.' Josh was busy typing something on his phone, only half concentrating.

Kate waited him out, used to his distractions.

He put away his mobile and finally looked at her. 'She's scared, that's for sure. Wouldn't take much for whatever she's fearful of to infect everything else. She starts seeing the bogey man in everything. The wind making noises outside – she's terrified it's a prowler.' He shrugged as

31

if to prove his point. 'If Ricci's involved and he left the conference for whatever reason to wander back home either yesterday or this morning, there'll be traffic footage of his car—'

He broke off, interrupted by a commotion at the head of the driveway. A large news van unable to find a parking stop appeared to have dinged a fellow reporter's vehicle while attempting a three-point turn, creating a mini-traffic jam. A crowd of mostly other journos had gathered to watch the hapless driver attempt to manoeuvre the vehicle, amidst much good-humoured catcalling.

'They're definitely gathering,' commented Josh. 'They'll be wanting a statement soon.'

Kate glanced at the media throng, who were for the moment at least distracted by something other than a story. She turned away.

'Might as well get it over with,' she replied. 'You can take this one,' she added, not reacting to the trace of surprise on his face. Without Skinner on the scene, she should be the one fronting up to the media as the case lead. She had never shirked from the task before and it wasn't something she could explain to Josh at the moment. 'Let's keep Mr Ricci out of it for now and focus on the timeframe,' she continued, avoiding his eyes.

He studied her but didn't pursue it. Together, they made their way towards the waiting news crews. As Josh took up position, Kate slipped unobserved past the reporters jostling for space. Only one set of eyes followed her with swift appraisal as she edged past. She thought she recognised his sun-ravaged face, looking more like one of the local cockies than a seasoned reporter. Richard someone. She couldn't remember his last name. Hadn't she heard somewhere that he had moved up the coast after working for years for one of the Sydney dailies?

Determinedly avoiding him, she continued on her way, past the packed vehicles, along the track to where it intersected with Elliot Pass. She had been informed where the koala toy had been discovered. Along the left-hand side of Elliot Pass heading north, approximately ten metres from its intersection with the track, at a small layaway. The forensic photos taken of the location had shown the toy discarded near a rutted section of bitumen.

She found the spot easily after a short walk: an informal gravel verge overrun by weeds and bordered by scrub, marked out by police tape. The going theory was that this was where the perpetrator had parked the car before making his or her way on foot, to and from the Riccis' place, dropping the toy on the roadside by mistake. She looked around her. The area was completely exposed to traffic. Vehicles flew past her on both lanes. She couldn't see it. To use the area as any kind of cover, unless in the dead of night when there was unlikely to be any through traffic, seemed absurd. And yet, this was where the soft toy had been discovered.

Her phone vibrated and she checked the incoming message.

This is Rayna Gardiner. The constable gave me your number. I need to speak to you in private. This is who Elissa's afraid of. This is Daniel's father and who you need to speak to about Sienna.

An image was attached to the text, capturing what appeared to be a photograph stuck within the plastic

33

sleeves of an old photo album. The time stamp indicated that it had been taken less than five minutes ago,
presumably from Mrs Gardiner's phone. Clearly, she had
been in a hurry as the shot was out of focus and partially
obscured by her finger over the camera lens. Kate stared
at the image, zooming in with her fingers to make out the
faces. The photo showed what looked like a high school
version of Elissa Ricci, dressed for a party or a formal, in
a flowing electric-blue halter-neck dress, smiling for the
camera. Something reared inside her, ice prickling her
skin as she focused on the young man standing next to
Elissa, also grinning cheekily into the camera, his head
turned slightly in profile. He wore his mousey-blond hair
long, which almost but not quite covered the beginnings
of an intricate tattoo stretching from the collar of his dress
shirt to his left ear.

6

'Tell me about Daniel's father, Rayna.'

'He's not a nice man.'

Now that she had Kate's attention, Rayna Gardiner seemed reluctant to speak. She closed her eyes and raised her face to the sky, seeking vain comfort in the pallid sunlight that was filtering through heavy-grey cloud banks.

Heedless of the cold, they sat outside. Kate had dispatched Constable Roby to accompany Elissa to Daniel's school to bring him home. She had left Josh inside directing traffic and chasing up Aaron Ricci, the elusive husband. It was now getting onto midday, almost three hours since Sienna had disappeared. Despite the urgency, the rapidly dissolving hours pulsating under her skin, she forced herself to remain still. She instinctively understood that rushing Rayna would achieve little.

They sat on a worn timber bench in the backyard facing the bush. Patchy kikuyu and an abandoned bright-yellow clamshell, empty of sand, ran into towering gums and scrub laced with lantana on the other side of a hip-height metal fence, the type Kate remembered from her primary school days.

It wouldn't be hard for someone to disappear in that scrub, Kate mused. It was the obvious exit route for an abductor and presumably the one the prowler had taken the previous morning. The dogs had been furnished with a selection of Sienna's clothes from the laundry basket, and Kate had watched as the dogs had sniffed the entire perimeter of the fence line, stopping at Rayna Gardiner's and Elissa Ricci's cars, both station wagons before moving on. So far, the dogs hadn't detected any scent tracks that gave a clue as to the direction in which Sienna may have been moved.

They were still in there, she knew, bush-bashing a five hundred-metre radius from the property boundary in concentric circles with a search team. A second team was scouring Elliot Pass outwards from where the soft toy had been found. She could hear the occasional bark from a dog or a call from one of the volunteers, blown their way by the wind.

'He liked hurting her.'

Kate glanced at Rayna, the silence between them snapping and stretching.

'She met him too young. He's twenty in that photo I sent you. That was taken at her Year Twelve formal. She was the only one with an older boyfriend. It gave her status amongst her friends—'

She faltered, absorbed in the past. 'I lost her to him. She moved in with him straight after school. Didn't look back… We lost contact. I lost contact.' A tremor shook her voice. She cleared her throat and continued.

'I had to move up north for work to Southport. I should have made more of an effort to see how she was getting on, but I was busy with a new job. I knew they were travelling around a lot, but she seemed happy whenever we met up… It took me ages to notice that anything was wrong. She was good at hiding the signs… and I was good at missing them, I guess.' She flicked her hand impatiently as if chasing away unwelcome thoughts, drowning out whatever dissenting voices were plaguing her.

'Elissa and me, it's always been the two of us. Elissa's father… he up and left when she was a toddler. And right from the start, she's been hell-bent on creating a perfect little family. Holding onto a relationship no matter what. I just didn't realise how much she was putting up with. By the time it became clear… well, it was too late.'

'Why too late?' Kate asked.

'She was pregnant with Daniel and by then she was trapped. She couldn't see a way out.'

'There are services that she could have gone to. We could have helped.'

She snorted. A sound of derision underscored by grief. 'The only reason she's alive today is because she didn't call you lot in. He would have killed her, you understand? Six years, she was with him. And he put her through hell. Beatings and cigarette burns and—' She broke off, turning away from Kate, unable or unwilling to elaborate.

When she resumed, her voice was scarcely above a whisper, quivering with anger.

'She thought it would get better once Daniel was born, but if anything it got worse. He hated that he had to share her with the baby. He was an animal. He did things to her in the bedroom… I don't… I can't talk about it.'

Unprompted, an image seeped into Kate's mind. A bedroom door swinging open and the musk of sex tinged with blood. Writhing flesh on a mounted large-screen TV; multiple men on a woman, who looked more like a child. Another woman sprawled in bed, handcuffed and unconscious. And Jason Veliu high as a kite.

'She only got away 'cause he was finished with her.' Rayna's voice broke into Kate's thoughts. 'He found someone else and discarded Elissa like a piece of garbage. Less than that. He kicked her and Daniel out when the bub was only a couple of months old, with just the clothes they were wearing. Didn't even let her take any nappies for Daniel. His own son! When I came and got them the poor little mite was a mess—'

'Kate—'

Josh was by her side, and by the look of him, he had news.

'Sorry to interrupt,' he continued with the barest of glances in Rayna's direction. 'Kate, it's Aaron Ricci. He's here.'

Kate glanced at Rayna and didn't miss the panic that seemed to flare across her face. She grabbed Kate's wrist as she made to stand, holding her close and whispering urgently into her face, 'Aaron is nothing like him. He loves Elissa. He would never hurt her or the children. He loves those kids. They're his life.'

7

'What was that about?'

'Nothing. I'll tell you later,' Kate replied. She followed Josh towards the house, rubbing her wrist where Rayna had gripped it. 'So, what's the deal with Mr Ricci?'

'Well.' Josh raised his eyebrows. 'I finally got onto him while you were with her.' He gestured over his shoulder to where they had left Mrs Gardiner, still seated in the garden. 'Turns out he's in Esserton, having returned from the conference early it seems. He reckons he had his phone switched off and only checked his messages not long ago. Apparently, he's been trying to call Elissa but it wouldn't connect.'

Kate exchanged a glance with Josh, neither of them convinced.

'He can account for his whereabouts this morning?' she asked.

'Swears he was at the conference.'

'Anyone confirmed that?'

'I've got Darnley there now, checking at the venue and with the firm.'

Kate nodded. 'Nothing from the neighbours?'

'Nothing yet. No one spotted his car.'

'We need to pull his phone records and the highway-traffic footage. Let's make sure.'

They stepped into the house, which lay in deep shadow, the sun having lost its battle against the clouds. Inside, the frigid air seemed concentrated, hoarded and amplified by the poor insulation and leaky ventilation. Kate's fingertips grazed the bare walls as they stepped through the gloomy corridor, feeling the chill seep through her skin.

The family was gathered once more in the sitting room off the kitchen. This time the tableau was made up of Elissa, a young boy in school uniform huddled at her side on the couch, and a man who was pacing the floor, agitated and upset. Once more Constable Roby stood guard, unobtrusive in the corner of the room.

Kate found her gaze instantly drawn to the young boy, recognising him from the photos on the wall. Daniel – Jason Veliu's son. She searched his pale, drawn face for any similarities with his father.

'Have you found her? Is there any news?' The words were a strangled cry from Aaron Ricci.

'Nothing yet, I'm afraid, Mr Ricci.'

Kate took in the missing child's father: a conventionally handsome face with the beginnings of a double chin that was emphasised rather than disguised by his smattering of facial hair. Aaron Ricci wore a well-cut suit in the vein of an overconfident real estate agent, but it was rumpled and dishevelled. His expression was a mask of stress, and his fingers dragged through his hair repeatedly, creating small ragged troughs. She noticed that the young boy's eyes were also on her, wide and staring. Only Elissa lay slumped, seemingly entirely withdrawn from the world.

'But the dogs? They must have found something. The scent of whoever's taken her?'

'The dogs are searching for Sienna's scent, Mr Ricci,' Josh interjected. He paused slightly to let the implications sink in. 'So far, they haven't found anything.'

Aaron Ricci stopped, his face collapsing as if punched. 'But it's been hours now. She'll be hungry. She'll need a feed and her nappy changed...'

'We're doing everything we can, Mr Ricci, believe me.' Kate's voice was gentle. 'We've got search parties scouring the bushland. We're not going to rest until she's found.'

'But are you sure you're looking in the right areas? I mean, this place is covered in bush. The bastard could have taken her anywhere—'

'The area is being searched systematically,' Kate assured him. 'Mr Ricci, I'm sorry if this is painful for you, but do you have any ideas on who may have taken Sienna? We've already spoken with your wife and we're wondering if there's any new information you can add?'

At the mention of Elissa, Aaron Ricci glanced back, his eyes shifting rapidly between his wife and stepson. Elissa remained crumpled and disengaged on the couch. She didn't appear to have heard a word.

'Mr Ricci?' Kate persisted. 'If there's anyone you can think of, we need to know.'

Aaron Ricci seemed to make up his mind. He motioned them towards the back door and the garden outside. Daniel's eyes, large and frightened, followed them out.

Outside in the darkened afternoon, the sliding door pulled closed behind them, Kate waited for Aaron Ricci to speak.

'My son, Daniel... He's not actually mine. I mean...' He sighed, his hands reaching once more for his hair. 'Elissa was with someone before me and they had Daniel.

She doesn't really talk about that time. She hates it when I ask any questions, so I don't anymore. I don't know anything about him. Just his name. Jason Veliu.'

Kate felt Josh stiffen beside her. Aaron Ricci, unaware of the reaction to his words, continued on.

'Daniel doesn't remember his father. He was two when I met Elissa and I'm all he knows. I've never met the bloke. Elissa told me he lives up north somewhere, up Burleigh Heads way…'

He seemed to catch something in Kate's face and his expression tightened. 'I never doubted her. Had no reason to… The only thing I know for sure is that he hurt her when they were together… She's got… There are marks on her body from that time.' His voice faltered and he swallowed hard before continuing. 'He treated her worse than an animal and she's afraid of him.'

'Do you know if your wife kept in touch with her ex-partner? Has Veliu ever tried to see his son?'

'No. Never. Elissa said he kicked them out when Daniel was only a newborn. Never accepted that Daniel was his son. He's never made contact or shown the slightest interest since. At least…' he hesitated, 'not as far as I know.'

'Do you know of any reason why he would come back now? Why he would want to hurt Sienna.'

'No. That's the thing. I can understand him doing something to Elissa or Daniel. But Sienna? I mean, what's the point? She's not his child.'

An image of Veliu, enraged and high on meth filled her mind. Nothing would surprise Kate when it came to Jason. A sudden fancy to torment an old victim by targeting what was most precious to her? A drug-fuelled urge to hurt and punish? It seemed entirely within character.

'How is your relationship with your wife, Mr Ricci?'

'What?' Ricci was momentarily thrown by Josh's change in questioning.

'You and Elissa. Everything good at home? We noticed Elissa is on antidepressants. That can't be easy for you. A new baby. No sleep. An unhappy wife.'

'She's fine. I mean, yeah, she got diagnosed with postnatal anxiety a few weeks ago. But she's been much better since she's been on the tablets.'

'Any side effects? I've heard some of those meds can have a bucket-load of reactions, until you get the dosage just right or you're on the right mix of pills. Was Elissa suffering any adverse effects, Mr Ricci? Moodiness, irritation, tiredness… lack of sex drive?'

'What? No. I mean, yeah, she was tired, but she's a new mum. Of course she gets exhausted from time to time.'

'So, it wasn't putting a strain on your relationship? You weren't thinking of leaving her? Taking a break, maybe? Taking Sienna away with you for a while?'

'Of course not. What do you mean? Do you think I did this? I would never hurt Sienna. I would never leave my family. What are you talking about?' His voice rose in disbelief and panic.

'Please, calm down, Mr Ricci. No one's accusing you of anything. We need to ask these things and consider all possibilities. It's part of the job.'

'Well, it's fucked. While you're wasting time looking into me, there's someone out there with my baby. Doing God knows what to her. Jesus, I can't believe this is happening.'

They waited until he had calmed himself.

'Mr Ricci, with your permission, we would like to access your mobile to check your call and location records as part of our investigation. This is about ruling out possibilities so we can focus on bringing Sienna home as soon as possible. As you can appreciate, time is of the essence right now.'

For a second, Kate thought he would refuse. He had gone very still. Then he nodded, reaching into his pocket and handing over his mobile. She noticed the lock screen was an image of his baby daughter. Only Sienna, not his wife or son.

'Do what you need to.'

8

'We need to bring Veliu in.'

'He's a distraction, Kate. I'm telling you. We should be focusing on Ricci.'

Kate and Josh were gathered in Skinner's office, having been called into his presence within minutes of stepping into the station. The incident room was humming with activity, and the air was charged with a palpable sense of urgency. Skinner had been fielding calls from the police media unit and the assistant commissioner's office. A press conference was scheduled for two hours. His expectant eyes were now trained on them, waiting for answers.

The room was hot, the heating overcompensating for the dip in temperature outside. Kate felt an overwhelming urge to scratch the site of her bullet wound, which she resisted, unwilling as usual to bring attention to her scar. Her eyes scanned the clock on Skinner's wall, ringed in by his various framed commendations and photos. Three-thirty. It was over six hours since baby Sienna had disappeared and they were no closer to bringing her home.

'Ricci's hiding something. I'm sure of it,' Josh continued. 'This feels personal. Maybe he didn't think Elissa was coping, or maybe they had some sort of fight and he removed the kid out of spite. But there's something not right there. We need to bring him in and tease out his movements.'

'Traffic's come up empty,' Kate reminded Josh, making an effort to win the argument.

She was referring to the available traffic footage from the intersections that fed into Elliot Pass. So far, no record of Ricci's vehicle had been spotted in the footage from that morning within the abduction timeline, or in the early hours of Thursday morning, covering the alleged prowler incident.

Josh waved a hand in easy dismissal. 'He could have been using a different vehicle.'

Kate swallowed her irritation as Skinner interjected, tired of their bickering.

'How sure are you about Veliu?'

'He made bail last night. So, he had the opportunity.'

'But what's his motive after all this time?' Josh interposed. 'The baby's not even his. Why go after his ex now after he's left her alone all this time?'

'We don't know that he has. Just that Elissa Ricci has never reported him, and based on her mother's account, I'm not surprised. She's petrified of him. For all we know, he may have been keeping tabs on her all this time.'

Josh shook his head. 'Why would he take the baby, though? It's too high risk.'

'I wouldn't put anything past him when he's cooked. You didn't see the state his partner was in the other day. He was fried and she copped the consequences. When he's in that state, I'd say he's pretty much capable of anything. He's found an opportunity to hurt Elissa in the worst way possible, and he's probably intending to make some money from it, too, if he can.'

'You think he's taken the baby to go after a ransom?'

'Why not? It's a way of showing Elissa that he can still control her, even after all these years. And it's easy money. Elissa will give him anything in return for Sienna, and she'll keep quiet about it, too.'

Josh shook his head. 'Ricci's far more plausible, in my book. He's got access, and he knows the layout of the property and all of Elissa's routines. He and Elissa are clearly having marriage problems. It's obvious.'

Kate bristled, holding her temper with difficulty. She met Josh's expression in a silent battle of wills. Why was he so bent on challenging her? Veliu was a solid lead that they should be following up. Was he so resistant to making space for her in front of Skinner? She had thought them friends who worked well together. He had seemed to genuinely care for her wellbeing following her injury. But something had switched the moment she had made her intentions about returning to work clear. She had felt his resentment flare and the cementing of his competitive edge. She could tell, he had not expected her back so quickly. He had just been getting established, acting in her position while she was on leave, and he clearly didn't appreciate having to surrender the role so soon. She felt a tug for her partner, though not enough to let him override her without a fight.

Skinner's gaze swung between Josh and Kate, settling on her. 'You sure you can handle him?'

She made herself hold his stare. Skinner was watching her, looking for any chink in her armour. It dawned on Kate that yesterday's small victory counted for nothing. This was the investigation that mattered. She would have to prove herself here and now – repeatedly if need be – that she was ready and able to see this through. Any weakness and Skinner would have no hesitation in again relegating her to the *not up to it* corner.

'If he's done this, sir, I'm going to nail him.'

–

Veliu sat draped across his chair, long and loose-limbed, a languid snake biding its time. A complacent smirk twitched at the end of his lips. His grubby shirt lay unbuttoned almost to his belly, his tatts and wiry strength on display. There was no lawyer today. It only half surprised Kate that Veliu had agreed without qualms to a second interview and alone. The ego and supreme confidence of the man had no bounds.

Constable Grant, gym-fit and muscles bulging, was sitting in on the interview, posted there on Skinner's orders to deter Veliu from trying anything stupid. Kate's irritation at being babied showed and the constable was doing his best to melt into thin air. Veliu winked at the hulking constable and batted his eyelashes, guessing it would infuriate him. Veliu cocked his eyebrows at her, waiting.

'How's Lena doing, Jason?'

'Raring to go, now that she's had a nice little rest.'

Kate swallowed her repulsion. She had heard that Lena Chalmers, Veliu's partner, had been released from hospital that morning. She had insisted on discharging herself and was refusing to cooperate with police on assault charges being brought against Veliu. Both of the children had been placed into the temporary care of Lena's parents.

'I understand that you weren't there to pick her up from hospital this morning? You had somewhere else to be?'

'Lena can look after herself. Plus, she had to visit her folks, didn't she? To see the kids after you lot dumped them there.'

Kate's mind flashed to the trembling dark-haired boy who had pointed a toy gun at her in an effort to protect his baby brother. There was not a word of concern from Veliu about his two children.

'But where were *you*, Jason? What were you doing all this morning while Lena was leaving hospital?'

His eyes narrowed and Kate cursed herself for showing her hand, too quickly. She was getting impatient.

'Why? What am I meant to have done now?'

'Just answer the question, Jason.'

'At home. Asleep.'

'You sure about that?'

'It's what I said.'

She sighed, frustration kicking within her. 'Can anyone verify that?' she pressed.

He regarded her, his eyes calculating. 'Yeah, I was at home when Lena got in. You can ask her.'

'And what time was that, Jason?'

'I don't fucking know. You'll have to ask her. She woke me up to bring in a sandwich for lunch, all right? Look, what the fuck is this about?' His tone had changed, wary now, knowing that the questions reflected more than just a follow-up interview to his existing charges.

'Are you sure you didn't happen to leave the house, Jason? This morning? Maybe take a trip along Elliot Pass?'

'Why would I visit that shithole?' His eyes had narrowed, his body suddenly tense and on alert.

'Have you spoken to your ex-partner recently, Jason? Elissa Gardiner or Elissa Ricci as she's now known?'

Kate's change of tack seemed to take him by surprise.

49

'What the fuck? What's that bitch got to do with anything? That was fucking ages ago.'

'She's married now, Jason. To a husband with a good job and a regular income.' She noticed the glint in his eyes at the mention of money. 'How are your finances at the moment, Jason? A bit slow going? Not like your ex. She's done well for herself since she left you—'

'I threw that whining bitch out. She never left me. They don't leave until I say so. I got rid of her.'

'Oh, I know. I've heard all about what you did, Jason. What a gentleman you were throughout your relationship. A bit like how you treat Lena now, isn't it?'

'Fuck off.' He dismissed her with a wave of his hands.

'Tell me, Jason. Have you spoken to Elissa since your breakup? Maybe visited her or your son?'

'He's not my *son*,' he interjected, suddenly furious. 'She was a fucking slag when I knew her. Spread her legs for anyone. You can't bloody pin that little bastard on me. Check his birth certificate. It'll tell you. I'm not listed as the father.'

Kate regarded him, refraining from pointing out how easy it would be to prove Jason's paternity. The reason that Elissa had never pursued Veliu for child support, or any kind of support for that matter, had more to do with wanting to create as much distance as she could from her violent ex-partner, rather than Daniel's paternity.

'Jason, I am going to ask you again. Did you happen to go anywhere near Elliot Pass in the last two days? We are specifically interested in the times between 8 am and 10 am this morning and between approximately 4 am and 6 am on Thursday morning.'

Something changed in his expression. A rush of recognition. 'Hang on. Elliot Pass. That was on the news today.

Are you saying the baby that's gone missing, that's Elissa's kid?' His eyes widened. 'What, and you're trying to pin that on me, are you? That's fucking bullshit.'

'Settle down, Mr Veliu.' Constable Grant leaned across the table in a gesture of warning.

'Don't you fucking touch me.' Veliu slapped Grant's hand away and rose from his seat in a swift movement. His chair crashed to the floor behind him. Grant surged forward, obviously glad for a reason to take Veliu on.

There was a knock on the door and it swung open to reveal Constable Harris accompanying a short, balding man, his stocky bulk bundled into a battered suit, a chunky gold bracelet looping his wrist. Kate recognised Veliu's cousin-cum-lawyer. He stood at the threshold, taking in the scene, his gaze traveling from Constable Grant, moments away from pulling Veliu into line, to Kate.

'This interview is over, Detective. I hope you weren't about to manhandle my client,' he added in Grant's direction. 'C'mon, Jason. We're leaving.'

'Mr Arnot, Jason's here of his own accord assisting us with our enquiries on an active investigation.'

'Get a load of this shit,' Veliu interjected. 'Now, they're trying to pin that missing baby on me.'

'Detective, unless my client is under arrest, this interview is done and we are leaving. If you wish to speak with Mr Veliu again, I would be happy to arrange a mutually suitable date and time.'

Jason slapped his lawyer on the shoulder. 'Fucking well done, Arney.'

The lawyer shook his head at Kate as Veliu skipped through the door – a wide grin playing on his face and his swagger restored. 'Not one of your better moments, Detective.'

As the two men walked out, Kate spied Skinner at the end of the corridor, his face set and unreadable as he turned away.

9

Her breasts felt rock hard, and painfully overfull. Finding a moment to slip away from the packed incident room, Kate escaped to the tiny and rarely used interview suite at the back of the building.

Locking the door behind her to protect against accidental intrusion, she set up her hand pump, sighing with relief as the milk squirted out. Once done, she would stash the filled bottles in the staff fridge encased in their protective pouch to deflect the curiosity and distaste of her colleagues.

She watched as the oat-coloured liquid steadily grew in volume, at once fascinated and repulsed by what her body could produce and how little control she had over the process. Her body was no longer her own. It was marching to its own primordial tune. She had as little mastery over her own flesh as a farmyard animal.

Without warning, she found herself weeping, heartsick over the baby that was out there somewhere waiting for its own mother's breast. Her failure with Veliu grated at her nerves, her fears over the case and her own limitations suddenly overwhelming.

She jumped as her mobile buzzed. Hastily wiping her tears, she reached for it with her free hand, recognising the caller ID on screen, her insides immediately turning to liquid.

Raising the phone to her ear, she answered the call. 'Dad.'

Static only and a series of scratchy noises.

'Dad? You there? Hello?'

Was it a pocket dial? Hanging up, she tried his number again, but it went directly to voicemail.

'Sarge, they're ready for you.' A quiet knock on the door and Darnley's voice outside.

'On my way, Greg. Two minutes.'

–

The lights of the cameras were bright on her face. Kate stood alongside Skinner behind a row of microphones, while the media liaison officer hovered at the edges of the gathered journalists. She was trapped in front of a dozen or more reporters. Any one of them could ask her a question about her father, and she would have nowhere to run. No way of escaping. In an instant, they could derail her position on the investigation.

She looked across the packed room. All the news channels had turned up, as had reps from the city dailies and radio stations. Kate shivered slightly. They would be making the metropolitan newscasts.

She felt the hum of anticipation in the crowd. The whiff of a big story that would almost certainly generate multiple articles and editorials. This was what they all waited for. A story with all the markers of tragedy and fear, the perfect ingredients for a media storm. Kate could tell they were champing at the bit to get in first with a question, to work out an angle to outfox their competitors.

A hush grew as the door to the conference room opened and Josh entered with Aaron Ricci. All eyes were suddenly on the beleaguered father as he walked, head down, to the waiting mics. Several heads craned and Kate could already make out the unspoken question in the raised eyebrows and murmured whispers: where was Elissa Ricci?

Kate shuffled to make way for Aaron, catching a whiff of crisp aftershave as he stepped in beside her. He had taken the time to shower and change, she noticed. A collared shirt tucked into jeans. His work clothes and luggage, Kate knew, had been handed over to forensics.

He looked fresh and presentable, an image that could go either way with the media. In her experience, journos expected parents of missing children to look unkempt and haggard, their entire world taken over by grief, uncaring of trivial matters like self-care and hygiene. It would all depend on Ricci's performance, she thought. He needed to project just the right mixture of grief and fear. Any perceived overconfidence, lack of emotion or off-beat note on his part, and he would be skewered alive by the waiting armchair pundits.

'Thank you all for being here today,' Skinner began. 'As you are aware, the Tweed-Byron Police District, headed by police from Esserton Station, have today commenced an investigation into the abduction of four-month-old Sienna Ricci. Baby Sienna was abducted from her home in South Esserton sometime between approximately 8.50 am and 9.10 am this morning. She was taken from her bassinet while her mother was in the shower. We believe the intruder entered the premises via the back sliding door, which was unlocked. No one else was at home at the time. An AMBER alert has been issued and we are appealing to the public who may have any information to come forward. A description and photo of Sienna is included in your briefing pack for media circulation.

'We are currently speaking to all residents who live along Elliot Pass. We are also interested in anyone who may have been travelling by car or by foot along Elliot Pass between the hours of 8 am and 9.50 am this morning, and also between approximately 3 am and 6 am yesterday – that is Thursday – morning. Any persons with dashcam footage who may have travelled along Elliot Pass during the specified periods are encouraged to come forward.'

Skinner paused, taking in the assembled faces that were hanging off his every word. He revelled in this stuff. Kate and Josh were there for effect, to make up the numbers and jump in only if requested. Skinner was in his element, rattling off his prepared remarks with practised ease.

'We understand that this is an extremely distressing situation for everyone involved, especially for the family. Our first and only priority is to find baby Sienna safe and well, and we are doing everything we can, with all resources on the ground, to make this happen. This includes coordinating with State Emergency Services and police search teams… I'll now hand over to Mr Ricci to say a few words before taking questions.'

He moved aside, making way for a clearly nervous Aaron Ricci to take up the vacated spot in front of the cameras. Ricci cleared his throat loudly, his eyes darting across the sea of faces before quickly looking down again. Unable to meet the camera's glare, he recited from his prepared statement, rushing and stumbling across the words, without once looking up, plainly wanting nothing more than for the ordeal to be over. A bad impression, Kate reflected.

'Our family has been devastated by Sienna's abduction. All we want is for our beautiful girl to be returned to us. We ask whoever has taken her to please show some mercy and bring her back. If you are too scared to come forward, please just leave her at a hospital or a medical centre so she can be cared for. She's only four months old. She needs milk and her mum...' Here, Ricci's voice caught but he held it together. 'If anyone knows anything, please just let the police know... We just want our baby back...'

Kate took in the room. Maybe it would have been better if Ricci had fallen apart, crying openly for the cameras.

'Thank you, Aaron.' Skinner deftly manoeuvred Ricci to a waiting constable who led him out of the room. The packed room of journalists watched him leave in silence, respectful for the moment, at least. Though no doubt, the unasked questions were swirling.

Where's your wife, Mr Ricci? Where were you when Sienna disappeared? Do you know who took her?

'Right, we have time for a few questions.' Kate grimaced as Skinner unerringly pointed to a shapely brunette in the front row for the first question.

'Alice Lawley, *Northern Advertiser.*' The woman was all business. 'You mentioned that you wanted people to come forward regarding the early hours of Thursday morning. Can you clarify why the police are interested in that time period prior to baby Sienna going missing?'

'We are looking into the possibility that there was someone at or near the property at that time who may be able to assist us with our enquiries.' Skinner's answer was ambiguous, aimed at not revealing too much of their current thinking: that the offender may have scouted the property on the Thursday ahead of the abduction.

The woman raised her hand again almost immediately, but Skinner had turned, bestowing his attention on another frantically waving hand.

'Serena Castilla, WIN News. Is there any indication that this could be a kidnapping? Have any demands been made?'

'All possibilities are under investigation, but at this stage we can confirm that no demands have been made.'

'Richard Markham, *North Coast Leader*,' a voice broke in before Skinner had time to make another selection. Kate looked up and fear slithered inside as she recognised the weathered face from the crowd that had surrounded the Riccis' house this morning. Those eyes full of calculation, which had followed her as she had tried to slip past the pack unnoticed. For a sickening second, she was sure that her time was up. Here was the moment that she had been dreading. A question unrelated to the case, which exposed her father's identity.

'Is the family or anyone known to the family under investigation?'

'The Riccis are assisting us with our enquiries, and as I said earlier, we are looking into all possibilities. No suspects have been established at this stage.'

Sheer relief flushed through Kate's body and she hardly heard Skinner's answer. The man concentrated on his notepad, not glancing her way.

The remainder of the press conference passed quickly with a dozen or so standard questions, parried easily by Skinner. Within minutes, it was over.

'Thank you, ladies and gentlemen.' Skinner dismissed the crowd and turned to leave, followed by Josh.

'One more question, if I may—' Kate froze and Skinner paused, irritated by the interjection.

'I wanted to ask if you had any comment on the allegations in this morning's news made by Mr Lahey about Minister Jackson's connection to a senior police officer in the Northern Region Command? There is conjecture that the police officer concerned may have worked at this station?' Richard Markham's eyes swung towards Kate, now openly roving her face for a reaction.

The journalists who had been in the process of packing up had suddenly stopped, their reporters' instincts pinging. Kate hadn't moved. Skinner's face hardened and his expression betrayed nothing.

'This press conference was called to discuss an ongoing investigation, Mr Markham. I have no comment to make on unrelated rumour and conjecture. If you have any pertinent questions relating to baby Sienna, please feel free to forward them through the police media unit.'

Skinner caught Kate's eye briefly before striding out of the conference room as an explosion of questions erupted in his wake.

10

The skies had finally broken and rain slashed at Kate's windscreen. Outside, rain–soaked paddocks were cloaked in grey mist, premature darkness setting in for the evening. Her headlights cut through the gloom, illuminating an empty country road; gnarled eucalyptus trees along the fence line providing shelter for patient cattle waiting out the wet.

She pulled into a gravel driveway, her tyres skidding for an instant on the slick mud. Her eyes flitted to her mobile as the vehicle strained up the rutted track. Three missed calls. All from Geoff. She knew she should be at home, the heaviness in her breasts once more nagging at her conscience. She shrugged away her guilt, silently seeking her husband and Amy's forgiveness.

She pulled up in front of the cottage, which was shrouded in darkness. Cursing, she ran through the rain, fumbling with the latch on the picket-fence gate and gaining the shelter of the front verandah. She rang the bell and pounded the front door. No light was visible through the drawn curtains and closed windows. The house was sealed shut. *Where the hell was her father?* She rang his mobile again. Straight to voicemail. *Fuck!*

Gaining the car again, she struggled out of her saturated jacket and turned up the heater, debating her options as she warmed her hands in the blast of hot air.

Scenes from that afternoon's press conference ran circles in her mind. She couldn't escape Richard Markham's face. That smug, self-satisfied smirk as he had landed his 'gotcha' moment, while she had just stood there.

Then there had been Skinner's questions afterwards.

'Have you spoken to Gray? Is this Martin shit going to be a problem?'

'It's just bullshit muckraking, sir. This stuff is ancient history.' As if she needed to explain any of this to Skinner: her father's old rival, next in line and snapping at Gray's heels for years, before finally gaining Gray's throne when her father retired early – encouraged or pushed out of the force when whispers of his involvement with the minister had become too loud to be ignored. What Gray and Martin had tried to build in their cottage on the hill had been an open secret in the upper echelons. Skinner had been the inheritor of the spoils when her father had left abruptly after Martin's death, all fight wrenched out of him.

Skinner was still waiting.

'I'll speak to him. It's not going to affect the investigation. I promise.'

'I don't give a fuck about Gray's personal life, Miles. But he headed up this station for years and he's your father. That means if he's compromised in any way, then it'll reflect on you. So, I'm going to ask you again. Is there anything dodgy here that I need to know about?'

She had managed to meet his eyes as she lied to his face. 'There's nothing. Sir.'

Nothing. Nothing at all. Just a gift. A gift of money that was propping up her mortgage.

Memory as sharp as a blade cleaved her mind.

Two days before her wedding over six years ago now. The wedding date, which had been brought forward by six months due to the oncologist's prognosis for her mother.

'Dad, this is too much. I can't accept it.'

He had waved away her protests, pressing the cheque into her hands. A cheque for $200,000.

She recalled that Gray had brought her out to this very spot. He had wanted her opinion on a property that had caught his eye. She hadn't thought much of it at the time. Her father had always waxed lyrical about buying a property one day to retire on, which had never amounted to anything. She had assumed the drive was an excuse by her father to escape the feverish wedding preparations underway at home. And she had been only too happy to oblige. To have a couple of hours alone with her father away from the stresses of event planning. The lightness in his face as he had gazed at the ornate miner's cottage surrounded by emerald-green paddocks, came back to her now.

Her own naivety sickened her. So overcome by Gray's attention. By his generosity. Enjoying the moment of father–daughter togetherness. Why hadn't she thought to question him? How could he have afforded a nest egg of $200,000 on his salary?

She had been so preoccupied by her own pre-wedding worries. A week of putting out one fire after another: organising a new MC because the one they had booked had broken his foot while mountain bike riding. A supply problem with the florist (was she happy to swap baby's breath for stephanotis?). Fielding daily phone calls from her over-hyped bridesmaids. Her mind had been a shamble.

She squeezed her eyes closed, trying to shut out the memories.

Was that the whole truth, though?

The reality was she had been dazzled by the cheque. The sheer size of it and the freedom it represented. She and Geoff had been so skint. The wedding had eaten into almost all of their savings; that much-longed-for house deposit an ever-more-distant dream. Tempted by the money, the relief of it, she had disregarded almost everything else.

Her mobile beeped and she glanced at the screen. She had set up a news alert and the screen glowed with a breaking headline. *EX-ESSERTON POLICE CHIEF LINKED TO DECEASED MINISTER SEX SCANDAL; POLICE DECLINE TO COMMENT.* The by-line read Richard Markham. Kate scrolled down the article, her eyes barely taking in the words before coming to a halt at the colour photo of her father in full police regalia standing alongside Martin Jackson and smiling into his face. A candid photo from one of the many public events the two men had attended together when Arthur Grayling had been in command of Esserton Station and Martin Jackson an up-and-coming local MP.

Kate stared at the photo as the rain drummed at her window and acid pooled in her gut, her mind trying but failing to find any wriggle room out of the mess.

11

Kate turned the door key and entered the sitting room quietly, taking care to step around the elaborate pile of Duplo set up next to the couch.

She breathed in the house. For the moment, no one knew she was at home. She took in the crayons, toys and cushions strewn all over the floor. The smell of burnt toast drifted from the kitchen, and bowls of half-eaten snacks and Milo-smeared toddler cups lay abandoned. She could tell it had not been an easy day.

She made her way through the room, picking up the various playthings and dumping them in the large toy box that took up the back wall of the family room. She picked up the food-crusted bowls and cups and carried them to the kitchen to join their cousins piled high in the sink, along with several used baby bottles.

'Mummy!' Archie had heard her fumbling in the kitchen. Her son flung himself into her arms.

'Hey, buddy. How are you? Did you have a good day?' She buried her head in his sweaty neck, squeezing him tightly. He wriggled away even as she tried to hold on. She noticed as he got older, his hugs were getting shorter and less frequent.

'Yep.'

Kate smiled. Oh, to get some actual words out of her son. 'What about the fire trucks? Did they arrive? Did you have fun?'

'Yep, but it was only one truck. And they didn't let everyone inside.'

'Did you not get to climb in the front?'

'No. Only Sasha and Ellie, and Nash and Henry got to climb up, because they were the room leaders today.'

Kate took in the frown on his face. She had clearly hit a sore point. 'That's a shame. What about the rest of the day? Did you have a better afternoon?'

'Yep, Daddy let me play Xbox when I got home. We played with Amy.'

'Did you now? How did that go?'

'Amy kept crying and dis-turbing us,' Archie stated flatly, pronouncing the unfamiliar word with care. 'So, we had to stop.'

'Oh, that's too bad, matey. But it's just because she's a baby and she doesn't understand. She'll cry less when she gets older.'

'Yeah, I know.' A lifetime of weariness behind the words.

Kate pressed her lips together, covering a smile. 'Is Daddy with Amy?'

'Yep. He's putting her to sleep.'

Kate swallowed her disappointment. She had been hoping to snuggle her daughter and get in a last feed before Amy went down.

'Okay, and what about you, Mister? Have you had dinner?'

He nodded emphatically. 'Daddy gave me Weet-Bix,' he said with a grin.

'Sounds yum. Okay, how about five more minutes of play and then it's time for a bath.'

'Ohhhhhhh.' His special whine that set her teeth on edge. 'Daddy said I could play Lego.'

'All right, how about ten minutes of Lego and then you can jump into the bath.'

'Fifteen! Twenty! Thirty!'

'Okay, Arch, let's calm down. We don't want to wake up your sister.'

'I want to stay up. No bath!'

'Archie. That's enough. Lower your voice, bud, or you'll have to go straight to bed.'

'Not fair! Not fair! Not fair!' Within seconds, her smiling four-year-old had switched into screaming, foot-stamping hysterics. Kate felt the familiar frustration build.

She heard a loud wail from the back of the house. They had woken Amy. *Fuck!*

—

Two hours later, Kate lay in the bath, trying to find relief for her sore breasts. She had skipped too many feeds during the day and her breasts were now too engorged to drain properly using the pump; her one attempt at work having been cut short. She had endeavoured to nurse Amy, in part to relieve her body, but also to try to settle her daughter, but Amy would have none of it, overtired and already full from the bottle, which Geoff had given her. It had taken Kate over an hour of walking with her screaming baby to finally settle her and to creep out of her room.

She had emerged to find the kitchen spotless and Archie in bed. Her husband sat nursing a beer in front of the TV, the baby monitor conspicuous on the coffee table. She could tell he was pissed off with her. For arriving late and for cocking everything up when she had finally come home. The ultra-clean kitchen was his passive-aggressive way of letting her know, if she was in any doubt, who was doing the parental heavy lifting in their household. While she was busy solving other people's problems, Geoff was at the coalface of their own family. Her performance with her children today just proved his point.

'You okay?' she had tried.

Geoff had faced her, exhaustion and weariness etched into the lines of his face. 'What do you want me to say, Katie?'

'I couldn't get away, Geoff. A baby's gone missing.'

'I know. There'll always be something.'

It was said matter-of-factly, but she had felt all the judgement in the world. The never-ending pressure of it. The feeling of always being a step behind, never quite able to perform either job to everyone's satisfaction. She had come home, while every other officer was still at the station, plugging away, leave and rostered days off cancelled. They would never say it to her face – always toeing the official line of work-life balance – but she knew what they thought. The furtive and not-so-subtle looks of frustration tossed her way as she had walked out were hard to miss. And for all that, home was no easier. She felt just as inadequate here as at work. Always scrambling, and never quite hitting the mark.

Geoff hadn't even bothered to ask after Gray. She knew her husband didn't have it easy. But fuck it, she contributed too. What other choice did they have? Someone had to pay the mortgage. Geoff's part-time job had disappeared out of the blue a couple of months ago, his old boss deciding, seemingly on the fly, to sell off his architectural business. An offer he just couldn't refuse. The new owner had immediately cleaved off all the contract positions. A business decision. Nothing personal. Geoff had been caught napping. He had always counted on the long-standing professional relationship to throw work his way. But now that avenue had dried up and Geoff was realising how hand-to-mouth the life of a freelancer really was.

Going back to the police force after her twelve weeks of paid maternity leave was the obvious solution. But Kate knew her decision had cost her husband, narrowing his work opportunities and binding him more tightly to the home front. Maybe she should have given him more time to find another position, made her leave stretch out on half pay, to see if anything eventuated from the multiple applications he had sent out. But her job had been there and waiting. An actual, regular income stream that would pay the mortgage and their bills if she chose to resume work. Not a hypothetical future prospect.

Picturing her husband's expression now, she felt the weight of all the decisions she had made. Sighing, she continued to knead her rock-hard breast tissue, willing the milk to drain. Bruise marks blossomed along the milk ducts where she had rubbed her skin into submission. *Jesus. Why did it have to be so hard?*

Fucking breastfeeding. She would gladly give it up if she could get away with it without feeling guilty. But it was tangible proof that she was bringing something vital to the mix as a parent; just as essential as Geoff. If she stopped, what did that say about her as a woman? As a mother? Not that Amy seemed to care either way. In the past week or so, Kate had noticed her daughter becoming increasingly impatient with the effort of having to suckle for her food, when the bottle gave her instant gratification.

She closed her eyes and a memory unfurled. Kate and her family on vacation with the Jacksons at a holiday park somewhere down the coast. Six-year-old Kate playing cards with the older and wiser eight-year-old Lesley Jackson in the dim confines of the Jacksons' caravan, while their two mothers sat out in the sun gossiping on lounge chairs. Kate recalled Lindsay Jackson, her skin boiling lobster-red in the sun, breastfeeding her newborn, Maya, while Kate's mum sat content in the chair opposite, her face tucked under a sunhat and her coffee-bean skin glistening with sweat as she sipped cask wine and played with Luke, then only three.

Kate recalled how much Lindsay had moaned and complained about what a bad feeder Maya was the entire trip, loudly proclaiming her intention of giving up breast-feeding as soon as possible. She thought back to the disgust and embarrassment she had felt about her best friend's mother constantly referring to her breasts. Kate under-stood now, too late, what Lindsay may have been going through, trapped by the overwhelming expectations of motherhood. It occurred to her that she had no memory of Martin or her father providing any sympathy or support to Lindsay. It had always been Aneesha, Kate's mother, at Lindsay's side.

A picture of her mother came to her now, the way Kate always remembered her: dressed in one of her favourite brightly coloured frocks, patterned with tropical-looking birds and flowers in rich reds and greens, sewed espe-cially for her by *Aunty Iris*. Not an aunt by relation, but a family friend, a Sri Lankan Burgher family living in nearby Murwillumbah, linked to Kate's mother's side through various family connections in the way things were in Sri Lankan households; *Burgher* being a catch-all term meaning Sri Lankans with Dutch, Portuguese or other European colonial ancestry. Aunty Iris and her husband, Uncle Elton, had been her mother's surrogate family when she had left the UK and landed in Whitlam-era Australia in the seventies with nothing to recommend her but her youthful confidence and a newly earned teaching degree. Two years later, she was married to a dashing young police constable stationed to a rural town in the middle of nowhere. Aunty Iris had been her only support when, as a young mother of two, Aneesha's own parents – Kate's maternal grandparents – had perished in a house fire back in the UK.

Kate thought with guilt that she had barely caught up with Aunty Iris since her mother had died. As quick with a smile as she was with a reprimand, and fiercely independent, in Kate's mind, Aunty Iris would be forever linked to lamprais, the intensely flavoured packets of rice and curry wrapped in banana leaf that were a speciality of Burgher cuisine and often involved overnight preparations. She recalled with sudden nostalgia sitting at Aunty Iris's kitchen as her mother and Iris bent over the stove, laughing and teasing, while the entire house filled with the smell of spices, fried silky eggplant and rich meat curries slow-cooked over hours.

Aunty Iris would be well into her nineties by now, Kate realised with a start. She had moved to a nursing home in Murwillumbah some years ago after the death of her husband. Kate needed to visit her and take the kids. Aunty Iris was the closest thing to family that remained from her mother's side and she needed to keep up that connection, before that too was gone.

With a dull ache in her heart, Kate wished her mother was here with her now. Aneesha Grayling, calm and competent, would have known what to do. With the kids. With her nursing issues. With Geoff. Everything.

She dipped her face under the water, holding her breath like she used to when she was a child, feeling the noise in her brain fade and her body melt into the water. One, two, three, four… seventeen, eighteen… She felt the familiar pressure build in her chest as her lungs grasped for air. Sixty four… sixty five…

'Kate! Jesus Christ. What the fuck are you doing?'

She felt strong arms reach under her elbows, warm water sloshing on the tiles as she was wrenched forcibly out of the bath.

12

Saturday

At the takeaway counter, the whirr of the coffee machine and smell of freshly ground beans filled the air. Kate's eyes were fixed firmly on the glass counter, on the glazed pastries and flaky scrolls and croissants, ignoring the daily newspapers, folded neatly and fanned out, ready for browsing by the café patrons. Constable Roby stood unnaturally still beside her, doing his best to ignore the unmissable. *HUNT FOR MISSING BABY ENTERS SECOND DAY! MINISTER'S NORTHERN LOVE NEST!* Each screaming headline worse than the other.

She glanced over to her constable, whose eyes skittered away guiltily, a blush travelling up his freshly shaved jaw, pink and goose-pimpled like a raw plucked chicken.

'Decaf skinny cap.'

Kate nodded to the barista, accepting her brew and walking out ahead of Roby. She sucked on her takeaway cup, trying to bury her sorrows in the warm, bitter taste, if not the caffeine. A concession to her nursing.

Roby, silent and jittery in the driver's seat, gunned the engine without a word, his bacon and egg roll sitting untouched in its paper bag by his side.

'If you have any questions, now's the time to ask, Constable.' Her gaze remained trained on the window, watching the businesses along the street opening up for the day. 'Maybe you can pry something out of me to take back to the staffroom. A juicy titbit right from the horse's mouth.'

She glanced at her companion. He didn't react, keeping his attention on the road.

Why was she needling the kid? He was not responsible for the state of her family. A flush of guilt, ripe and raw, spiked through her. She swallowed it down with her coffee.

At the Ricci house, Kate dodged the clamouring journalists and barrage of questions. *I am not the story*, her mind screamed as she ducked and weaved and broke from the crowd into the Riccis' front lawn, the stationed uniformed officers preventing the reporters from encroaching any further.

Around the side of the house, past the carport – empty of Aaron Ricci's car – they made their way to the back door and the kitchen. The glass door slid open easily.

Kate stepped into the dimly lit room, the all-pervasive chill once again striking her first. Did the family ever use a heater?

'Hello? Mrs Ricci? It's Detective Miles. Anyone home?'

A shadow moved in the gloomy kitchen and shuffled forward, revealing itself to be Elissa Ricci, still in her clothes from the day before. For a second, Kate wasn't sure the woman recognised them.

'Mrs Ricci? Is your husband at home?'

'What?' Her eyes struggled to find purchase, landing finally on Roby. 'He said he needed to get out of the house...'

'What about your mother, Elissa? Are you alone? Where's Daniel?'

'Daniel stayed over at Mum's. She thought it best.' Her face melted into a wordless cry, her shoulders shuddering. Roby led her to the couch, placing a box of tissues beside her and returning to the kitchen to fix a cup of tea. Kate waited as he fussed over the woman. She wondered where Aaron had disappeared to. How had the family thought it appropriate to leave Elissa alone at home in this state?

'Have you… did you find her? Is that why you're here?' For a second, Elissa had managed to shrug away the fug enveloping her. She looked terrified of receiving an answer.

'No, Elissa. I'm sorry. We haven't found Sienna yet.'

Elissa's face fell with disappointment, but also, Kate noticed, a sliver of relief that she had been spared worse news. She sat down in the chair opposite.

'We're pursuing a number of leads and the public appeal will start bringing in information. Someone would have seen something. Your husband did well last night.' She reached out to clasp Elissa's hand in comfort, and felt her stiffen.

'Actually, Elissa, we're here to go through a couple of matters with you. To help clarify some things for us.' Kate waited a beat, making certain Elissa had heard her.

'When we spoke yesterday, you said you couldn't think of anyone who would want to hurt you or your family. What about Daniel's father, Elissa? Would Jason Veliu want to hurt you?' The mention of Veliu's name, without warning, was unfair. But Kate wanted to shock the woman out of her haze.

Elissa paled, what little blood remained in her face draining away. 'Don't mention his name,' she hissed. 'He... That was a long time ago.'

'Have you come into contact with Jason since you broke up? Has he tried to see Daniel or harass you in any way?'

She shook her head, adamant. 'He doesn't know where we live.'

'You're certain of that? You've never seen him hanging around? A strange car or a passer-by that you thought you recognised that could have been Veliu?'

'No. Never. Nothing like that.' She met Kate's eyes and looked away, doubt and fear competing within their depths.

'We know the type of man he is, Elissa,' Kate pressed on. 'What he's capable of. Your mum told me how he treated you and Daniel. He sounds like someone who would hold a grudge.'

'He's not Daniel's father.'

'I'm sorry?'

'Daniel is not Jason's son. There's no reason for him to come after us.' Elissa turned to Kate, her expression desperate. 'You don't believe me, but it's true. I never told Mum that Jason was Daniel's father. She just assumed it, like everyone else. Even Aaron. I just never corrected them.'

'Okay, so what about Daniel's biological father? Is he currently in the picture?' Impatience snapped at Kate, making her short with Elissa. So, Veliu had been telling the truth, after all.

A harsh, guttural sound, somewhere between a laugh and a sob, escaped Elissa. 'I don't know who Daniel's father is. There were so many...' The last words were barely audible.

A shudder of warning charged through Kate. Elissa was tearing at the seams and she had the power to stop it, to end this conversation. She could feel Roby's gaze on her, willing her to stop. But then what about the investigation? What about Sienna?

'Elissa, I know this is difficult. Who Daniel's father is, it's none of my business. We're not here to judge you or your past. The only reason I need the information is so we can eliminate people from the investigation. So we can find the person who took Sienna.'

'I didn't... You think I was sleeping around?'

'Elissa, it doesn't matter what I think—'

'Fuck you, you sanctimonious bitch! Do you really think I could do anything behind Jason's back even if I wanted to? He made me do it. To pay off a debt. An *agreement* that they had come to. I don't fucking know which one of them made Daniel. I wasn't keeping count. You want a list of suspects, go ask Jason!' Her words rang through the silent house.

'Elissa, I'm sorry. I didn't mean to cause you pain—'

'Get out! Get out! Get out! Go and find my daughter!' she screamed, flinging the cushions from the couch at Kate.

'What's going on? What's happening? Elissa, what's wrong?' Rayna Gardiner had emerged via the back door. Kate caught a glimpse of Daniel, pale and anxious behind his grandmother.

'It's okay, Elissa. I'm here now. It's okay.' Rayna had taken charge, striding over to the couch and enveloping her daughter in her arms. She stroked Elissa's hair and rocked her slowly.

Roby glanced over at Kate. 'It's okay, Sarge, I'll stay with them.'

She was being dismissed by a junior officer. Kate retreated, making for the open door. She took up Daniel's unresisting hand and led him outside, away from the house and the upsetting scene, into a sunny patch of lawn.

She glanced down at his drawn face, his hand a small, warm bundle in hers. Had he heard his mother's words? Had he understood? For his sake, she hoped not.

'Your mum's a bit upset, matey. This has all been really difficult for her.'

'I know.' A soft voice, sounding younger than she would have expected for his age. 'Have you found Sienna? Is that why you're here?'

'Not yet, buddy. But we're looking so hard.' The inadequacy of her words tore at her, but the boy accepted them without comment.

'Is Mummy still angry at me?'

'About what, matey?'

'I wanted to play with Sienna after school, but Mum didn't want me in her room. She said I mustn't wake her.'

Kate smiled, thinking of her own battles with Archie, trying to keep him from disturbing Amy.

'I'm sure she's not cross at you, Daniel. She's just really sad at the moment—'

'Daniel. Time to come in now.' Rayna was at the door, motioning her grandson inside.

He waved to his grandmother before turning to Kate, his expression tight. 'You're going to find Sienna, aren't you?'

'We're going to do our very best.'

He plucked his lip, sensing the ambiguity of her answer. 'Promise?' he asked, holding out his pinkie.

Kate ignored the sinking feeling that enveloped her and wrapped his finger with her own. 'I promise.'

13

Kate watched the minute hand tick 10.45 am on the wall clock. Her eyes were always drawn to the oversized time piece, a *Star Wars* Millennium Falcon silhouette. The only original object in the room, otherwise decorated entirely in psychologist-bland, non-descript upholstered furniture, charcoal carpet and off-white walls.

Fifteen minutes to get through before she was free to leave, her obligation to her husband met. Geoff had insisted on booking in an emergency session after last night's bath incident, even though she had been at pains to explain that it hadn't been what he thought it was. This was not like those first few days and weeks straight after her accident and Amy's birth, when self-condemnation and torment had squeezed her lungs and drowned out all reasonable thought. She had come so far since then, learning how to keep the panic at bay – most of the time, anyway. That period of her life felt like a fevered dream to her. Something she had moved on from. But Geoff had not forgotten. It was either this session or he would speak to Skinner.

She had fobbed Roby off with an excuse, getting him to drive her to the centre of town, a block away from where she needed to be, and had run-walked the rest of the way.

'I know you don't want to be here, Kate. You feel it's a step backwards. But this is not a linear path. You will need to manage this for the rest of your life. Whether it's me who supports you or someone else is a matter for you. But you're not going to get there alone.'

Kate turned back to meet the kind grey eyes of her interrogator.

Pip Hutton comforted her and irritated her in equal measure.

Kate knew it was her youth that she objected to the most and the clichéd expressions she often resorted to. The hackneyed phrases that sounded like they had been lifted from every therapist sitcom ever made. Pip was easy to dismiss, until she wasn't. Kate had found that out to her cost in previous sessions. There was a sharpness in there and deep compassion, behind all the stock phrases of her trade. Without warning, she could pierce Kate's defences, all of the carefully constructed scaffolding that she had erected to safely navigate the counselling sessions.

Pip's probing had at times made Kate open up more than she had intended, lulled into revealing her soft under-belly. Glimpses only, yet more than was safe. Geoff's growing dissatisfaction. Her own ever-present fear of losing her hardwon career. Her father's long shadow. Even her feelings towards Darryl Murchison. They had touched on it all. Always, she had tried to give enough to show that she was making progress but not enough to matter. Sometimes she succeeded. Sometimes, Pip surprised her.

The psychologist had helped her, it was true. But she was a means to an end. A gateway back to the police force, a hurdle which Kate had successfully scaled. She couldn't afford to falter now. She had to keep Pip happy and convinced that she was on top of things if she had any chance of getting on with her job.

She pasted a look of deep weariness onto her face. 'I told you already. Geoff made a mistake. I was holding my breath underwater. I wasn't trying to kill myself.'

Pip let her words sit in silence. But that trick didn't work on Kate. She was used to waiting out difficult suspects in interviews. A little quiet made no difference to her.

Pip broke first. 'Your husband is worried about you, Kate. You're leading the most high-profile case of your career under a media storm that's now become personal, all with a brand-new baby. That's a lot of pressure for anyone to carry, let alone someone who's been through what you have.'

Been through what she had. The reverberations of a gunshot that she couldn't escape, that broke into her consciousness at all hours, felling her with what could have been. Her job could have cost her everything – her family, her life – and yet it was what she ran to every single time. What did that say about her? Where was Pip on that particular pickle? Her fingers flexed, reaching for her abdomen to sooth the guilt. To the place where they had cut Amy out, an emergency caesarean on the night. At the flicker in Pip's eyes, she stilled her hands and wrested her attention to focus on the problem. She had to give Pip something. Something that didn't sound trite. She had to earn a pass mark so she could get back into the real world. To her real work.

'This case is important, Pip. It's not like anything else. There's a child involved. A baby. I was given a second chance. Now I get to do that for another family.'

The psychologist's face softened and contempt curdled within Kate at the woman's sentimentality. So, it would be as easy as that.

'There is no tab, Kate. There is nothing you can do to balance the scales of what could have happened. One day you'll have to learn to come to terms with that.'

–

'Does she know we're coming?'

'I called her this morning.' Roby gave her a quick sideways glance. 'Veliu's not with her. He's at home.'

Kate grunted, annoyed that Roby had so easily intuited what she had been thinking.

They were on their way to meet Lena Chalmers at her parents' home in the north-east of town, where the Veliu children were still being housed, though Lena herself had returned home at Jason's insistence. Kate understood from Child Protection Services that Veliu was yet to visit the kids.

In the outskirts of town, they pulled up outside a tidy fibro cottage elevated on struts against flooding and bordered on either side by unpruned plumbago hedges, grown wild. Timber slats covered the underside of the house like a valance.

Lena was waiting for them, sitting on the steps of the front porch with an older woman in sweatpants and jumper, presumably her mother. The baby lay on a rug in the grass surrounded by soft blocks and toys. Lena's eldest son, who only moments ago had been absorbed by his toy cars on the footpath, retreated to his mother's side on their arrival.

Walking up the driveway, Kate waved at the boy – she had been told his name was Charlie – but he hid behind

Lena's skirt without acknowledging her, their previous encounter still too fresh. The baby made a cackling, gurgling sound on his mat, drooling and sucking enthusiastically on his toes as they approached. His mother smiled and lightly tickled the bridge of his nose.

'It's good to see you, Lena. You're looking well.' It was true. Lena looked freshly scrubbed, adorned in a brightly coloured loose-flowing skirt and a close-fitting top, the long sleeves hiding the remnants of the ligature marks on her wrists. Her shoulder-length hair was brushed and shiny, and a lick of make-up had been applied to her face. Kate noticed the children were similarly well presented, bathed and in clean clothes.

Lena was clearly putting her best foot forward, doing everything she could to retain access to her kids. To her, Kate and Roby were the authorities and she needed to pass the test.

'What's this about? I don't have much time. Brayden will need a feed soon.' An act of bravado and indifference to hide her nerves, though Kate didn't miss the red-raw fingernails and apprehensive glance towards her mother. The older woman peered up at them through runny, soft-boiled eyes, making no move to speak.

'We won't keep you long, Lena. We just need to ask you a few questions to clarify a couple of things.' Kate nodded in the direction of Lena's mother without any luck. The woman was making a point of not acknowledging their presence.

Lena hesitated for a second and then nodded, bending down to speak softly in Charlie's ear. The boy shook his head fiercely, tightening his grip on his mother's skirt.

'It's okay, bud. Just stay with Grandma for a few minutes, okay? I won't be long.'

Releasing Charlie's hold of her skirt, she followed Kate and Roby back down the driveway to stand on the grass verge at the front of the property, out of hearing of her mother and son. She faced them, her arms crossed and ready.

'How are the kids doing?' Kate asked gently. 'They seem well.'

'The kids are fine. They're great. You don't have to worry about them. They like being at Mum's.'

'And how are you, Lena? Are you recovering okay?'

'I'm fine. Everything is fine. Like I said before. It was just sex, okay? I told you people already, I'm not testifying. Can we just drop it?'

'Lena, he had you handcuffed to the bedpost. You were unconscious and bleeding when we arrived. We got called in because your neighbour could hear screaming—'

'He's a bloody perve over there at number four,' Lena interrupted, her voice rising. 'You can't believe what he says. He watches the neighbours with binoculars. Did you know that? He's the one you should be arresting.'

'Lena, the point is you weren't in a good way when we arrived,' Roby cut in. 'The kids were alone and hungry. If your neighbour hadn't called us, anything could have happened to them.'

'No! You don't get it,' she said, facing him. 'It'd be worse for them if I don't do the things he wants. He's happier afterwards, all right? He's nicer to the kids and it's easier for everyone.'

'But what about the next time, Lena?' Roby asked. 'And the time after that? What if he really hurts you or the kids? Child Protection will keep getting involved. Again and again.'

Her face crumpled. 'No! I'm a good mum… You can't take them away from me. Please.'

'Nobody wants to take your kids away,' Kate intervened. 'But you know the only way you and the kids are going to be safe is if we put Jason away. You can't keep doing this, Lena,' she continued. 'He's not going to change. You may think you can keep adjusting your behaviour to satisfy him, but he'll just demand more. That's how he works. He'll grind you down until there's nothing left.'

Lena shook her head, trying to shut out Kate's words.

'Do you have money, Lena?'

She didn't reply and Kate didn't press her, guessing the truth.

'I can't go against him. I just can't.' It was a whisper wrenched out of her. When Lena looked up, her expression was desperate. 'It's not all the time. He's good with the kids most of the time. It's just the pressure of everything. He just needs a release, that's all. I can't just leave him.' Her voice was strained, trying to convince herself as much as the police officers.

Roby went to speak once more, but Kate stayed him with her hand.

'It's okay, Lena. You don't have to make a decision right now. But please think about what we've said, okay?'

The woman nodded, a small movement of indecision.

'Lena, we also need to ask you a couple of questions about Jason's movements over the last few days and we need you to really think about your answers, all right?'

Lena raised a questioning glance to Kate and Roby, wariness creeping into her eyes.

'Can you tell us if Jason was at home when you got back to the house on Friday after the hospital?'

'Yesterday? Why does it matter what happened yesterday?'

'Please, Lena. Just answer the question.'

'I took an Uber straight from the hospital to Mum's. I got here around ten-thirty, I think, and stayed here for most of the day. I only went home around two, I think. Jason was in bed and he wanted a sandwich, so I made it for him.'

'Did it look like he'd been out at all?'

'I don't know. He was in bed in his jocks like always. Look, what's this about?'

Kate ignored her and continued with her questions. 'What about Thursday, Lena? Before the police arrived at the house. Had Jason been at home all day with you? Did he stay the night?'

Lena stared at her, completely confused. 'No, he hadn't been at the house for a couple of nights. He takes off sometimes and doesn't tell me where he goes. He came home around eight o'clock in the morning while Charlie was having breakfast. And that's when… well, you know… he took me upstairs.'

'Thanks, Lena. You've been really helpful. Just one last thing. I'm sorry if this sounds impertinent, but do you know if Jason kept in touch with any of his past girlfriends? We are particularly interested in a woman called Elissa Ricci or Elissa Gardiner. Have you ever heard Jason speak about her?'

Lena stepped back like she'd been slapped. 'What the fuck? Isn't that the woman in the news? The one who lost her baby? I mean, how the hell do you do that?' A wail rose from the garden behind them and Lena turned towards the sound. 'Look, I've got to go. Brayden needs a feed.'

'Lena, you didn't answer the question. Has Jason ever spoken about Elissa? Do you know if he still keeps in contact with her?'

'I don't know. You'll have to ask him—'

'Lena, the baby needs you.' A loud shout from Lena's mother.

As if on cue, another sharp, irritable cry escaped the baby.

'Look, I need to go. I don't know anything about this. Just… just leave us alone, okay?'

They watched her run back towards her children and scoop the crying baby from the mat. Kate noticed the grandmother had made no attempt to comfort the baby, remaining impassive in her spot on the steps.

'Lena reminds me of my aunt. My mother's sister in Adelaide. She was with a bloke like that. Scared shitless of him but unable to get out.' Roby glanced at Kate and away again, answering her unspoken question.

'He got put away eventually, but not before he bashed her so hard she ended up with a permanent brain injury. She's on a disability pension now.'

14

'Sienna Ricci. Four months old and missing since approximately 9.00 am on Friday morning. So far, no signs of
disturbance or violence has been uncovered at the Ricci's
residence, and the dog squad has come up empty in their
searches of the surrounding bushland, meaning no indication of human remains or a dump site. We are proceeding
on the basis that Sienna is alive and that she was taken
by an external party, very likely someone known to the
family. We have an infant who is out there somewhere
and it's our job to bring her home.'

Back in the incident room, Kate surveyed the faces
of her assembled team, alert and hanging on her every
word, the atmosphere taut with anticipation. Kate felt the
power of it. Directing an investigation, a high that coursed
through her body like a drug.

'Jason Veliu has no alibi for Thursday morning when
Elissa Ricci thought she heard a prowler in the yard, or
for the abduction on Friday. We know he has a history
of violence and drug abuse. Those of you unaware of his
activities, make sure you familiarise yourself with his file
for the edited highlights. He has a past with Elissa and
she's terrified of him, just like his current partner, Lena
Chalmers is right now. Neither wants to risk speaking out
against Jason and we need to do that for them.'

A shiver ran through her as she clocked Skinner taking up the rear corner, unobtrusive and at the same time the most conspicuous of all. It was now more than twenty-four hours since Sienna had disappeared. He needed to see that Kate was on course. That they were close to a result.

'We need to check any available traffic and dashcam footage for Veliu's vehicle. If his car is caught anywhere near Elliot Pass, I want to know. We also need to chase up all his known associates. He must have palmed off Sienna to someone. My guess is he's biding his time before seeking money from the Riccis. We should keep track of the Riccis' accounts, too, make sure there are no discrepancies. Veliu's movements and his associates are our priority today. By this afternoon, I'd like us to be in a position to seek a warrant to search his house and put in a request for his phone records.'

Her body hummed with anticipation, knowing in her very core that she was on the right track. Veliu was within her grasp. She could feel it. She was going to get the smarmy bastard, whatever it took.

She turned to Constable Darnley standing by her side, awaiting his turn. 'Darnley, an update on where we're at?'

'Sarge.' Darnley looked down to consult his notes. 'We are chasing a number of leads from the information line. We've had reports of a sighting in Tweed Heads and Pottsville, but so far they've both been accounted for by local families. All the area hospitals have been alerted along with crisis centres, charities and GPs. Again, no reports of anyone bringing in infants fitting Sienna's description. Three child sex offenders registered as living within twenty kilometres of the property, have been interviewed and their whereabouts confirmed for the relevant times.

'…In addition, all interviews with neighbours within a kilometre of the Riccis' property are now complete. Unfortunately, no one's reported seeing anything suspicious either on the day of the abduction or of the prowler incident. So far, there've been no sightings of Aaron Ricci's car at or around those times on either day. In terms of the search teams, we've got officers from Tweed Heads and more volunteers from SES joining the search again today. Apart from the soft toy found yesterday, they have no further updates.'

The door swung open noiselessly and Kate noticed Josh enter the room followed by Constable Vickie Harris. It irritated her that he couldn't be bothered making it to the briefing on time. She watched him whisper something into Harris's ear, wondering what job he had got her doing for him.

She forced her attention towards Darnley, feeling childishly peeved that Josh had entered just when Darnley was listing all the investigative threads that had yet to pan out.

'Thanks, Darnley. Anything new from forensics?'

'They're still running the fingerprints lifted from the house. So far, nothing that shouldn't be there. And as you mentioned, Sarge, no blood residue or signs of violence. A preliminary report should come through this afternoon.'

'Thanks, Darnley. Okay, everybody, that's it for now. You know what to do.' She dismissed the crowd.

'Actually, Kate, I've got some additional information on Aaron Ricci that I think you would be interested in. May prove more important than Veliu.' The officers who had been in the process of dispersing stopped, their gazes wavering from Josh to Kate.

Kate frowned. Trust Josh to bring up the information at the last minute to make the biggest splash. She kept her gaze firmly on him, resisting the urge to clock Skinner's reaction.

'Let's hear it, then.'

'Constable Harris and I were going through the traffic records last night looking for any signs of Ricci's car.'

Kate glanced at Vickie, who refused to make eye contact. 'The traffic footage around Elliot Pass has already been reviewed,' she countered. They had been through this. 'There was no sighting of Ricci's vehicle.'

'That's true, but we followed up on the highway footage and it shows a different story. Ricci's version is that he's been at a conference in Broadbeach since Wednesday. That he only drove home on Friday – yesterday – after the morning session, getting to Esserton just before midday.' He paused for effect, smiling, knowing that he had the entire room's attention.

Kate felt herself itching to slap the self-satisfied smile from his face. 'And?'

'And… There's no highway footage of his car travelling towards Esserton anytime on Friday morning. But then we come to Thursday. That night, we've got his car heading south and taking the Tweed Valley Way turnoff at 7.42 pm and then the Esserton exit at 8.06 pm. We have no record of him heading back up north to Broadbeach later that evening or anytime on Friday. That means he was lying about where he was and he's right in the frame for the abduction yesterday morning.'

'Hang on,' Kate persisted, not ready to concede. 'Are we sure it was him using the car? Could he have lent the vehicle to someone? I thought we checked on Ricci's conference attendance with the venue? Darnley?'

'I did, Sarge,' replied Darnley, 'but like I indicated in my report, the sign-in procedures are fairly rudimentary. There are sign-in sheets for each session and his initials are on Friday morning's session. Who did the actual initialling is another question. I spoke to a number of conference attendees and a few thought they'd seen him around on Friday morning. But he was the only person attending from his firm, and not sure how many of the others really knew him by sight. They could have easily got the days mixed up.'

Shit! She had missed that completely. She was yet to read Darnley's report. There were so many things sitting on her desk, awaiting her review.

'It's not only the traffic footage,' Josh continued, unperturbed. 'I also put in a request yesterday to the phone tech company for Ricci's mobile location data to build a timeline. The info just came through.' A glance towards Skinner. The request had clearly received priority. Josh held up a series of printouts, his expression trying but failing to mask his triumph. 'His last recorded phone GPS location is Broadbeach on Thursday evening at around 6.47 pm. After that, there's nothing until just before midday on Friday when his mobile places him at Leigh Road in South Esserton at 11.48 am. He's clearly switched off his location services, or likely turned off his phone entirely.'

'It's reflected in his call records as well,' Josh went on, referring to his notes and plainly relishing the opportunity to display his thoroughness. 'Nothing to and from his phone during that period. The last activity on his mobile is a four-minute call to Elissa on Thursday evening at 6.38 pm. Then radio silence until 11.51 am on Friday, when Ricci calls his messaging service. According to Elissa, she tried ringing Aaron on Friday morning just after Sienna disappeared, but she couldn't get onto him. The messages went to voicemail. Our attempts to contact him also went straight to his message bank, until Aaron finally answered his phone at 11.56 am on Friday, and then he fed us a story about having just arrived in Esserton, after driving back from the conference. I call bullshit.'

A buzzing sound had started to envelop Kate's ears, heat crawling under her skin. She forced herself to address Josh. 'Anything else?'

He held her gaze, disdain snapping in his eyes like a whip. 'Well, the Leigh Road location is interesting, don't you think? That's where his phone places him on Friday, and it's just south of town, maybe ten or twelve minutes from Elliot Pass. I'd say that's a pretty curious fact.' Without waiting for a response, his eyes moved to take in the gathered team, and Skinner, his real audience.

'I strongly believe there's a second mobile he's not telling us about. We received permission from Mrs Ricci yesterday to access their financial records. They hold a joint account, but according to Elissa, Aaron is the one who takes care of the bills. I thought it was worth checking their statements to see if any transactions pointed to the purchase of a second phone.' He paused, knowing he had the entire room hooked.

'I think we've got something. A purchase from an Optus store, about seven months ago. Harris will chase the records. If Ricci bought a SIM package at the same time as the phone, then we've got a mobile number and we can pull call records and contact details from the service provider. We'll know who he's been communicating with.'

His words hung in the air, their significance clear to every police officer present.

The sheer volume of information was irrefutable. All of which Kate had missed with her single-minded pursuit of Veliu. While she had gone home on Friday night, Josh and Constable Harris had stayed on and done the leg work. She could feel Skinner's eyes boring into her.

She nodded to Josh. 'We need to speak to Ricci. Bring him in.'

Kate scrambled out of the door and into the rear carpark, almost falling in her haste to get out. Heat swarmed underneath her skin, her breath coming in short, panicky spurts. The effort of maintaining control until she had escaped the incident room making her weak with anxiety. She had to get away. Away from the questions, the averted knowing expressions, the doubt she saw written in all their faces.

The air felt raw and chilled her sweat-bathed skin. The sky was crisp and diamond-sharp, streaked with fine cloud lines that filtered in light but little warmth. She leaned against the station wall, her hands clammy on the rough brick exterior, breathing deeply, fighting for composure. She squeezed her fists, concentrating on calming her mind, on slowing her breathing.

'You all right there?'

She looked up and panic flared. Richard Markham had materialised out of nowhere and was staring at her. She could feel him taking note of every shortened breath and goosepimple, every sweat stain and tremor. *Jesus*, that was all she needed, an article detailing her mental health difficulties, witnessed first-hand. That would be the final blow.

She wiped her face. 'I'm fine. Just needed some air.' She turned away, buying time, trying to still her shaking hands.

'You look like you need a drink. I've got some water here if you want it.'

'I told you I'm fine. What are you doing here, anyway? There's no scheduled briefing today.'

'Actually, I was hoping to find you, Detective. I wanted to get your comment on a separate matter to the Sienna Ricci case… But maybe I've caught you at a bad time.'

She closed her eyes, concentrating on her own pain and willing the man to disappear. *A separate matter.* How diplomatic. Like she didn't know exactly which mud he wanted to shovel.

The silence lengthened and she wondered what he was waiting for. Painting a proper mental picture, no doubt, getting all the details down perfectly. She felt the tension grow to breaking point within her.

Her eyes snapped open and she found herself completely alone. A solitary magpie fluted at her from an adjacent tree. She looked down to find an unopened bottle of water placed carefully at her feet.

15

There was no point in dwelling on the failure. Yes, Josh had scored a win. But it was a single battle, not the war. Kate needed to produce something from her end. Something just as compelling. It wasn't about showing Josh up. It was about regaining the respect of her team. To show them that she was willing to put in the same amount of work as she expected of them. To feel that they could trust her judgement.

Ensconced in the rear interview room that she now considered her own ad-hoc office, breast pump in hand, Kate pulled up Lena Chalmers' history on her laptop. Searching the police database, she brought up the all-too-familiar catalogue of DV call-outs over five years, spanning multiple police districts up and down the north coast. Veliu obviously liked to move around, dragging his family with him, ensuring that Lena never got too settled in any one place, put down roots or created connections. Kate recognised the depressing pattern of incident-based policing with limited follow-up or connecting the dots to build an overall picture of systematic abuse.

It made for sobering reading. Snapshots of suffering that spilled through, despite the orderly veneer and brevity of formal police language. *Old bruising was observed across the victim's arms and upper torso. The victim was found unconscious on the dining-room floor, sporting contusions to the left side of her face and head. An infant (male, eighteen months) was discovered in the backyard, alone and in distress in soiled clothes. Multiple holes were observed in the walls of the house where the plasterboard had been broken through by the assailant's fists. The victim refused medical attention. The victim refused to make a statement. The victim states that her injuries were sustained as a result of a fall.*

Since returning to live in Esserton some eight months prior, Veliu's household had already clocked up several police call-outs, including Kate's encounter with the family two days ago. And they were the matters that got reported. Who knew what Lena put up with behind closed doors? Kate noticed that in each case, Lena had refused to pursue the matter, deflecting responsibility away from Veliu wherever she could. Kate knew it was a pattern of behaviour that reinforced the most ingrained beliefs within the police force. *You can't help someone who doesn't want to be helped.* The well-worn maxim that she had heard a hundred times before; both a genuine expression of frustration and an excuse to look away.

The older DV records that Kate had managed to pull up for Elissa Ricci – then Elissa Gardiner – from a decade ago, showed a similar nascent pattern of control. The records were scarcer. Kate had only managed to unearth two incidents. Either Veliu had shown more restraint or Elissa had been willing to put up with a lot more in silence. Neither incident had led to any charges being laid, Elissa having refused to implicate Veliu in any way. The power that Veliu held over these women appeared inviolate.

It was all down to fear. If she could just convince Lena that this time they had a fighting chance. Proving a connection between Veliu and Sienna Ricci would change everything. It would send Jason away for good, not just through a revolving door of magistrate appearances. Lena would be free of Veliu without needing to battle through Family Court or risk losing custody of her kids; better than an uncertain future lived behind the toothless tiger of an apprehended violence order, constantly watching her back.

Studying the details of a couple of the most recent call-outs to Veliu's address, Kate noticed that the calls to triple zero had been made by Lena herself. She was getting braver. She just needed to be shown an avenue for escape.

Another name also stood out: Frank Stanton, who had called in several times complaining about the noise from Jason and Lena's. She recalled a sharp set of eyes behind dirty spectacles, a weather-worn face and stooped body. Veliu's neighbour, who had rung in the incident that Kate had attended. Lena had called him a perve, someone who watched the neighbours with binoculars.

Finishing up with the pump and collecting her things, Kate made for the staff kitchenette. After storing her milk-filled cooler pouch in a corner of the fridge away from the officers' various packed lunches, she headed out to her car. In less than fifteen minutes, she had arrived at her destination. Her mobile rang as she pulled into the kerb.

Josh's voice came through the handsfree, overloud and full of feedback. 'We can't find Ricci.'

'What do you mean?' she asked, distracted, her hands searching for the dial to turn down the volume.

'I mean he's not at the house. Elissa and her mother have no idea where he is. I reckon he's done a runner.'

'How long has he been away?'

'According to Elissa, he left the house this morning around eight. Hasn't called or been seen since.'

Kate recalled that Ricci's car had not been at the house when she and Roby had visited Elissa earlier. 'Okay, let's not get ahead of ourselves. He could be anywhere; at the pub or with a mate. Have we tried any of his contacts?'

'Elissa gave us a list of names, which we're following up now.' The suppressed annoyance in his voice was clear; she didn't need to tell him how to do his job. 'Apparently, he has no family nearby. According to Elissa, his closest relatives live down the south coast almost at the Victorian border.'

At the opposite end of the state, Kate noted. She heard a muffled voice through the speaker saying something to Josh. Of course, he had said *we*. Harris was there with him.

'How did Vickie go with the second mobile?'

'We just got confirmation from the Optus store. Ricci definitely bought a pre-paid phone and SIM pack back in January, just a basic flip phone. No internet. It's been activated. So, we have a number to chase up with the provider. The details should be in your inbox. I emailed it through a few minutes ago.'

'I'm not at the station.' She ignored the loaded silence that greeted her statement. 'Can you put the request through for the call records when you return? Call me as soon as you have something. That was good work, by the way. Well done—'

Josh grunted and hung up, cutting off her final words. They fell flat, sinking unheard inside the overheated confines of her car.

Exiting the vehicle, she shook away the feeling that she was once again on the wrong side of the case. Three in the afternoon and it felt closer to dusk. The skies had closed in, sapping light from the day, and the wind had picked up, blowing frigid drafts of air that went right through her. She shrugged on her jacket.

Number four Ryder Close comprised a brick bungalow set within an unfenced corner block at the junction of Denman Drive. A single gum tree stooped in the lawn, surrounded by grass mowed to surgical precision, sloping down to the kerb. Kate noted that the house sat up on a slight rise with prime views of the properties on both adjoining streets. She took in the wide bay window at the head of the house geared for exactly that. Three doors down to her left on Denman Drive, she could make out a section of Veliu's rental, partially shielded by shrubbery.

She saw movement at the window as she walked up the neatly brushed path. The front door opened without her having to knock.

Frank Stanton stood at the doorway barring entry, as if she intended to force her way inside. He wore a version of the same jumper and sagging tracksuit pants that he had on a couple of days ago, clearly a uniform of sorts. The difference between his personal attire and the military precision of the yard was striking. She wondered if he got help around the house and with the garden. The eyes that met hers held the same look of distrust coupled with distaste that she recalled from their earlier meeting. Warm, stale air, cat piss laced with body odour, seeped through the open doorway.

'Mr Stanton. It's Frank Stanton, isn't it? We met on Thursday when the police responded to the domestic disturbance at number thirty-three.'

'No one's Australian anymore. Even the GP at the bloody medical centre is Chinese.'

She ignored the jibe and continued. 'I'm Detective Kate Miles, Mr Stanton. I believe you called in the incident on Thursday? I was wondering if I could ask you a few follow-up questions?' She held up her ID for inspection.

'Kate, is it? Is that your real name or one of those put-on names because no one can pronounce your real one?'

She suppressed a sudden urge to laugh. 'It is my real name, Mr Stanton,' she replied, maintaining a straight face. She had been named after the women in her family: Kathryn, her grandmother from her dad's side, and Aneesha, her middle name, a permanent connection to her mother.

He stared at her for a long moment. 'I knew a Kate once. Went to school with her. Runt of a thing. She died of pneumonia in third form.' When Kate made no response, he went on. 'I see he's back.' He motioned towards Denman Drive. 'No point in my speaking to you people, if you keep letting him go.'

'We're working on that, Mr Stanton. That's why I'm here. I'm hoping you can clarify a few things regarding the family, based on what you may have observed.'

'She's worse than useless, that girlfriend of his. She calls herself a mother. That boy's left to his own devices more often than not, while she's inside with him doing God knows what. The kids would be better off without either of them, I'll tell you that for nothing.'

A bite of anger whipped through her, but she managed to control herself. There was no point getting into an argument with the man. He was set in his thinking, and nothing she could say would shift his views. She didn't need to defend Lena to this man. She just needed to extract what information he may have on Jason.

She tried again. 'Mr Stanton, we're interested in Veliu's whereabouts. Did you happen to notice if Jason was at his house on Friday morning? Did he go out for any period of time that you saw?'

'How the hell should I know? I'm not their bloody security guard, am I?'

'I understand that, Mr Stanton. It's something we'll be checking with all your neighbours. I've come to you because I know how much you care for those boys. How diligent you've been with calling in any incident, to make sure those kids are protected. You're observant and you notice things. That's why I came to you first.'

There was a momentary pause, indecision playing on his face. An internal battle was clearly raging: his instinctive reluctance to help someone of her ilk versus his own sense of self-importance.

'He never came home on Thursday night after you lot arrested him. For a second, I thought you might have finally put him away. But then I saw him driving back yesterday. Just after midday, it was.'

And there it was, confirmation of her suspicions. 'Are you sure about those times, Mr Stanton? Are you sure that he was definitely not at the house for all that time?'

'I just said that, didn't I?' he sneered at her. 'I don't sleep very well, all right? At my age, I'm lucky to get a couple of hours straight. When I can't sleep, I come out here.' He gestured behind him. 'I sit in the front room and watch the street. There's always something going on if you're willing to wait.' He pointed to the eucalyptus in the yard. 'There are two possums that live on that tree and a couple of owls that visit most nights. If I get bored, I can put the telly on.'

He pointed his finger at her emphatically. 'I know what I saw. He hadn't come home by the time I went to bed on Thursday night. Around eleven is when I normally turn in. I managed a few hours before coming back out around three in the morning. And then I sat up until dawn. I can tell you, their house stayed silent and dark all that time and there were no signs of life in the morning, either. I was at the mailbox getting my post, when I saw him drive in. The dickhead hooted at me and waved.'

That sounded like Veliu. He wouldn't have been able to help himself, making a point to the busybody who had called in the police.

'And you're sure it was him?'

He clicked his mouth with impatience at her apparent obtuseness. 'Of course it was him. I'm not likely to miss that bloody great Ford Ranger, am I?' He muttered something under his breath about stupid bloody women.

Kate held her temper and thanked him sincerely before leaving. She felt his eyes follow her until she had left his property and climbed into her car. Only then did she see his door close.

She smiled. He might be a racist and a chauvinist, but he had come up with the goods as a witness. Tomorrow, she'd get an officer – preferably male and white – to follow up with Mr Stanton and obtain a formal statement. But for now, she had enough to bring Veliu in. He had lied about his whereabouts and this time she wouldn't fumble her chance. She needed to check with Roby where they were up to with the CCTV searches. If Veliu's four-wheel drive had been snapped up somewhere near Elliot Pass, it would be the smoking gun.

She grabbed her phone, clocking the multiple missed calls on screen. *Fuck.* She dialled the station number, and it was picked up within seconds.

'Sarge, where are you? We've been trying to contact you.' Roby sounded subdued, like he was trying to keep his voice down. Kate could hear people in the background.

'Sorry, had the phone on silent. Listen, Roby, where are we with the CCTV? Did you find any matches on Veliu's Ranger?'

'I haven't had a chance, Sarge. We've been focusing on trying to find Aaron Ricci.' He ploughed through her grunt of frustration. 'Sarge, the inspector's been looking for you—'

There was a pause and she heard a scuffle of voices before a new voice came through the line: Skinner, pissed off.

'Where the fuck are you, Miles? Ricci's done a runner and I just had the Gardiner woman on the phone throwing a bloody tantrum.'

'Sir, I'm at Denman Drive interviewing one of Veliu's neighbours. He confirmed that Jason definitely wasn't home at the time of the abduction. That means he was lying and he's right back in the picture for Sienna. I want to bring him in again.'

'What neighbour?'

'A Frank Stanton. He's a pensioner and lives three doors down. According to Mr Stanton, Jason never came home after he made bail on Thursday evening. He didn't come home until after midday on Friday, though he said he was home the whole of Friday morning.'

'Have we confirmed if he could have been somewhere else?'

'No, we'll need to check that—'

'Anything on CCTV or traffic cameras that places him near Elliot Pass?'

'Not yet, sir. I've got Roby checking.'

'So, we have nothing but the word of one pensioner. And what, he stayed up all night did he, so he could stake out when Veliu drove in and out of his property?'

Kate gritted her teeth. 'Sir, Stanton's old, but I think he's a reliable witness. Veliu's story is a mess. He's got form and he's got a motive. We need to bring him in.'

'What bloody motive? There hasn't been any demands for money made to the Riccis. I agree, he's a sick fuck. But you are not taking him on again, unless you have something more solid than the word of one bloody neighbour. I'm not having the same debacle as last time. Ricci's our focus. Get back here and help find the man.'

The phone went dead and she stared at the screen. *The same debacle as last time.* Skinner's words buzzed in her ear like blowflies on a carcass. Of course he wasn't going to let her forget her previous run-in with Veliu that easily.

She turned on the ignition and made her way slowly onto Denman Drive. Passing number thirty-three, she glanced at the house automatically, wondering if Lena was at home. She caught movement from the corner of her eye and instinctively applied the brakes, an expletive rising from her lips.

16

'You should see the other guy.'

The joke fell flat. Aaron Ricci's wan smile was a grimace behind his mangled face. One of his eyes was swollen shut, his nose reduced to a bloody pulp. The entire right side of his face had ballooned into a grotesque approximation of his features. A paramedic was by his side, probing the damage.

Even as Kate kneeled beside him, she could smell the bundy fumes issuing from him like a haze. Courage from a can.

'Aaron, this was not a good idea.'

'I had to do something,' he mumbled. 'Look at him. He just gets to live his life after everything he's done. You know, he's the reason Elissa can't function, right? She can't even fucking look at me...' His voice broke and he swatted away the paramedic's hand.

'Mate, you have to sit still so I can examine you.'

'I just wanted to smash him. Pummel his fucking head into the wall and watch it splatter. He's taken everything from us. He's taken Sienna. God, he's taken Sienna.' He tried to scramble to his feet and Kate helped the ambulance officer to hold him down.

'Aaron, you need to calm down, all right? You're in enough trouble as it is.'

Once she was certain that Aaron was in hand, the fight deflating out of him almost as soon as it had begun, Kate glanced over to where Veliu was being sequestered in a separate corner of the garden, chaperoned by a couple of officers. He looked untouched, sporting an afterglow and sweat sheen like he had just finished a particularly good gym session, Ricci's attempt at violence having hardly left a mark. Veliu was hyped and shirtless, unheeding of the cold, and enjoying the attention of a female paramedic, flirting and play sparring. Across his bare back, an inked tiger sprang in mid-pounce, pulsating with each of Veliu's movements, its body coiled and glistening. Jason caught her staring and winked.

It seemed that Kate had arrived just in time. She had managed to pull the men apart but not before Veliu had made a point with his fists. He had been brutal and efficient, making light work of Ricci's compact frame and non-existent defence skills. Ricci had been cowering on the footpath – a discarded cricket bat lying useless in a nearby flowerbed – when Kate had run into the yard, shouting at Veliu to stop. She placed a cautious hand to her cheek, gingerly moving her mouth and feeling a dull pain radiate along her jawline. She had taken a glancing blow off Ricci as he had attempted a final retaliatory swing against Veliu, only succeeding in hitting his rescuer.

Lena, she noticed, stood hunched beside Veliu, in her husband's shadow. She assumed Lena had been inside the house the whole time but had only emerged when the noise of the police and ambulance vehicles had become too obvious to ignore. She watched as Lena's gaze skipped over her, refusing to acknowledge her presence.

Evening had fallen quickly and the media had arrived, establishing a cordon of light along the front of the property, illuminating the gathered first responders and rubberneckers. She thought she recognised the stooped silhouette of Mr Stanton leaning into a microphone held aloft by a reporter, the camera's glare highlighting each aging fold of his face.

'Is he right to be questioned?' Josh's voice was impatient. He had arrived quickly, this time without Harris in tow. He accosted the paramedic who was helping Aaron towards the waiting ambulance parked in the driveway.

'We need to take him in, mate. You've seen his face. He's probably got a couple of broken ribs as well.'

'Five minutes,' Josh persisted.

The paramedic relented and Kate joined Josh at the open ambulance doors. Inside, Aaron Ricci was being strapped upright into the stretcher.

'He's groggy,' the paramedic warned, moving aside to allow them access.

'I know I shouldn't have. But Rayna told me what Veliu did to Elissa and I just saw red.' Ricci's voice was muffled like he was speaking through a mouthful of marbles. A strangled laugh escaped him. 'Fat lot of good it did me.' He hesitated, clearly struggling to voice the next words. 'Have you arrested him? Has he told you where he's holding Sienna?'

'We're still pursuing all leads, Mr Ricci.' Josh's face gave nothing away. 'We'll be looking into Mr Veliu's involvement in detail. But at the moment, we're also interested in confirming your own movements.'

A spasm quivered across Aaron's face. Was it fear or pain from his injuries? 'What do you mean?'

'We know you weren't at the conference yesterday, Mr Ricci. We know you drove back to Esserton on Thursday night. Are you sure you've told us everything? About where you were? Where Sienna is?'

His undamaged left eye, which had escaped Veliu's ministrations, widened in shock. 'What? What are you talking about? The bastard's right there. He's right outside. Just arrest him. He's the one who's taken her. You're not seriously wasting time on me, are you?' He was getting agitated, his voice rising and his arms starting to swing.

'Mr Ricci, you need to calm down.' The paramedic was at Ricci's side again, shouldering past Josh.

'Where is she, Aaron? Your daughter needs her mother. Isn't it time you dropped the act and told us the truth?' Josh was pushing too hard.

'Josh—' Kate's rebuke fell flat.

'Fuck you, you bastard,' Ricci spat.

'Right, that's it. You're done. We're leaving.' The paramedic pushed Josh bodily out of the way and pulled shut the ambulance doors.

Josh shrugged off Kate's restraining hand. 'All right. I said all right.'

Cameras clicked and she heard the raucous laughter of Veliu in the background.

–

Kate waited by her vehicle as Josh directed the remaining officers and handled the media. Sometime during the evening, the balance of power between them seemed to have tipped even further in his favour. She fought the feeling of rising panic, of scrabbling within quicksand. She was being sidelined and she felt powerless to prevent it.

Veliu was insisting on pursuing charges. Though he had suffered not a scratch in the skirmish, Ricci's intent upon entering Veliu's property, bat in hand, was undeniable. It was all a laugh for Veliu, something to complete Ricci's humiliation. Kate had willed herself to not react as he'd mouthed words about defending himself and being in fear for his safety. He hadn't bothered to hide how much he was enjoying himself.

The situation was playing into Josh's hands. Ricci would be arrested and held for questioning. His car had been impounded for forensic testing. So far, the initial search of the vehicle had not uncovered the elusive second mobile. Kate had called Elissa to inform her of her husband's whereabouts, though she doubted that the substance of the phone call had sunk in. Aaron Ricci would be helping the police with their enquiries: that blandest of statements that said everything and nothing at all.

Josh was with her at last. An uncomfortable silence expanded between them as he concentrated on his mobile without looking at her. She took in his aloof form, the tension apparent in the tightness of his jawline. It occurred to her that he was under as much pressure to deliver a result as she was.

Since returning to work, they had been on opposing teams. Pitted against each other by circumstance. No doubt he thought she was being shown preferential treatment by Skinner, fast-tracked into leading an investigation when she wasn't ready. It was clear that he believed himself better equipped to run the case. To handle the pressure. She could see how it looked from Josh's standpoint. She had returned to work within months of an almost life-ending firearms incident, and with the responsibilities of a new baby on top of everything else. To Josh, she was a liability. But he didn't see the work she had put into getting here, how much it had cost her, how much it was still costing her. How many strings and provisos and conditions were attached to every small victory. How she had to prove herself, repeatedly, just to maintain a place at the table. He was right, it wasn't fair.

'You okay to bring him in?'

Kate chewed the inside of her cheek, controlling the urge to snap at him. 'I think I can manage driving between the hospital and the station, yeah.'

He looked up. 'I meant the press will be there.'

'It's fine. I'll call you from the hospital if there's a problem.'

He hesitated, about to say something, but seemed to think better of it. Instead, he motioned to his phone. 'Harris just messaged about the request to the mobile carrier. We should have the call records shortly. Latest by the morning.'

Kate didn't reply. She had no equivalent message from the constable. Josh and Harris seemed to have established their own lines of communication. She waited to see if there was anything else before turning away. She opened the car door, impatient to be gone. As she started the engine, she heard him call out something and wound down the window.

'I just wanted to ask how Gray's doing. You know, with everything…' his words trailed off. She could tell it was an apology of sorts. A downing of weapons.

She had wondered when he would ask. After all, Josh had met her father numerous times. She had thought them on good terms. His deliberate silence on the subject had been another sore point festering between them, unacknowledged and ignored.

'He's gone to ground. Not answering my calls.'

'What about Luke? Can he try?'

Kate grimaced, her attention abruptly diverted to the other complicating factor in her life. Her brother enjoyed an even more dysfunctional relationship with her father than she did. Kate had always been the conduit between Luke and Gray, and she had no doubt that Luke had made no attempts to contact Gray. It was up to her, as it always would be.

'How are you holding up, though? I saw that bloke from the *Leader* at the station again today.'

She froze, suddenly wanting nothing more than for the conversation to end. She had no wish to dwell on Richard Markham. She was still on tenterhooks, expecting their encounter from that afternoon to be written up in the paper.

'Yeah, I saw him around, but we didn't speak.'

'It'll pass, you know. They'll find something else to write about. Fuck, who gives a shit what they did in their private lives. They're both consenting adults, aren't they? And they call *us* pigs.' He shook his head in disbelief.

She half smiled and began pulling away from the kerb. Josh meant well, but how quickly would his views turn if he had an inkling of the whole story. If only Gray's involvement had stopped at sex. She had no illusions about how quickly her father's legacy would crumble and her reputation by association. The police would turn on them in an instant, eager to cut off a limb to save the whole.

The weight of her father's shadow trembled above her. She would need to make a decision soon. Find a way to come up with that bloody money.

17

Kate nodded at the duty nurse and slumped against the hard plastic chair, a takeaway coffee in her hand. The waiting room of the emergency ward with its near-constant chorus of the sick and injured hummed around her. She sipped through the slit in the takeaway lid and instantly regretted it as the molten liquid bled across her tongue, a blister blossoming immediately. She set the cup aside and squeezed her eyes, feeling equally drained and anxious.

It was getting close to thirty-four hours since Sienna had gone missing and she felt the walls closing in. The spectre of failure – of never finding the baby – something which she had never seriously contemplated, felt like a real possibility. She had let the case unravel. Lost control of its direction. What if Skinner was wrong? Even now, the trail that led from Veliu to Sienna was running cold. His movements at the time of the abduction were just as unaccounted for as Ricci's. They should be looking into both men, not picking and choosing. And yet, Skinner had reined her in. She hadn't been able to convince him. A wave of guilt rolled through her. Her fingers hovered over her phone screen and dialled the number for home. The call was picked up after a dozen rings. She heard the clutter of the receiver and the sound of a mouth breathing. No words.

'Hey, buddy.' Kate guessed it was Archie. Geoff had to be busy with Amy. She felt an irrational stab of relief that she wouldn't have to explain herself to her husband.

'Mummy! There's no ice-cream in the fridge. Can you bring home cookies and cream or chocolate? Please. Please. Please.'

'Matey, I'm going to be late home tonight. I can definitely pick up the ice-cream, but it won't be for tonight, okay? How about you have double helpings tomorrow?' she tried to head off his disappointment.

'Ohhhhhhh.'

'Hey, you know what? I think there may be some of the chocolate biscuits that Grandpa brought over still in the pantry. Maybe you can have that for a treat tonight, instead?'

'Yay, yay, yay!'

'Hang on, bub, before you go—' But she was too late. The receiver had been abandoned and he was off.

She hung up and sent a text to Geoff.

Her eyes scanned the waiting room, searching for a distraction, alighting on the wall-mounted TV, which had its volume off and was flickering silent moving pictures from a news broadcast. With a jolt, she realised that she recognised the dark-haired woman, prematurely faded and stretched into early middle age, mouthing soundless words onto camera. Lesley Freeman née Jackson. Kate hadn't seen or spoken to her childhood friend in years and marvelled at the changes racked by time. As she continued to watch, she thought she could still trace the original lines of the girl she had once known. The footage changed to show Lesley escaping from the cameras in a black BMW.

Kate was surprised by the ache of loss that still cut through her. After all these years, she should have got over it by now. Lesley Jackson at sixteen – black-clad and glamorous in chunky jewellery, a cigarette balanced on her red-streaked lips – supremely confident. She had been Kate's idol, growing up. Until, of course, her father and Martin had changed everything.

The familiar anger coursed through her, slick and oily. Every time she thought she had no more emotion to expend on her family, she seemed to find an untapped vein of vitriol to breach.

'Detective Miles? He's ready for you.'

A nurse stood behind a wheelchair, where Aaron Ricci sat bandaged and stitched up, a pile of discharge papers and what looked like prescription painkillers on his lap. Ricci's face, what little she could distinguish, was stony and he refused to look at her. Kate nodded to the nurse as Ricci rose gingerly, declining any assistance.

The registrar Kate had spoken to earlier had confirmed that Ricci's encounter with Veliu had earned him two broken ribs, a hairline fracture to his right cheekbone, severe facial bruising and mild concussion. In his opinion, Ricci would be in pain once the medication wore off in a few hours but was able to be questioned, which was all that concerned Kate.

She led him towards the hospital exit in silence.

–

'This is a waste of time. You should be helping our family, not arresting me.'

Aaron Ricci looked exhausted. It was past 8 pm and Kate could see the first signs of pain pinching the sides of his face, though he made no complaint. His skin looked grey under the interview-room lights. He leaned against the thinly padded couch, trying to find a more comfortable position. The interview was being conducted in the station's family room as a concession to Ricci's injuries.

'Mr Ricci. We're here because your movements are unexplained during the same period that your daughter went missing. We have traffic footage which shows that you drove back to Esserton on Thursday evening, even though you were meant to be at your conference. So, where were you, Aaron? Where were you when your daughter went missing?'

Josh was unrelenting and insistent. They had been at it for more than an hour. The same questions being asked over and over without result. So far, Aaron had remained impassive, refusing to answer anything directly, but fatigue was setting in and his resolve appeared to be waning in the face of Josh's persistence.

'You're not listening. I'm not the one you should be hassling. It's that bastard Veliu that you should be going after.'

'So you say, Mr Ricci, and yet you're the one who's not answering our queries.'

'I didn't take my daughter, Detective. That's all there is to it. *I* didn't touch her.' Aaron's voice was pleading and Kate didn't miss the emphasis on the pronoun. Did that mean he knew the person who had and was protecting them?

'Mr Ricci, you can keep avoiding the question and I'll just keep asking,' Josh pressed on, undeterred. 'We all want to get out of here, just as much as you do. Just tell us where you were and we can all move on.'

Aaron clasped his head in frustration. 'I went for a drive on Thursday night, all right. I don't like being cooped up, so I just drove for a few hours and then went back to the motel. I was at the conference on Friday, like I said.'

Kate shared the slightest of glances with Josh. And there it was. The crack in the dam they had been waiting for.

'So, you drove all the way to Esserton and then drove all the way back?' Kate's tone was mild, but her disbelief was clear. 'Did you think to drop in on Elissa or the kids while you were here?'

Aaron blinked. 'No, I… I didn't want to disturb them. I knew Elissa would be tired and it would be the kids' bedtime… Anyway, I'd called her earlier to check on them…' he trailed off.

'Oh that's right, I forgot about your four-minute phone call to Elissa. Well, that certainly explains it.' Kate allowed the seconds to stretch to let the deficiency of his words to linger.

'The thing is, mate,' Josh took over smoothly from Kate. 'We've checked the highway traffic footage from Thursday night and from Friday morning and we couldn't find any record of your car returning to Broadbeach. Only footage of you heading into Esserton on Thursday evening. Are you certain that you made your way back?'

Aaron hesitated but only for a second. 'I didn't use the highway. Only local roads. There's more than one way to get to Broadbeach, you know. Like I said, I felt like a drive.' He jutted out his jaw in defiance. He had committed himself to the story now and was obviously going for broke.

'This conference you were attending, Mr Ricci,' Josh continued. 'According to Elissa and also your boss, whom we spoke to, you were booked in for both days, Thursday and Friday. You drove up to Broadbeach after work on the

Wednesday, spending the night at your accommodation, ahead of the conference the following day. Is that right?'

He nodded, wary, sensing another trap.

Josh made a show of consulting his notes. 'On the morning of your daughter's disappearance, Elissa told us she tried calling you around 9.40 am after she couldn't find Sienna. After arriving on the scene, we also tried your phone several times, but we were unable to reach you. All our messages went to voicemail. When I finally got through at – let me see, it was at 11.56 am – you stated that you had your phone turned off and had only just listened to your various messages. So, to be clear, Aaron, you had already left the conference *before* you were aware of Sienna's disappearance and had reached Esserton by the time we spoke just before midday. Is that correct?'

They were at the crux of it now. Kate could feel the tension in the room. Ricci's lies were closing in on him. She could sense his mind scrabbling, trying to find a way out.

His eyes strayed to the door, seeking escape, before he made himself answer. 'Yes, that's right. I stayed for the first session only – 9.30 to 10.30 am. All the later sessions were on legislation and HR and not really applicable to the sales work I do. So, I thought I would head off early and try to get some work done before heading home. It always piles up when I'm away from the office,' he stumbled and stopped abruptly.

'Tell us about Leigh Road, Aaron.' Josh's voice was steely.

'I'm sorry?'

'Leigh Road, that's where your phone GPS places you on Friday morning after you switched your mobile on again. Not really anywhere near your office, is it, Leigh

Road? But you just said you were heading to your office and that's in the middle of town, isn't it? Imagine our surprise, Aaron, when your GPS data places you instead at the southern end of Esserton – ten or twelve minutes from your house, where your daughter was abducted.'

Aaron blanched as he struggled to stay in control. 'This is fucking bullshit! I just went for a drive, is all. I like being in the car. It helps me think. There's no bloody law against going for a drive. You're just twisting everything. I didn't do anything wrong.'

Kate met Josh's eyes and took over. 'You sure about that, Aaron? At the very least, you've pissed off your boss. I wonder what he'd say to paying all your conference expenses only to find you didn't attend a major part of it just because you didn't feel like it. It's almost like you used the conference as an excuse to be somewhere else.'

'Fuck! How many times do I need to say this? I was there, all right. My signature is on the attendance sheets.'

'Yes, we've checked the sheets. Pretty basic sign-in procedures, I thought. Easy to take advantage of. We noticed you signed in with your initials rather than your signature for all of your Thursday sessions. Nice and easy to forge. Just get a friend to write A.R. down for the Friday and it'll be like you were there all along. Leaving you free to be wherever you wanted.' She paused, letting the words sink in before continuing. 'I wonder how quickly this friend would come forward, if they knew they were being used as a cover for child abduction.'

'I fucking told you, I didn't touch Sienna. Why aren't you listening to me?'

'Which conference session did you say you attended on Friday, Mr Ricci?' Kate resumed, her voice sharp and insistent.

'It was something about social media branding for small businesses. How to build and maintain a customer base. The presenter was Sarah something.' He looked up at her, defiant.

'Anything stand out to you about the session? Any key points that you remember? What was the presenter wearing, out of interest? A skirt? A suit jacket? Did she wear her hair up or down?'

He bit his lip and looked away. 'I didn't notice. I can't remember. My mind is a mess with everything that's happened.'

Kate nodded. Aaron's recollection of the session was little more than a line lifted from the conference program. Once more she let the silence lengthen before signalling for Josh to continue. She had forgotten how good they were together. Riffing off each other's cues, knowing when to hold back and let the other take the lead. It was time to jolt Aaron out of the fantasy he had constructed.

'Mr Ricci, we'd like to speak to you about your mobile.'

Kate saw Ricci stiffen, suddenly alert. Josh hadn't missed it, either.

'You turned off your mobile for a significant period from Thursday evening until just before midday on Friday. Do you make a habit of switching off your phone for long periods so you're uncontactable during emergencies?'

'I just forgot, that's all.'

'By the time you switched it on again on Friday, you were back in Esserton, is that right?'

Ricci nodded, his mouth drawn tight, his eyes watchful.

'So, here's the thing, Aaron. You can spin it any way you like, but we know you weren't at the conference on

Friday. There's no traffic footage of your car driving to Esserton on Friday morning. Now, I know what you're going to say.' Josh held up his palm as Ricci went to speak. 'You're not a highway person. I get it. You like the back roads where there are no pesky traffic cameras. But the thing is, we'll be taking statements from the conference attendees and looking at the building's CCTV. And I'm willing to bet there'll be no sign of you on the Friday.' He stared Ricci down.

'We know you drove to Esserton on Thursday night. You didn't drive back to Broadbeach using any local roads. You stayed in Esserton. Very likely, somewhere near this Leigh Road. It's what you were planning to do all along. You had already organised a friend to cover for you at the conference by writing in your initials on the Friday attendance sheets. You wanted everyone to think you were at the conference all of Friday. That's why you had your mobile switched off from Thursday night, so your location wouldn't register.' Josh's voice was a steamroller, remorselessly laying down one fact after another.

'When you handed over your mobile to us on Friday, you knew we'd be looking into your location history. You couldn't pretend to be in Broadbeach when your mobile GPS placed you in Esserton on Friday. Hence this bullshit story about leaving the conference early on Friday morning after the first session.'

Josh removed some papers from his file and slid them across the table towards Ricci. 'These are photocopies of Friday's attendance sheets from the conference. One name seems to have been scribbled out from the sign-in sheets for all but the morning session. It almost looks like someone signed in for you and then had to go back and cross out your name when it became clear that you couldn't possibly have attended the later presentations. Who did you call, Aaron, to cross out the names for you? A mate, was it? As a favour to you?'

Ricci had collapsed into himself as the words rained down on him, relentlessly cataloguing the inconsistencies in his story. Kate could see the fear in his eyes. But it wasn't enough. They needed to break him. So far, their evidence was circumstantial, built mostly on supposition. If they were to charge Ricci, they needed a confession.

As she watched, Josh leaned in for the kill, his voice deliberate and slow. 'More importantly, Aaron, what did you use to make the call? Was it a second mobile, maybe?'

They were close now. Ricci had the trapped look of a man who had reached the end of his resources. His tongue darted, wetting his lips in quick, skittish movements.

'We know you purchased a second phone and SIM package in January, Aaron. It's right there in your credit card records. Pretty brazen, I thought. Although we all make mistakes, don't we? We've got the mobile number and we're just waiting on the call records to come through from your provider. It's time to stop the lies, Mr Ricci. You need to tell us what you did to Sienna. Your vehicle is undergoing forensic examination as we speak. We're going to find out anyway, but it would be much better for you if you just dropped the pretence and told us where she is.'

Ricci's answer was strangled. 'You really think I did this, don't you?' His eyes moved wildly from Josh to Kate as if finally realising the depth of the hole he had dug for himself. 'I want a lawyer. I'm not talking to you again until I get a lawyer. This is wrong. You're making a huge mistake. I didn't kidnap Sienna. I love my daughter. I would never hurt her.'

There was a knock at the door and Constable Roby entered, his face set. Kate suspended the interview for the purposes of the recording and rose with Josh. At the doorway, she took in Roby's words, her eyes glancing across to Ricci. He seemed to read something in her expression.

'What? Is it Sienna? Have you found her? What's happened?'

She ignored his question. 'Mr Ricci, you'll be free to leave once the custody sergeant arranges your bail conditions. Constable Roby here will look after you. We'll need to speak to you again and I strongly urge you to remain at home and contactable. You may want to take this time to organise that lawyer.' Leaving Roby to deal with Aaron Ricci, she exited the interview room with Josh.

The screen door is open. Why is it open? So easy for an intruder to slip in and do whatever they want. To take whatever they want.

The house is a mess. Piles of clothes partially folded. The remnants of breakfast scattered across the kitchen. A half-finished mug of tea. Milky cereal bowls mixing with baby bottles in the sink. The smell of toast lingers in the air. The toaster is still warm to the touch. Crumbs litter the countertops. My finger presses on a stray Weet-Bix shard, crushing it into cereal dust. A few more crumbs won't make a difference.

Slovenly. It's a good word for this house. I move the word around my mouth, liking the feel of it and the images it conjures: of sweat and rotting fruit, unwashed clothes and dirty floors.

My fingers itch to open the cupboards and peer inside. In the kitchen and the wardrobes and the bathroom. To catalogue each sign of ragged domesticity. To discover what they hide from view. Their pathetic little secrets: Metamucil, haemorrhoid cream, lube.

But I need to be quick. Move through the rooms. Quickly. Quickly. Mustn't touch. Only look.

And there she is, snug in her bassinet. Waiting for me. Her eyes are open as if she knew I would be coming. They are huge, a vast ocean of marble blue. They find mine and her lips crinkle into a smile. Her chubby legs kick the air and she gurgles softly as a line of drool drips from her wet, gummy mouth.

I bend down closer. Our noses are inches apart and I can smell her sweet bath-oil scent, mixed with a ripe hint of something else. Her nappy needs changing.

'I don't have much time, little one,' I whisper. I tuck my present into the folds of her blanket. A tiny pink-and-grey koala. I spotted it at the newsagency of all places and couldn't help myself. But maybe it will be noticed? I take it back and instead place it in her overflowing toy box. What's one more amongst the crush of teddies and fur?

I kiss her forehead, allowing the soft strands of her whip-black hair to tickle my skin. And just for a moment, I let myself imagine what it would feel like if she were mine.

18

Kate picked her way along the rough dirt track towards the artificial lights illuminating the rise up ahead. Her torchlight stabbed at the bushland crowding the trail on both sides, dense and dark; her breath steaming the frigid air. Needles of she-oak snapped back at her, scraping her clothes as Josh forged ahead. She paused for a second, taking in the landscape. A dozen or so metres below, she could just make out the parking area of the nature reserve where they had left their vehicles alongside other first responders before continuing uphill on foot. At least the terrain and distance would provide a natural barrier against any intrepid journalists.

As they gained the top, several forensic officers wearing plastic overalls came into focus, crouching beside a temporary cordon of lights set up around a section of scraggly scrub directly ahead. What lay beyond was hidden from view by their powder-blue-sheathed figures. A large rock overhang thrusting into the sky provided the back-drop for their activity. She could hear the rush of water, a creek somewhere close by.

Kate's eyes found three teenagers in dark hoodies and jeans, two boys and a girl around sixteen or seventeen, she figured, watching on from the edge of the clearing. The kids who had called in the police. She was surprised they had hung around. They looked fearful and out of place, shoulders hunched and arms folded across their chests, or hands pressed deep into pockets, their eyes continually drawn to the activities of the forensic team. She recognised Constable Darnley, a solid and calm presence amidst the confusion. He was speaking to them in turn, ushering each teenager a few metres away from the huddled group to take down their individual statements. They were in good hands with Darnley.

Donning the required protective gear, Kate moved with Josh to the SOCOs forming a ring around the cordoned-off area. The sharp smell of urine mixed with damp, rich earth caught her nose. One of the forensic team called out something that she didn't catch, but it raised a smile from Josh and he leaned in closer towards the woman. A flash from the police photographer's camera flared and Kate felt herself stumble. Light-headedness surged like a wave. She turned away, hardly taking in the balled-up discovery that was partially buried amongst the soil and leaf litter.

'I'm just going to take a look around.'

Josh didn't look up at her words. Turning, she collided hard into the photographer's shoulder. Mumbling an apology, she moved away, her breaths coming in shuddering gasps. She felt her skin prickle with damp as she struggled against the rising tide of panic, conscious of the curious eyes that glanced her way. Every synapse was firing red-hot needles as tendrils of heat rose and closed in around her throat. Dread, thick and tar-like, swamped her thoughts and movements.

'Sarge…' Kate's eyes snapped open to find Darnley, quiet and reassuring by her side.

'I've finished with the kids. I can take you to the cave, if you like.'

When she didn't respond, he motioned towards the expanse of rock that formed a natural boundary along the ridgeline. Kate followed numbly, aware only that he was protecting her, steering her away from prying eyes until she had regained control. Gratitude stirred within the soup of her scrambled emotions.

Darnley led her to the side of the rocky outcrop. What she had at first glance taken to be a solid rock barrier, revealed itself to be a narrow entrance into the monolith. The opening was little more than a slit in the rock, shielded by thick scrub and only visible when viewed directly. Kate bent her head as she squeezed in after Darnley.

The crawl space opened up almost immediately into a wide cavern worn into the rock over time. Kate took in the space, illuminated in fragments by the beams of their torches. The rock wall was dry to the touch and provided shelter from the elements on three sides. Beyond its rocky ledge, the ground fell away down a vegetated embankment into the thick foliage below. The sound of water was clearer from here. The creek had to be running somewhere below. During daylight hours, the outcrop no doubt provided expansive views of the reserve; a perfect spot to escape the world for a time.

She took in the evidence of recent occupation: tagging on the cave walls, discarded chip packets, drink bottles, and cigarette stubs. She could smell the distinct tang of cannabis smoke lingering in the rocky enclosure, a combination of sweet grass and fetid musk. As her eyes began to catalogue the space, she could feel her breathing slow, her mind starting to unclench.

Darnley spoke quietly without requiring any response or reaction from her.

'They come here quite often, apparently, the three friends. Mostly on the weekends, they reckon, and also to wag school, I expect.' He raised his eyebrows at Kate. 'But they reckon they haven't visited all week. They all swear they didn't notice anyone tonight, along the trail or hanging around the cave. Not that they'd see much, if they were hidden in here the whole time,' he observed.

'Max, the sixteen-year-old, is the one who needed to go for a piss. Scared the living crap out of the poor bugger. Not sure if they'll be coming here as often anymore.' He glanced at her sideways before continuing. 'Couldn't find any weed on them, of course. They'd had plenty of time to get rid of it before we showed up. But I don't think they're lying. I think they're genuinely affected and are trying to help.'

They stood together in companionable silence and Kate felt her body still. She touched him lightly on the shoulder. 'I think I've seen everything I need, Greg. Thank you.'

Crouching low, she followed Darnley out through the gap in the rock. Breathing in the sharp, icy air, she contemplated what lay ahead of her: the task of notifying Elissa and Aaron Ricci.

19

Sunday

Kate concentrated on adjusting her left breast so Amy could attach properly. She winced as her daughter suckled greedily, unintentionally biting the cracked edge of her nipple. Kate breathed through the pain and waited for her daughter to get into a rhythm. Her eyes felt scratchy from her poor night's sleep, and a headache was starting to radiate from deep within her skull.

She could hear Geoff in the kitchen unstacking the dishwasher with unnecessary clamour. Plates and mugs were banged into cupboards and the doors slammed shut.

Arriving home in the early hours, she had collapsed on the couch. Deep in sleep, she hadn't heard her daughter's cries when Amy had woken at daybreak. Geoff had attended to her and settled her, giving Kate another half an hour of shut eye, before Amy had become too agitated with hunger to distract. Beyond handing Amy over for a feed, Geoff had barely spoken to her this morning, his frustration clear.

The toll the past few months had taken on Geoff was obvious. He looked older and heavier, his skin dulled and his face set to a permanent expression of resentful acceptance. Guilt, acrid and bitter, reared inside her.

It had all been so different with Archie. When she had returned to work after her firstborn, Geoff had been happy and looking forward to being a full-time, stay-at-home dad, pressing pause on his own successful architecture career. It had all been a novelty. An adventure.

Kate had assumed they could go back to the same arrangement with Amy, without really checking if anything had changed on his side. She had underestimated how much Geoff had enjoyed being back at work part-time while Archie was at day care. And that was before all the complications with the shooting and everything that had precipitated from it.

Now everything was fraught and fractured, without any real way out, without one of them losing. It wasn't as if she could reduce her hours even if she wanted to. And it definitely wasn't an option as far as she was concerned. Apart from their financial situation, she hadn't worked this hard, sucked up to Skinner and jumped through multiple work health and psychologist hoops to give it up now.

Her mobile buzzed as if on cue, but when she glanced down on the screen, she saw that it wasn't work, but her brother, Luke. She had been meaning to call him to discuss the fallout from their father, but she hadn't found the time. The thought of dissecting it all now felt intolerable.

'Hey.' His standard greeting.

'Luke, I can't talk now. On my way to work.' A white lie. Unnecessary, yet it had tripped out.

A pause, as he evaluated her words. He was well aware that she was trying to avoid him. Like father, like daughter, like brother.

'They're talking about dodgy deals now. Funny money,' he pressed on.

She sighed, closing her eyes. She had seen the latest online news reports. Accusations of financial impropriety by Minister Jackson. Allegations that he had used insider knowledge of coastal developments for financial gain with the very strong implication that those closest to him had benefited too. She had raced through the story, searching for her father's name, skimming across the words like hot sand grains on the beach in summer that could burn her soles if she lingered too long. No names had been mentioned and for that she was grateful, but the trail of breadcrumbs was clear for anyone to follow. And where was her father in all of this, she wondered for the umpteenth time. Where had he disappeared to? Ducking for cover while she fronted up to the rabble.

'Have you spoken to him?' Luke's voice sounded again in her ear.

'Not yet,' she replied shortly. *Why don't you talk to him for once? Why is it always up to me?* The unsaid words hung heavy and potent in the distance between them. *You know why.*

'All right, well I need to get going, so...'

He hung up before she had the chance to finish her sentence.

Amy stirred and there was a shout from the sitting room. 'Mum, I want *PJ Masks*.'

'Coming, mate.' She buttoned up and rose with Amy on her hip to attend to her son and the TV remote.

—

'Thank you, ladies and gentlemen, for being here today. We have called this morning's press briefing to provide further details on the events of last night.'

Skinner was in solemn *community leader* mode, ready to disseminate the unpalatable news to the waiting crowd, the message tightly controlled and regulated. He was primed and, underneath his calm exterior, relishing every moment in front of the camera.

Standing behind him, Kate felt all the weight of her fatigue, layer upon packed layer of exhaustion dragging her down. She knew she looked drawn and frayed, the opposite of camera ready. Puffy bags sagged under her eyes, and she had deliberately chosen a heavy jacket to mask her milk-heavy chest. She was so sick of the side-eyes, and the beat-too-long stares grazing her body at the station. The last thing she wanted was a figure-hugging suit when fronting the press.

She recognised Josh taking up a position at the back of the room. Skinner had picked Kate rather than Josh to accompany him on the podium, and she could feel his fury even from this distance. She knew what he was thinking: this was yet another example of Skinner paving the path for her. She had seen it in the curl of his lips, and the burn of unfairness that had sharpened his features when Skinner had announced his decision. She would have laughed aloud if the whole situation hadn't been so ridiculous. Bloody men and their fragile egos. Kate knew her boss. She was on stage with Skinner because having a woman and person of colour by his side would play well for the cameras and place Skinner in the best light. She wished it was otherwise but there it was.

At the lectern, Skinner was continuing with his statement. 'We can confirm today that a body was recovered from Layton Reserve at approximately 9.25 pm last night, which we believe to be that of Sienna Lillian Ricci, the four-month-old daughter of Elissa and Aaron Ricci, who was reported missing on the morning of Friday the twenty-fourth of August.'

Kate could feel the shiver of shock run through the crush of reporters, as Skinner paused to let the news sink in. Seasoned as the journos were, she knew that crimes involving children were the worst of the worst, the most horrific and least palatable of all news stories, equally likely to draw in or turn punters away.

'As you can imagine, the family is devastated. They will make a statement in due course but have asked for some time and privacy to process this terrible news.'

The understatement of the year. Kate had accompanied Josh to inform the Riccis the previous night, and it had played out as badly as she had anticipated. At first, Elissa had not seemed to take in the news. She had thanked them for finding Sienna, as if they had found her daughter safe and sound rather than a body buried in the forest. Kate had been forced to repeat herself multiple times, until the message had finally pierced through. Elissa had launched herself at Kate in despair, a dry-eyed, open-mouthed keening. She had been adamant that she wanted to view the body immediately, while they had to explain that it wouldn't be possible until after the postmortem examination. The manner in which Sienna had been found automatically ruled the circumstances as suspicious, meaning that the formal procedures of forensic examination would need to come first.

Kate had held Elissa, half supporting her, half carrying her to the couch, where she had sat with her until Elissa had calmed down, eventually drifting off into an exhausted sleep like a child.

Josh had been less patient with Aaron. Ricci had reacted in shock, spewing beer-laced vomit, mostly in the kitchen sink, but also on the tiled floor where it had splashed on Josh's leather brogues. Josh had been left to clean up the mess while Kate dealt with Elissa. Ricci had stunk of booze, hardly able to stand, the stench of alcohol rising off the man like steam. It had been clear how Aaron had chosen to spend the hours following his release from custody. At least their son, who was staying over at his grandmother's, hadn't been there to witness the scene. Kate shook away the memory as Skinner's voice broke in once more.

'We are currently appealing to members of the public with any information to come forward. In particular, we are appealing to anyone who may have frequented Layton Reserve for bushwalking or mountain bike riding or any other recreational activities in the last forty-eight hours. We would like to speak to you if you recall any incident or anything unusual in or around the reserve. Any and all information is welcome and a confidential one-eight-hundred number has been set up for people to call in.

'Moving forward, the case is being investigated as an unexplained death and a task force has been set up, led by Detective Sergeant Kate Miles.' He motioned briefly to Kate. 'Detective Miles will be happy to take a few questions.' Skinner stepped aside, letting Kate front the bank of microphones.

She knew this was coming and yet her heart rate spiked as multiple hands shot up like bolts. Would they stick to the story at hand or would they derail her with questions about Minister Jackson's proclivities? She chose a reporter from the front in a neatly pressed shirt and tie.

'There are reports that the baby was discovered by a group of teenagers. Are they being questioned in relation to Sienna's death?'

She breathed out. An easy lob that she would have no trouble dispatching.

'The body was discovered by three young people, who called it in. And we are very grateful to them for acting so responsibly. It wasn't an easy sight to witness. The teenagers are not being considered persons of interest at this stage and counselling has been offered to each of them.'

She motioned to a reporter in the middle of the pack sporting a brightly coloured pant suit and boots.

'Have you got any theories at this stage of who may be responsible? Are you looking at Aaron Ricci as a possible suspect?'

'We'll of course be pursuing all avenues. As you can well understand, we need to speak to the family on an ongoing basis and Mr Ricci has been helping us with our enquiries. As has the whole family.'

'Has Mr Ricci been charged in relation to yesterday's altercation with Mr Jason Veliu?' she persisted. 'And can you confirm if that matter is in any way linked to Sienna's case?'

'I can confirm that assault charges have been laid against Mr Ricci. He was released last night subject to bail conditions and is due before the magistrate later this week. Any links to Sienna will be considered if found to be relevant.' Kate ignored the reporter's attempts to insert a further follow-up question and directed her attention to a journalist at the back.

'Detective, just to be clear. Are you saying Mr Veliu is being investigated in connection to the case?' They weren't going to let her get away with it that easily.

'As I said, we are looking into all pertinent avenues. My duty is to Sienna and finding the person or persons responsible for her death. It is not for me to pick and choose a suspect. If you choose to print any names, that information would be uncorroborated.'

'Detective, do you have any concerns about the fact that Sienna's abduction has escalated into homicide? Do the public more broadly need to be worried about the safety of their children?' A journalist from the front row again, projecting his voice to gain Kate's attention.

Kate paused, annoyed at the blatant attempt at sensationalism. Her answer was sharp and to the point. 'To be clear, Sienna's death has not been established as homicide. Her body is yet to undergo postmortem examination to establish a cause of death. To answer your question, while we are pursuing all possibilities, we don't believe there to be any risk to the general public. Thank you, ladies and gentlemen, I think that's it for now. We will keep you updated as the investigation progresses.'

20

Morning, Gail. How are you? Hope the kids
are well. Wondering if you have time this
week (tomorrow or Tues) for a quick chat?
Wanting to get your opinion on some refin-
ancing options. I'm on my mobile. Cheers,
Kate.

Kate hovered the curser over the 'send' button. The short,
innocuous missive had taken her an age to draft, as she
had endlessly deleted and rewritten the email. Gail was
their mortgage broker and Kate pondered the wisdom
of approaching her before broaching the subject of an
increased loan with her husband. She was aware though
that she needed to do something. The problem of her
father's money was a dead weight on her chest, the anxiety
squeezing her breath every time her thoughts strayed too
close. Whatever it took, she was determined to come up
with the money that would free her from her father's
mistakes. She would not be dragged down by his actions.

A discreet cough told her that Josh was waiting and
had sent Constable Roby to hurry her along. The case
briefing was about to begin and she was needed in the
incident room. *Fuck it.* She pressed 'send'.

'Our priority today is Aaron Ricci. The witness statements and CCTV from the conference, forensics on his clothes and vehicle, and analysis of all of his electronic devices. Get on the blower and hurry up anyone you have to. I want this bloke charged by the week's end.'

Kate clamped down on her teeth, controlling herself with difficulty. Skinner was on a roll and there was little point in interrupting. To call attention to the fact that she had been briefing the team on the same matters that Skinner was now enumerating, before he had walked in and summarily taken over, would be less than useless. They had already gone over all of this. Frustration spat and bubbled under her skin like water on hot oil. Why had he put her in charge if he was going to undermine her at every possible opportunity?

Skinner's voice rolled on. 'He killed his fucking child, and we weren't quick enough to stop him...' The barest hint of a pause as Skinner's eyes found hers so she had no doubt of who he believed to be responsible. 'We have things to make up for. The media is on our back and the AC's office is on this. We need a quick, clean result. No fuck-ups.' Though his words were directed at the team, Kate felt their sting like a slap to her face.

Kate could feel the charged atmosphere of the room. Skinner was stamping his will on the investigation, tacitly directing the team on the outcome he expected, leaving no room for questions. This type of politicking was what she hated the most. The bending of resources towards a pre-ordained result. The silent closing of doors, the picking and choosing of which avenues to pursue.

'Do we have anything on his second mobile yet?' Skinner finally paused for breath and Josh answered without waiting for Kate.

'We do, sir. The information came through first thing this morning. The call records are very specific. Phone calls only – no texts – and almost exclusively to a single phone number. A mobile ending in eight-five-zero, registered to an A.N. Garrett. The listed address is Florence Street in South Esserton, an approximately ten-minute drive from Elliot Pass and around three streets down from Leigh Road.' He paused a beat to acknowledge his own win. 'We have a call from Ricci's mobile to the eight-five-zero number at 7.36 pm on Thursday night and also two calls made at 9.07 am and 9.09 am on Friday morning.'

'That's it? No other calls?'

'Nothing else, sir. No other calls have been made or received on Ricci's second mobile since Friday. It looks like it's been turned off, so we don't have the option of tracking a location. Calls just go to an automated voice-mail. So far, it hasn't turned up at the Riccis' house or in his vehicle and he's not admitting to it. There's every chance that he has already disposed of it.' Josh hurried on as Skinner grimaced. 'At the moment, we're proceeding on the basis that Ricci stayed overnight at this Florence Street address. Our priority today is visiting this property and finding Garrett.'

Skinner nodded, partially appeased. 'What about Ricci's laptop. Anything yet?'

Josh shook his head, as if reluctant to concede another negative result. 'The techies have only done an initial screening. His internet history shows a scattering of porn sites, but there's nothing involving minors. There's also folders of photos. Lots of Sienna but of the rest of the family, too. Nothing that would raise any alarms, but they'll keep digging,' he added.

'Any preliminary forensics?' Skinner's questions continued to be directed at Josh.

Kate forced herself to speak ahead of him. 'The vehicle is being analysed and all of Ricci's clothes from his conference trip are also with forensics. We expect traces of Sienna's DNA to be in the car and on his clothing, of course. Forensics will be focusing on any anomalies. Any concentration of body fluids – blood or DNA – where we wouldn't expect it, like in the boot of the car. Or conversely, any indications that the vehicle's been cleaned. They are also looking for any matches to the soil and leaf-litter samples collected from where Sienna was found last night.

'The SOCOs also believe they've found the original dump site, a shallow grave close to the creek, which was around twenty metres away from where she was discovered, up the embankment. They believe she was most likely moved, dragged from the original site by an animal. Possibly a feral cat or a fox.' She paused, seeing the flush of horror that passed through the assembled faces. It wasn't a pleasant thought. She pushed past the detail, not wanting to focus on it. 'The Sydney labs are supporting and we're getting priority, so we should get some results on his car and personal effects soon. Also, the autopsy is scheduled for tomorrow,' she added before Skinner could ask.

Skinner nodded and before he could start up again, Kate barrelled on, addressing the assembled team. 'We also need to make sure that we don't give up on our current leads. We can't forget that Veliu has no alibi for Sienna's abduction on Friday.' She could feel Skinner's derision at the mention of Veliu but refused to back down. 'We have a statement from one of the neighbours indicating that Veliu didn't get home after his release from custody on Thursday, that he only returned home after midday on Friday. That means his movements need to be followed up and pinned down. Ricci's our priority, but the CCTV and other checks on Veliu's movements and his associates should also continue, including checking in with that cousin of his who's also his lawyer,' she finished firmly.

Skinner resumed where he had left off, as if she hadn't spoken.

'I'd like to have something for the press today. There'll be another media briefing this evening.' He dismissed them without reference to Kate.

The officers dispersed, the developments overnight lending fresh purpose and urgency to the team. Kate had already assigned their tasks before Skinner had deigned to intervene, so there was nothing more to add. Still, she felt short-changed having not been allowed to run the meeting on her own terms. Her eyes followed her boss out of the room, resentment cementing, cold and hard.

'Ready?' Josh raised his eyebrows, impatient to get going. She nodded, swallowing her discontent as far as it would go, and followed him out.

–

They drove without speaking, each busy with their own thoughts. The noise from the radio filled the car, a limp skin of music and inane chatter coating the silence between them. They were heading to the southern edge of town on the foothills, where modern subdivisions with views of Mount Nullum were spreadeagled amongst rural pastures and abrupt pockets of thick bushland. Neighbourhoods which, just three or four years ago, had been raw, hard-edged new builds, fresh out of construction, had grown into fully fledged suburbs with mature landscaping and houses settling into homes. They drove past dog walkers, head-phoned joggers and kids making slow laps on their bikes. The unseasonal chilly weather had cleared overnight and the neighbourhood was taking advantage. The mid-morning air sat crisp and still, basking in the late-August sunshine. A return to the more usual winter conditions they were accustomed to.

'I think it's in here.' Josh turned into a villa complex, pulling to a stop in a designated visitor car space. 'Pretty flash,' he commented, taking in the immaculately trimmed hedges and squares of mown lawn separating sleek townhouses.

Kate agreed. The complex sported a Hamptons beach vibe: all shuttered windows, pediment roofs, and weatherboard exteriors in understated modern colours, white and blue-grey. Though only a twelve-minute drive from Elliot Pass, this was a world away from the isolated bush cottage that Ricci lived in with his young family. A.N. Garrett, whatever their connection to Ricci, presumably didn't want for money.

'Lots of neighbours,' she pointed out as they made their way along a row of homes to their left. If Ricci had stayed here, she thought there was a good chance he could have been spotted.

'Where the hell is number twenty-two?' They had reached the end of the line of homes without finding the one listed as Garrett's residence. They looped back, walking slower and checking each number, until they reached the very end of the complex, where a metal-and-timber-panelled fence separated the homes from a bush reserve. Two knee-height bollards stood diagonal to each other along a break in the fence line, marking the transition between ordered residential living and bushland. The paved footpath within the complex gave way to an informal gravel track leading to the scrub, no doubt used by the residents for walking and bike riding in the reserve. It also provided an ideal means for accessing the complex unnoticed. A person could park on any one of the side streets and access the complex via the bush reserve with very little chance of being noticed by its residents. *Shit!*

She turned sharply to Josh. 'That bushland, do you know where it leads to? Does it link up to Elliot Pass?'

Josh's eyes widened, immediately connecting the dots. On her phone, Kate clicked onto Google Maps, locating the bushland that formed the north-western boundary of the Florence Street complex. Taking in the terrain, she held up the screen to Josh. The map showed uninterrupted green spanning from the site to Elliot Pass, across some 2.4 kilometres of rugged downhill terrain.

'What do you reckon? A twenty, thirty-minute hike from here?'

'And back again.' Josh nodded. 'But doable, I'd say.'

An elderly woman, slim and erect in exercise gear, her skin bronzed a deep copper, emerged from the bushland path, moving in the long, confident strides of a practised jogger.

Kate approached her with a smile. 'Sorry to bother you, but we are trying to find the property of an A.N. Garrett. Number twenty-two?'

'Oh, yes, that's Allison's place. No one can ever find it. It's through there.' She pointed to a paved path just visible behind a lattice privacy screen that appeared to lead around the row of residences they had been searching. The entrance to the path was heavily obscured by densely packed foliage and potted plants. Kate realised that they had walked past the spot not a minute ago, mistaking it for the side yard of the townhouse next door. Ms Garrett was clearly averse to prying eyes.

'Just follow the path and her place is tucked in behind.' The woman smiled.

'Thanks so much. Do you know if Allison's around today?'

'No idea, love. I live in the complex across the street. Just come through here to access the walks. I only know Allison to say hello to. She's probably in, being a Sunday and all.' The woman nodded and continued on her way, displaying no curiosity at their presence.

Following where the woman had pointed, they squeezed past the various planters and cascading vegetation to reach the front door. The front portico stood in shadow, cut off from the sun by the profusion of plant life, jungle-like and wild. The excited squeal of a child playing somewhere in a neighbouring property floated in the air. The sound seemed far away and out of place. The home looked unoccupied and shut away: the blinds down at each of the windows, and the front door locked and secured. There was no garage. Allison Garrett presumably used one of the car spots designated for residents along the main driveway. There was no response to Josh's insistent knocking.

'Could be out for the day. We should try the neighbours.'

Kate didn't respond. They would need to go through the motions with the neighbours, but she had the sinking feeling that they were too late. From the set look on Josh's face, she suspected that he felt the same. Allison Garrett had fled, most likely tipped off by Ricci after his release from custody last night. If that was the case, he had made a monumental mistake because it would be another nail in his ever-expanding coffin.

21

Aaron Ricci sat in the interview room, subdued and watchful. Yesterday, he had been all defiant bravado. None of it was in evidence today. The gravity of his situation had finally sunk in, or more likely had been pummelled into him by his lawyer. He sat silent, letting his lawyer do the talking. His raw, bruised face – a deep blood-purple, the colour of aging beef – was directed to the floor, refusing to meet anyone's eyes.

Across the interview table, Kate and Josh waited in silence for Ricci's lawyer, Adriano de Matteo, to finish his opening preamble. Grizzled and sharp-eyed, he was one of those commanding men who made their presence felt with the aid of a well-cut suit, an above-average height, and an air of assumed authority. The heater whirred, pumping tepid air across the room. Kate could see a bead of sweat starting to pool along the lawyer's hairline. This was her least favourite interview room, being too close to the station amenities and bearing an ingrained essence of Pine O Cleen and old plumbing. She surreptitiously popped a tab of Mentos into her mouth, breathing in the sweet, fruity tang, as the sugar flooded her tongue.

'As I mentioned before, Detectives, my client is here voluntarily to make a statement to assist you with your enquiries. In particular, he is here today to clarify certain statements he made to you last night regarding his whereabouts from approximately 7 pm on Thursday night to around midday on Friday—'

'You mean the lies he told?' Josh interjected.

'I assure you, Detective, that if my client had been encouraged to avail himself of legal representation – his legal right – prior to speaking with you last night, this confusion could have been prevented, and you would have been free to pursue more pertinent avenues.' The lawyer shrugged. 'But as it is, here we all are.' De Matteo had the mannerisms of an old-fashioned orator, wordy and grandiose, guaranteed to get under Josh's skin, just as they were meant to. Kate could almost feel his enjoyment as he pitted his considerable intellect against Josh.

'Mr Ricci was informed of his rights last night.'

'I'm sure he was.' De Matteo raised his palms in a conciliatory gesture that nevertheless came off as mocking. Josh bristled and Kate directed a glance of caution his way.

'Mr de Matteo, shall we get on with it?' Kate's voice was mild.

'Yes, of course. As I was saying, my client categorically asserts that he has no knowledge of, and took no part in his daughter's abduction or manner of death. He wants nothing more than for the monster responsible for Sienna's death to be brought to justice. The reason he's here today is so that questions regarding his own movements can be put to bed, so the police can focus on who really did this and not be sidetracked by irrelevant, shall we say, distractions.'

'Your client's refusal to account for his movements during the exact period when his daughter went missing hardly counts as an irrelevant distraction, Mr de Matteo,' Kate retorted. 'I think we've wasted enough time on unsupported assertions, don't you? If Mr Ricci has something to say, let's hear it, shall we?'

De Matteo inclined his head to Ricci, a sign that he was finally permitted to speak.

When he began, his voice was hoarse and scratchy, possibly the result of the previous night's alcohol binge. 'What you said before, you were right. I—'

Josh interrupted him harshly. 'Louder, so we can hear you, Mr Ricci.'

Ricci started nervously and de Matteo raised an eyebrow at Josh. 'Let's all try to be civil, shall we, Detective? When you're ready, Aaron. Just a bit louder, if you can.'

Ricci started again.

'What I told you last night, it's not what happened. I did leave the conference a day early, like you said. After the last session on Thursday, I stayed for a couple of drinks and left around seven.' He paused, his neck and jaw rigid with tension. 'I drove back to Esserton, but I didn't go home. I wish I had. I mean, maybe if I'd been there, maybe none of this would have happened.' His voice cracked, and he waited for the emotion to pass before breathing deeply and resuming.

'The place I stayed at… I mean, who I stayed the night with… she has nothing to do with all of this. I want her name to be kept out of this.'

'That's not something we can agree to at this stage, Mr Ricci,' Kate countered. 'It all depends on the information you give us.'

Ricci held her gaze, appealing for understanding before breaking away. In slow, stilted bursts, he resumed.

'Ally… Allison Garrett, I met her about seven months ago. At another conference, actually.' He let out a

149

strangled laugh. 'She... we started seeing each other. That's who I was with on Thursday night. At her town-house on Florence Street.' Kate pictured the residence deliberately hidden behind its veil of deep green. A touch of the theatrical like an off-kilter fairy-tale, had been her first impression of the shrouded dwelling. Her curiosity about the owner of the property sharpened as Ricci continued.

'...We were planning on being together all of Friday. Actually, it was Ally who got it all sorted. She knew one of the conference organisers, so she was able to get my initials added to the Friday attendance sheets. We hardly ever get more than a few hours together and she was excited about us finally being able to spend the night without me having to rush off...' Kate noticed that he hadn't counted himself as looking forward to the rendezvous. Ricci was already creating distance between the two of them.

'But then on Friday morning, around eleven-thirty, we saw the news on TV. And there was footage of you holding a press conference outside my house.' He gestured at Josh. 'It was like a nightmare. I just jumped in the car to drive home. I turned on my mobile in the car – actually, I'd left it in the console overnight. Forgot about it the night before. Anyway, there were all these missed calls from you and Elissa. I was driving back from Ally's when you rang.' He nodded at Josh.

'Just so we have the timeline straight, Aaron, you left Broadbeach around 7 pm on Thursday evening and stayed overnight at Ms Garrett's townhouse in Florence Street, South Esserton. You say you left Ms Garrett's house the next morning, Friday before midday, after you saw news of Sienna's abduction on TV.'

'Yes, that's right.' Ricci nodded.

'Did you or Ms Garrett leave the house at any other time during your stay? Particularly, anytime during Friday morning from say 8 am to 10 am?'

'No. I mean, yes. I mean, I did leave the house but not on Friday. I went to get some takeaway on Thursday night. It was late, around nine, maybe. We were really late ordering and they had finished their home delivery by then. Ally stayed at home. You can check with the restaurant. We ordered from Thaiphoon on Cromer Street. But we never left the house on Friday. We were home all morning until I left Ally's at a quarter to twelve or something like that.'

'Are you absolutely sure of that, Mr Ricci? You can account for Ms Garrett's movements for the entire morning? You didn't sleep in, for example, while Ms Garrett went out for a bit? Maybe for a morning walk in the bushland at the back of her place?'

Ricci's face screwed up in confusion and Kate saw a grain of alertness cross his lawyer's eyes. 'What? No. What do you mean? Ally was with me the whole morning. We didn't get out of bed the entire time, if you must know. So yes, I can account for our bloody movements.'

'And would Ms Garrett be willing to confirm that, Mr Ricci? To provide a statement about where you stayed from Thursday night until midday on Friday?'

'Yes. Definitely. I'm sure she would.' There was a slight hesitation there. The barest hint of uncertainty.

'So, why not tell us all this yesterday, Mr Ricci? You seem to have a foolproof alibi,' Kate observed without irony. 'Why all the lies?'

'I don't want Elissa finding out. She wouldn't under-stand. It would kill her if she knew. This thing with Ally, it's just sex. Elissa and I, we have a life together, you know? She's family. I would never hurt her.'

Kate swatted away the irritation she felt at his words. The professed love for his wife as he betrayed her. His absolute conviction of the effect of his actions on his wife, with not a feeling spared for Ms Garrett. Jesus, the cheating husband. It was all so bloody clichéd.

He must have seen something of her feelings in her face because he was quick to press the point. 'You must think I'm an arsehole. Just another man who can't keep it in his pants.'

'Your personal life only concerns us as it relates to the case, Mr Ricci. Beyond that, it's really none of our business.'

'I never went looking, you know?' he pleaded, a platitude, to justify his actions to himself. 'And Ally knows I would never leave Elissa.'

At their lack of response, he pushed on. 'Elissa's not normal. What that man did to her, it's fucked her up. She finds it hard to be intimate. To let me even touch her sometimes. Ally… she's just so free. It's a relief, you know? Not having to ask or feel guilty. Fuck… I don't know why I'm telling you all this. It's not like it matters.'

The silence stretched as Ricci retreated into himself, embarrassment and shame fast replacing the moment of revelation.

Josh exchanged glances with Kate. It was time to change tack.

'Your relationship with Ms Garrett, Mr Ricci,' Josh began, 'you say it started approximately seven months ago. Tell me, how did you two communicate with each other?'

Ricci looked up at Josh's voice. He hesitated, reddening slightly at the knowledge of what Josh was asking.

'I bought another mobile so I could call Ally without Elissa finding out. Not that Elissa ever went through my phone or anything. She trusted me.' His voice gave way again. 'But it felt cleaner this way... Separate... Ally was the only one I contacted on that phone.'

'And where is this mobile now, Aaron?'

Ricci glanced over to his lawyer and de Matteo intervened. 'It appears that my client left his second phone at Ms Garrett's when he left her place on Friday. He has not been in contact with Ms Garrett since that day and I also understand that Ms Garrett has not attempted to contact Mr Ricci in that time. Have I got that right, Aaron?'

'Yes, that's right.'

'That's convenient,' Josh muttered. 'You sure you didn't call her after leaving the station last night, to give her a little heads-up about our interview? Any emails or private messages? It's easily checked, Aaron, so we strongly suggest you're honest with us. Are you friends with Allison on any social media platforms?'

'Look, I'm telling you, I haven't contacted her and she hasn't tried to contact me. Not by email. Not by bloody Facebook. Nothing. We kept our lives separate. I only ever used that mobile to call her and I forgot to take it with me on Friday in all the rush. Right from the start, we made an agreement to not complicate things by connecting on social media. It's just too messy.'

'Would it surprise you to learn, Aaron, that Ms Garrett seems to have left her townhouse.' Josh went on, 'A strange coincidence, don't you think? We tried visiting her today and we were informed by a neighbour that she apparently left her house in a bit of a hurry last night, around 10 pm. Packed her car with a couple of suitcases. Seems she's made the decision to go away for a while. Do you know anything about that, Mr Ricci? Did she happen to tell you about her plans?'

'I told you, I haven't spoken to her. I don't know anything about her going away or where she could be.'

'We'll need to find her, Mr Ricci,' Josh's voice was firm. 'Any information you can provide that would help us track her down, would be to your benefit. Do you know any of her friends or family? Anywhere you can think of that she could have gone to?'

'I wouldn't have a clue. All I know is that she runs her own business in event management, and she mainly works from home. We didn't really talk about our personal lives and families. We just didn't go there, all right?' He shrugged like the matter should be obvious.

'The thing is, Aaron, without Ms Garrett available to corroborate your story, what we have is just that: a story.' Josh marked Ricci with a glare. 'You had your mobile switched off, so we can't confirm your movements via your GPS data. And so far, none of the neighbours we've interviewed from Florence Street remember seeing you or your car at the complex on Thursday evening or on Friday morning—'

'I was having a bloody affair! Of course, I didn't park at the complex. I parked in the next street down. It was Gilford or Gilmore Place or something. Ally told me to use the bush track at the back of the complex so there was less chance I would be seen, and that's what I did.'

'Be that as it may, Aaron, at the moment your movements are unaccounted for.' Before Aaron could interject,

Josh pulled a sheet of paper from his file and slid it towards Ricci and his lawyer.

'I want to go back to your second device, Aaron. These are the phone records we obtained from your service provider. I want to draw your attention to two calls you placed to Ms Garrett's mobile at 9.07 am and then again at 9.09 am on Friday morning. Can you explain to us, Mr Ricci, why you needed to call Ms Garrett from your mobile if, as you say, you were with Allison at her town-house in Florence Street?'

'I don't know what you're talking about. There were no calls. I don't remember making any calls.' Aaron had paled visibly beneath the crimson pall of his bruised skin. He turned wildly to his lawyer for assistance.

De Matteo ignored his client and examined the prin-tout of the phone records. 'Detective, I'm sure there's a very simple explanation for these records. Potentially even innocuous pocket dials. This doesn't prove that Mr Ricci was any place other than where he says he was.' De Matteo's tone was matter-of-fact, but Kate suspected that for the first time in the interview, the lawyer was on less certain ground and on guard.

'Well, I'm sure you can argue that in court, Mr de Matteo,' Josh observed dryly. 'Right now, what we know for a fact is that the bushland reserve behind Ms Garrett's property leads to Elliot Pass. In fact, it joins up with the exact bushland that Mr Ricci's property backs on to. It's a bit of a hike from Florence Street, but it can definitely be done.' He paused to let the information sink in.

'So, let me tell you what we think happened.' He eyed the two men in turn. 'Mr Ricci, we believe that you and Ms Garrett together planned and carried out the abduc-tion of your daughter—'

'No! That's not true.' Ricci's voice was a bewildered cry.

Josh ignored him and continued as if he hadn't spoken. 'You organised the cover of the conference to ensure you had an alibi for the day. The location of Ms Garrett's townhouse provided the perfect means for accessing your property, without the need to use your car, which may have been recognised by your neighbours—'

'No. No, wait. This is bullshit.'

'—you know your family's routine. You have a key to the house. You knew exactly how to get in and out without making a sound. Sienna's your daughter. She's not going to cry out when she's cuddled by her father.'

Ricci's face was ashen. He shook his head in disbelief as Josh's words continued to crash over him, unrelenting.

'But something went wrong and Sienna died. Maybe it was an accident and you didn't mean for it to happen. Whatever occurred, you or Ms Garrett disposed of the body. And you went after Jason Veliu to distract us and pin it all on your wife's ex.'

'I didn't do this. I swear, this didn't happen.' Tears were starting to bubble up and he sniffled into his hands.

Josh observed Ricci with dispassionate interest. 'I must say, last night's interview was a master stroke. Stringing us along to see how much we knew or had worked out. Not even a hint about Allison Garrett until you had the chance to speak with her and make sure she got away. And suddenly, here you are today, being so forthcoming and honest about your relationship.'

'It's the truth. This time I've been telling you the truth.' He turned a desperate, tear-stained face to Kate. 'Please. I'm not lying. I didn't hurt Sienna. I didn't kill my daughter.'

22

Through the automatic doors, Kate stepped into a crush of people; teenagers in languid groups, families treating their kids after weekend sports, backpackers and truckies looking for their fast-food fix.

The tang of salt, fat and sugar hung heavy in the air and recalled the previous occasion that she had been at this very spot, when the room had featured paramedics and a group of frightened employees. So many of the locations and places in town had that effect on her, carrying the mark of her police work. A veiled second town touched by violence and tragedy that shimmered under the skin of the familiar places and people everyone knew. Her eyes wandered towards the counter – no one familiar on shift.

She stepped past a young mother negotiating chip portions with her twin toddlers in high chairs. One of the little girls howled in protest as her mother grimly doled out the fries between the two.

'Ten chippies each. That's what I said, Molly. You have to share with your sister.'

'No! My chippies!' She swung her legs and kicked at her mother.

'Molly! Stop that right now!'

Kate hurried past as Molly's voice rose in a wail. She neatly dodged a uniformed employee mopping up the spilled remains of a Mc-something next to the entrance to the toilets and made for the party room at the back of the restaurant.

She had made it. Or at least she hadn't entirely missed the birthday party of Lachie, Archie's newest friend from preschool who was turning five today and celebrating with fourteen of his friends, all boys. Archie had made a point of reminding her before she had left that morning, and she had made a supreme effort to make it in time before the party ended at four. Partially to make up for the fact that she had forgotten the ice-cream she had promised Archie over the phone the previous night. He had checked the freezer first thing in the morning, the turkey, and was yet to forgive her lapse.

Her husband was another reason she had made the effort. Like her, Geoff often found himself at sea at these events, struggling to remember parents' names and topics for small talk. They usually made a point of tackling such gatherings together as an act of solidarity. Given how things were at home at the moment, she had more reason than ever to be here.

She pushed open the heavy glass door and found herself amongst a scrum of whooping boys of all different ages, who were following a slightly overwhelmed-looking party host dressed in costume and carrying a cake. She spotted several older boys still entwined in the multi-level play equipment that rose to the sky inside the glass-box play-room. Either they hadn't noticed the cake being brought out, or they were too absorbed in their own games to bother having to stop to sing 'Happy Birthday'.

Her eyes roved the room for her son, not seeing him. Parents stood at the back of the room chatting in straggly groups. She saw Geoff, seemingly deep in conversation with an athletic-looking woman in skin-tight jeans and a delicately embroidered boho-style top. The woman was leaning in to catch what Geoff was saying, her shoulder brushing up against his and strands of her hair threading against his jumper. He smiled and gestured animatedly with his right hand, his other hand resting on the handle of their daughter's pram like an afterthought. Kate presumed Amy lay sleeping inside. She shrugged off a spike of irritation. Geoff clearly didn't seem to be having trouble making small talk on this occasion.

'Mummy!' A sweat-tousled head barrelled into her legs and Kate kneeled down to scoop her son into her arms. She had been worried about how Archie would fare at the party, seeing that he had always preferred dress-ups and craft over soccer and monkey bars. His friendship with Lachie was a recent development. The youngest of four sporty and rough-and-tumble brothers, Lachie was loud and strident, the opposite of her quietly spoken and earnest son. Kate couldn't see the attraction and had taken an instant dislike to the boy, which she knew was petty but couldn't help herself. She had been particularly unimpressed with his parents' boys-only party invite, which seemed unnecessary, given all the pre-school friends they shared.

'Are you having fun, buddy?' She kissed his red face, shiny with sweat.

He wriggled away but stayed close. 'Yep. I climbed right to the top level.'

'Did you? Wow! That's great.'

'I waved to Daddy from the top.'

'Good job, Arch. Did you want to keep playing or have some cake?'

'Mmm. Have some cake.' She noticed he hadn't let go of her hand.

On cue, the room broke into song. 'Happy Birthday' followed by three raucous cheers led by a musclebound man in cargo pants and an Adidas print shirt who Kate presumed must be Lachie's father. Lachie, surrounded by his three brothers and his Instagram-perfect mother, crowded around a Superman-themed birthday cake. Five blue candles were blown out as a dozen or so phones recorded the moment.

Kate waited for the crowds to thin before obtaining a slice of cake for Archie and accompanying him to the corner, where Geoff was now standing by himself beside Amy's pram, sans the boho lady.

'You made it,' he said, brushing his lips across her cheek. He smelled of nuggets and strawberry milkshake, and she couldn't help wondering if his good mood was the result of his earlier conversation with the svelte lady, rather than a reaction to seeing Kate. Still, he was speaking to her again, which was something.

'Yeah, Josh has things under control.' She didn't elaborate and he didn't ask. It had not been a good time to leave, straight after the Ricci interview. She had sensed that Josh had wanted to talk, to tie off loose ends, to finally discuss the case as colleagues rather than combatants. But as with everything in her life, the timing was off.

Ricci had left with his lawyer, distraught and shell-shocked. Formal charges would not be laid until they had shored up corroboration in the form of physical evidence. Kate had left Josh to deal with the warrant for Allison Garrett's home and to coordinate the search for her whereabouts, including chasing up traffic records for her vehicle and following up on any financial activity, social media, and contact with work colleagues. With any luck, the autopsy next week and the forensic searches of Ms

Garrett's home and Ricci's car would furnish the physical evidence they needed to tie Ricci and his lover to Sienna's abduction. It would, of course, all be cold comfort to Elissa, whose loss would be compounded once she found out who was responsible.

Kate shook away the thoughts of Elissa's grief and focused on her own family.

Peeping inside the muslin wrap covering Amy's pram, she checked to see if her daughter was awake. Amy lay relaxed in deep slumber, her tiny chest moving up and down in steady beats. Kate smiled. Like all babies, Amy slept better in the presence of a steady hum of background noise rather than in pin-drop silence, where even the slightest sound was likely to startle her awake. The beginnings of a thought flickered in her mind and then died again.

'Can I go back to play, Dad?' Archie had finished his cake and his eyes were fixed on the play equipment, which was once more crawling with boys from the party.

'You go.' Kate motioned to Geoff. 'I'll stay with her.'

Kate's attention returned to her daughter as Amy whimpered softly in her sleep. She placed a hand on her baby's warm body, shushing her, and Amy wriggled and settled once more. Feeling the soft, firm weight of her daughter beneath her fingers, she experienced the familiar roll of guilt twisting her gut, her mind flooding with images of another time, another place. In hospital, staring through the plastic walls of the incubator unit at the tiny spectre of her daughter, born pre-term, crisscrossed with tubes that were keeping her alive. The sickening camera roll of *what-ifs* that her brain hoarded away and served up as punishment at every opportunity. The joy of her daughter would always be coloured by the violence of her entry into the world. The result of her mistake. Her arrogance. Shame rushed through her and nausea rose.

'She's beautiful.'

Kate looked up to find a grey-haired woman in a twinset, presumably a grandmother of one of the kids, who had stopped to catch a glimpse of Amy. Her hands were bent with arthritis and foundation caked her crepe-paper skin.

Kate nodded, her reply sticking in her throat. The woman smiled, kind eyes surveying her from behind old-fashioned glasses. After a moment or two of silence, she moved away. Kate exhaled. She waved and caught Geoff's eye, motioning that she was taking Amy for a walk. She wheeled the pram outside into the cool air with relief, retreating to a quieter end of the carpark away from the drive-through line.

'Detective?'

Turning, she found Lena Chalmers, her arms heaving with brown paper takeaway bags and a packed drink holder. Her eyes blinked at Kate in shock.

'Lena. Hi. How are you?'

'I… I'm good. I'm getting food to take to Mum's for the kids… What are you doing here?'

'My son's inside for a party. I was just getting some air.'

'Oh… Of course.' She laughed nervously.

The seconds ticked by and Kate's attention sharpened, aware that Lena was still standing there, unmoving.

'Is there something I can do for you, Lena?'

'I heard on the news… About the baby… I can't believe it. It's just so awful.' Her eyes moved to the pram beside Kate.

'It is awful. The family is devastated.' Kate observed Lena, taking in the other woman's obvious agitation.

'I need to talk to you. To tell you something.' Lena's eyes slid away, unable to hold her gaze. 'I'm sorry, I should have spoken about it before...'

'It's okay, Lena. You can tell me now. Is this about Jason?'

She nodded.

Kate's spirits rose. Lena wanting to speak about Jason was a good sign. Maybe she had finally decided to provide a statement about what he had put her through on Thursday? Could she be thinking of leaving him? Kate's mind flew to her contact at the local women's refuge. The refuge director, Kate was sure, could find some space for Lena and the kids even at short notice. Or at least, she could help Lena set things in motion.

'I think Jason was there,' Lena's stricken voice broke through her thoughts. '...that day when the baby disappeared.'

Did he see me? Did he recognise me? This is what keeps me up at night. It was only a couple of seconds, but he had glanced my way. It wouldn't have meant anything to him at the time. But now...?

Once he had thought about it and made the connections. Would he realise? Would he forgive me? Or would he punish me? Would he make me suffer for everything I've done?

Sienna.

Her tiny crumpled body that had somehow felt heavier afterwards. Like the burden of my lies had added to her weight. I remember her lying in the crook of my arm, snug and doll-like, yet cold. Placing her down on the wet forest floor. How I had dug into the soil and litter. My hands scrabbling the earth. Interning Sienna in that place, despoiling her face and limbs with dirt and mud.

I can no longer bear the thought of gardening. My fingers buried in soil, thick with worms, it fills me with horror. The smell of damp earth and wet leaf litter takes me back. To that night. To that moment. When I scurried through the darkness, afraid of the thing I carried. Afraid of going through with it and yet knowing that I had to.

23

Kate had timed well her arrival to the Northern District Base Hospital at Tweed Heads. Entering the mortuary suite, she was in time to hear Graham Barlow, the hospital's resident forensic pathologist, bark a final instruction to his assistant who was wheeling a morgue trolley back out to cold storage.

Kate's eyes skated past the undersized body bag that lay marooned on the trolley, knowing full well its doll-like contents: Sienna Lillian Ricci, sewn up after her post-mortem examination. Kate had chosen to miss the autopsy. She knew that it could be interpreted as weakness on her part, but she didn't care. It was a matter of self-preservation. She had viewed her share of decaying bodies and uncompromising forensic scenes. But she had never dealt with such a situation with a child of Sienna's age before and that first glimpse of her at the reserve had been enough. Caked in soil and dried blood, and with the sour whiff of urine from the unfortunate teenager who had chosen to relieve himself at that particular spot. Kate didn't need any more images in her head of this child than she had already absorbed. The autopsy file and its photos, which would be landing on her desk soon enough, would be plenty.

Her eyes moved to Barlow, observing the stooped silhouette of the pathologist. His gaunt, cigarette-ravaged body was masked by morgue scrubs. She had been expecting some sort of mocking comment at her obvious no-show, but he acknowledged her with no more than a silent nod. Even Barlow, she realised, brittle and battle-scarred as he was, had his limits. Today would not have counted as an easy day at the office for any of the team.

Barlow moved to the sink, where Kate joined him. She watched as he lathered and scrubbed his hands with an intensity of focus, the clouds of yellow antiseptic soap draining down the sink.

'I hear you're about to arrest the father.'

'Aaron Ricci is definitely up there on our list.'

His eyes narrowed, not missing the note of hesitation. 'Ha. Always guarded. Just like your old man.' He wiped his hands and threw the crumpled paper towel in the bin. 'Your colleagues don't seem to share your reserve, Miles. Got a call from your boss this morning. Only interested in any forensic material on Sienna that can be matched to Ricci: his clothes and car or something from his girl-friend's house. You know that'll take time, don't you?'

Kate nodded. The search warrant had come through last night and a forensic team had descended on Florence Street that morning. Ms Garrett's whereabouts were still unknown. Her car had been traced through CCTV and traffic cameras heading north through town, but the trail had gone cold on the outskirts. There was every possibility that Allison Garrett had made it across the border on the back roads. They were currently coordinating with the Queensland police. Financial records and mobile tracking requests were also in train to try to get a lead on her location.

Her phone buzzed. She ignored it, letting it go to voicemail. 'Anything you can tell me?'

'Physically, she seems well nourished for her age. There are signs of some congestion in her nasal tissue, indicating she was likely suffering from an upper respiratory infection, a cold or something similar, around the time she died. No obvious sign of trauma or disease, apart from the bite marks and lacerations around the torso, neck and limbs, of course, but they are all postmortem. I'd say the work of a feral cat or fox. Foxes are known to bury their surplus food and that's consistent with the shallow re-burial site she was found in. But we'll have to wait for forensic veterinary confirmation on the bite marks. The multiple grazing across her body is also postmortem, likely from being dragged or moved along the ground by whatever animal it was. I'll need to wait for toxicology to confirm anything in her system, drugs or medication.'

'So, you don't have a cause of death for me?' The words were out before she could catch them.

A shadow crossed Barlow's face as his eyes hardened.

Kate remembered too late the diplomacy required to deal with Barlow. He had become even more difficult to navigate since the findings from his office had recently come under challenge in a widely publicised coronial enquiry that remained active. The same case that had led to her firearms injury. Kate herself would be expected to front up to a reconvened inquest in a few months' time. She had since heard rumours that the Health Service was trying to use the case to push Barlow into early retirement. He was still here, so it appeared they hadn't succeeded. Yet.

'Must I remind you, *Detective*, that not all cases come with a ready-made map showing *X marks the spot*,' he spat.

'It's about ruling out improbabilities based on the evidence available to you. I try not to reach for unicorns in the presence of horse manure.'

Kate sighed. This was clearly about their previous case. She had inadvertently picked a scab that was still weeping. Refusing to engage, she ploughed on. 'But we have a time of death?'

He shrugged. 'It's difficult with babies. With limited musculature, there's usually no demonstrable sign of rigor mortis in infants. The classic thirty-six to forty-hour cycle of rigor development and disappearance for adults doesn't apply here.' He was lecturing her now, his preferred mode of communication.

'There are minimal signs of bloating, but then the cold temperatures over the last few days would have helped slow things down, especially if she's been out in the reserve all that time, noting there's not much weight on her to retain heat.'

Kate felt a stab for the lone body left out in the rain and cold.

'My best guess is that she was deceased for at least twenty-four hours from when she was found at the reserve, most likely considerably longer. I'll be able to provide more details when I forward through my report,' Barlow finished.

Kate curled her lips. *Considerably longer.* What the hell did that mean? Barlow was being obtuse and deliberately unhelpful. Why couldn't he just give her a straight answer? Sienna had been reported missing around 9 am on Friday and located at Layton Reserve close to 9.30 pm on Saturday night. Being deceased for at least twenty-four hours from the time of discovery meant Friday night-time. So, Sienna had been killed sometime in the twelve hours between going missing on Friday morning and around nine to ten o'clock that same night. There, she had done the maths for him.

Her phone sounded again and she registered a second missed call from the station.

Barlow pumped a bottle of hand cream, working the moisturiser into his skin. 'A preliminary report will be emailed to you, Detective.' Words of dismissal.

The hospital doors slid open and Kate exited the stale, recycled air into the crisp sunlight outside. Her stomach growled and she ripped open the chocolate bar she had collected from the hospital vending machine on her way out. Ahead of her, an elderly man adorned in perfectly ironed formal slacks and a collared shirt was making his way up the entrance ramp, pushing a wheelchair housing a tiny brown-skinned woman wizened by age. For a moment her heart stilled, the mouthful of chocolate and nougat congealing on her tongue. But no, it wasn't who she had thought it was. Of course, it wasn't Aunty Iris, her mother's adopted family, and the man navigating the wheelchair wasn't her long-dead husband. Kate stepped aside, allowing the couple to move past her. The woman broke into a smile, and in her wrinkled countenance Kate thought she saw the ghost of another face, patient and undemanding. Regret rose, hard and sharp. There were so many obligations that she wasn't meeting.

Swallowing the mouthful of confectionary, her appetite suddenly lost, she reached for her phone.

Constable Roby came on line, his voice static-filled and tiny. Cursing the terrible connection, Kate tried to make out what he was saying. The words slowly slotted into place and she felt herself go rigid.

'Sarge, we got it… traffic footage… like Lena said.'

24

A shiver of unease ran through Kate as Constable Roby knocked on the front door. She almost stopped him but resisted.

They waited in silence on the unkempt front porch, the winter sun bearing down like the last few days of frigid cold had never happened. Kate could feel beads of dampness swell in her armpits. Empty beer cans and cigarette butts littered the bare cement slab, and old webs caked in dust adorned the external siding. A punching bag hung suspended from a ceiling beam. Next to it an armchair slumped, grimy with stained upholstery, alongside a neatly stacked pair of children's gumboots. Beside the front porch, in the car port, sat a gleaming dark-metallic-grey Ford Ranger. Clearly, money was available for some things.

For a brief moment, the wisdom of doing this without Skinner's authorisation scuttled through her mind, but she shook it away. She had also failed to run it past Josh, but then he had been busy at the Garrett house. She had spoken to him briefly after returning to the station from the autopsy, but he had been irritable and preoccupied, annoyed that the search of Allison's home had not produced any immediate results. So far there was nothing to indicate the house had ever accommodated a small child; no wipes or nappies in the rubbish, no bottles or other baby paraphernalia. She gathered that the forensics team had commenced searching the communal garbage-bin area in case Allison or Ricci had disposed of anything in one of their neighbour's bins. Josh had rung off before she'd had the chance to acquaint him of the new developments with Jason Veliu.

Yesterday, Lena had hesitantly informed Kate that one of Veliu's regular drug clients lived near Elliot Pass, noting that Jason had been making weekly visits to the area for well over six months. According to Lena, Jason had spent considerable time cultivating that particular client's business. As Veliu had put it, the man was a rich knob from Brisbane, who had set up digs in an out-of-the-way property. Lena didn't know the customer's name, only the fact that Veliu had on several occasions spent time partying at the man's property off Elliott Pass and was, without question, familiar with the area.

The admission of drug supply hadn't come as a surprise to Kate. Veliu had long been on their radar as a small fry in the methamphetamine supply network operating along the north coast and across the border. But it was the Elliot Pass location that had pinged her interest. If Veliu had been visiting the area for months, he had undoubtably discovered where his ex-partner now resided with her brand-new family. Of that Kate was certain. Had he been terrorising Elissa all this time? A cat toying with a mouse, just because he could, with Sienna ending up the unwitting casualty of that campaign.

With everything going on with Ricci, Kate knew that Veliu's movements had received little to no priority. She had assigned Roby to the task of reviewing the smattering of CCTV and the surprisingly large amount of dashcam footage that had been donated by members of the public in response to the information call-out. What Roby had uncovered was indisputable: dashcam footage that showed the back of a dark-grey Ford Ranger bearing the same licence plate as Veliu's turning left into Ridge Road, one street up from Elliot Pass at 8.42 am on Friday morning. The timing was too great a coincidence to let slide.

But it was not just that. When Kate had arrived at the station following the autopsy, a stack of phone messages had been waiting at her desk. All from Rayna Gardiner. When Kate had returned her call, Rayna had been distraught. Gone was the straitjacket reserve of a few days ago. News of her son-in-law's second questioning by the police had clearly unnerved her, badly. Her shock and disbelief had been palpable. She had been adamant in her defence of Ricci, unwilling to hear any information to the contrary, and had practically screamed at Kate over the phone.

'Where Sienna was found, that's one of Jason's favourite fishing spots. He used to go there as a kid. When he and Elissa lived in town, he would go there almost every other week, sometimes camping overnight. I remember, whenever I planned on visiting, Elissa would time our meetings during one of Jason's fishing trips. It's Veliu you should be looking at, not my daughter's husband. I told you that on the very first day. Why won't you just do your job and arrest the bastard? Aaron didn't do this!' She had hung up before Kate had got a word in and her attempts to call Rayna back had gone unanswered.

Skinner had been out and Kate had made the call. So here she was, once again at Veliu's doorstep.

In response to Roby's second round of loud knocking, the door opened a crack, revealing a sliver of Lena's face. Though she lay in shadow, a dimly lit hallway stretching behind, they could still make out a new rose-coloured swelling flowering above her left eye. The bruising had definitely not been present when Kate had spoken to Lena yesterday. It was clearly a fresh addition to the tapestry of violence that already marked her body. Lena's eyes widened in dismay on seeing them, her expression fixed on Kate, trying to convey a wordless message. She gestured a silent forefinger in the direction of her shoulder, an infinitesimal movement, carefully shielded by her body. Kate understood. Veliu was somewhere behind, hidden in the darkness of the house.

'What are you doing here? What do you want? Can't you just leave us alone?' her voice rose in volume.

'We're sorry to bother you again, Ms Chalmers, but we need to speak to Jason. Is he in?'

The briefest pause and she shook her head. 'No. He went out. I don't know where he is.'

'His vehicle is in the carport, Lena. You're sure he's not in?'

'A friend picked him up. He's not here.' Her voice rose again. She wanted Veliu to hear that she was saying all the right things. If they were to gain entry to the house, they would need to do it without her assistance.

'Look, you can't come in, all right. I told you, Jason's not here.' Lena attempted to close the door, but Kate wedged her foot in, holding it in place. Up close, she could see the faint tremble in Lena's hands, the nervous tick in her forehead. The woman was terrified. She wondered if Veliu had a weapon inside.

'Did Jason do that to you, Lena?' Her voice was a low whisper.

Lena's hand landed briefly on her injured face and away again. 'This? This is nothing. I wasn't looking and walked into the bathroom door.'

Kate stared at Lena and came to a decision. Her voice rose firm and loud. 'Ms Chalmers, we need to speak with Jason in connection with an ongoing investigation. I believe he is inside the house and I need you to step aside, right now—'

Her eyes caught quick movement in the shadows of the corridor followed by a scuffle of footsteps and the sound of the screen door slamming.

'Go. Go… Around the back!'

Roby was already away, sprinting down the porch steps and around the side of the house to cut Veliu off. Kate plunged into the darkened house, tearing past Lena, who flattened herself against the wall with a cry. Through the kitchen she slammed past the screen door, still swinging open on its hinge, her weapon drawn, taking in the neglected yard, searching for signs of movement.

An empty hills hoist creaked in the wind amidst uneven patches of lawn, and a ramshackled metal shed sagged at the bottom of the garden, half hidden by overgrown shrubbery.

Roby joined her from the side of the house. He shook his head, confirming that Veliu had not escaped that way. Kate nodded and motioned to the shed, indicating for him to follow. Apprehension surged through her as they approached the structure, every muscle taut with tension as she steeled herself.

Staying close to the shed wall, the metal sheeting cold against her skin, Kate edged forward, listening hard for any sounds, her own breathing loud in her ears. She stopped. *Was that something?* She thought she had heard a creak inside the shed, or had it just been her imagination? She swallowed the rising panic; her entire body screaming at her to run the other way. She could see the door was unlocked and slightly ajar. Signing for Roby to cover her, she rounded the corner and in a swift movement swung the door wide, her Glock rigid and ready, aiming into the darkened space.

It revealed nothing. The shed was empty apart from a rusted handheld lawnmower and a tower of water-stained storage boxes. *Shit!*

Kate's eyes roved the thick shrubbery concealing the fence line. Could Veliu have had time to scale the fence, or was he still concealed out here somewhere watching them, hiding in plain sight? Her head snapped towards the house. Or maybe he was still inside? The open kitchen door a ruse to distract her, so he could depart through the front while they were dicking around in the backyard. *Fuck!*

'Roby, the house. Check it room by room. Make sure he's not hiding inside.'

She raced past him, skidding along the side of the house to get to the front yard. As she rounded the corner, she heard the revving of an engine. Ahead of her, Veliu was at the wheel of his Ford Ranger ute, reversing out of the driveway at speed, Lena a terrified hostage in the passenger seat.

'Jason, stop the car!' Kate screamed, her arms raised and taking aim.

The vehicle jerked and slowed momentarily as Veliu caught her eyes. His free hand reached out to grab Lena by her hair and pull her towards him, using her as a shield. His lips flared into a savage snarl, daring her to pull the trigger.

Kate hesitated and Veliu accelerated. Without pause, he drove straight into the patrol car they had arrived in, parked on the opposite kerb, ramming with a sickening crunch into the side of the driver's cab. The ute tray of the Ranger smashed into metal and glass, crumpling the patrol car like paper. He glanced at Kate in triumph.

While Veliu was distracted, hands busy on the steering wheel and the gear stick, Lena seemed to take her chance. The passenger door flung open and Lena propelled herself forward, only to get jagged by her seatbelt. She desperately tried to untangle herself, but the split-second delay was enough for Veliu to catch hold of her arm. The car accelerated and Kate watched in horror as Lena's body was dragged half in and half outside the vehicle. Her feet scrambled to keep up with the moving car, being hauled off the bitumen by its momentum, her body wedged in by the open door. The car veered into the kerb, and the momentary slowing of the vehicle was enough for Lena to wrench herself free, slamming into the ground, her body rolling and her head ricocheting off the cement footpath.

Kate began to sprint towards the vehicle, hollering again for Veliu to stop. With a scream of rage, he accelerated and sped away, the open passenger door swinging as he careened around the corner, tyres squealing.

'Lena... Are you okay?' Kate reached down to help the woman lying prone on the grass verge, but Lena recoiled from her. The smell of burnt diesel fumes hung in the air. Kate heard the sound of Roby pounding down the driveway and swearing at the sight of their ruined transport. Bystanders were starting to gather, phones out, concern mixed with excitement.

Lena sat up unsteadily, her hand protecting the brush-stroke of bloodied skin marking the side of her face.

Flinching from the gaze of the onlookers, she turned on Kate, her eyes wild, her voice a frantic plea.

'The kids. He's going to go after the kids. You need to stop him.'

25

Kate waited alone in Skinner's office. She could hear the murmur of voices in the incident room outside, the low rumble of Skinner's voice occasionally interrupted by Josh's quick, clipped responses. She couldn't hear what they were saying, but she knew the subject of their conversation.

She trained her gaze to the window, to the last vestiges of coral-hued light streaking the sky, the familiar landmarks of concrete and brick morphing into shadow. She took in a couple of patrol officers emerging from the side carpark, their movements measured and relaxed. Snatches of their laughter and conversation floated up to her as they passed through the entryway below, swallowed into the florescent glow of the station building.

She heard the door being closed behind her.

'Josh must be happy,' she said without turning, the bitterness escaping before she could stop herself.

Skinner ignored her, taking his time to settle into his chair before regarding her. 'Ellis will be handling operational decisions going forward. You can stay on the case or take on alternate duties. It's your choice.'

Kate seethed at his use of the word *choice*. Like she had any say in the decision. She made an effort to curb her rage from spilling out and giving him further ammunition.

'I'd like to stay on the case, sir, if it's all the same to you.'

Skinner shrugged, indifferent. 'Whatever you think you can handle.'

There it was again. A quick barb at her mental state, because that's what it boiled down to. Any failure, any misstep on her part would always come down to that. The ready excuse that Skinner could turn to whenever he needed. *She wasn't coping. She wasn't up to it. It was too much, too soon.* She could see his reasoning writ large. He had given her a chance and she had blown it. Skinner didn't agree with her handling of the investigation and now she was being sidelined, the role of case lead being handed over to Josh. The entire Veliu mess laid directly at her door. To her lack of planning. Her lack of preparedness. For letting Veliu get away. For getting sidetracked and creating a whole new problem that the team had to deal with when their attention should be on building a case around Aaron Ricci.

'What about Lena and the kids? Has anyone followed up?'

'Take it up with Ellis.' Skinner waved his hand in dismissal.

The incident room felt different, as she stepped out. Kate was suddenly hyperaware of her colleagues, her skin ablaze and alive to their every reaction. Their determined busyness so as to avoid meeting her eyes. The hurried glances hiding embarrassment or pity or both. Only Darnley and Roby met and held her gaze, a small gesture of solidarity.

She headed directly for Josh, feeling the room hold its breath, expecting a confrontation. He was in conversation with Vickie Harris, the constable in the middle of a sentence. Kate cut across without apology, caring little as Harris lapsed into purse-lipped silence.

'What's happening with Lena Chalmers? Have we checked on the kids?'

Josh's reply was unhurried, lifted from the same playbook as Skinner's. 'Is there a problem with the children?'

Kate exhaled, refusing to play the game. 'Lena raised the issue of Veliu going after the kids as payback.' Her thoughts flew to the crumpled figure on the side of the street, shaking uncontrollably, all bravado gone. The split second of super-human courage it had taken to escape from her oppressor falling away in the face of the possible consequences of her actions. Of what he might do to exact his revenge. Lena's entire focus had been on her kids begging Kate to check on them at her mother's place before Veliu could get to them first.

Kate had called it in along with the general call-out on Veliu's vehicle. But with the general confusion at the scene, Lena being transported away by ambulance, the media descending, and her own endless questioning over what had occurred, she feared that the request had fallen by the wayside.

Kate knew that Veliu's Ford Ranger had been found abandoned a few blocks away from the house, which meant that he was on foot – or more likely in possession of another vehicle via one of his many petty-criminal associates, given that there had been no reports of stolen vehicles in the vicinity. So, that meant Veliu was on the run in an unknown vehicle. They were checking his known contacts through the system, but it was going to take time. The risk to the kids, she felt, was real. She had believed Lena's fear without question. There was no telling what Veliu, rage-fuelled and thwarted, was capable of.

The look Josh gave her was pitying. Once again, she was imposing sentiment onto their operational decisions, letting her overwrought emotions as a new mother colour her thinking. Another example of why he was a better choice to guide the investigation. 'I doubt the kids will be his first priority at the moment. More likely to be lying low right now, don't you think? Can't really spare anyone anyway with everything that's going on…' He eyed her meaningfully, not letting her forget the origin of their extra workload. 'But if it makes you feel better, I'll get a patrol to drive past.'

'I'd feel better going and checking myself.'

He nodded, no doubt glad of an excuse to get rid of her brooding presence from the incident room. 'If that's what you want.'

26

The detour to check on Lena's kids had made her late getting home. Even later than she had promised, when she had called Geoff from the station earlier. Kate was expecting a scene when she stepped inside. Geoff's patience with her was increasingly on a knife's edge, the heaviness in her chest overfull with milk, a relentless reminder of her tardiness.

Still, the trip out had been the right decision, if only to settle her own mind. Despite Lena's mother's obvious displeasure at seeing her. Her objection to having Kate inside her house, the unnecessary fuss. Kate had insisted on sighting both children, walking through the squalid home, to a dank room at the back, where she had spotted Charlie asleep on a mattress on the floor beside the cot with his baby brother. She had passed a silent, bearded figure moulded onto a fraying couch, his eyes glued to the TV, presumably Lena's father. He hadn't turned or seemed to even notice her presence in the house.

Kate had tried her best with Mrs Chalmers, explaining what had occurred that afternoon and impressing on her the potential threat Veliu posed; the need to be on guard, to notify Charlie's day care for the coming days. There had been little reaction from the woman, even to the news that her daughter remained in hospital under observation for head trauma after her escape and fall from Veliu's car. Whether she was already in communication with her daughter and aware of the day's events, Kate couldn't tell. Lena's mother had given her nothing. Kate had felt a deep pall of helplessness driving away, unable to tear the last image of Lena's children from her mind.

Pulling into her front drive, her heart sank at the sight of her father's beaten-up ute parked in her usual spot. She was too tired to have to take on her father tonight. She swore and reversed, parking alongside the kerb.

Inside, she moved through the house, bracing herself at each threshold, feeling her unease grow with each empty room. She heard a squeal, recognising Archie's excited whoops from somewhere out the back. *Of course, they were outside on the deck.* She paused at Amy's door, knowing she risked disturbing her daughter if she stepped in, yet not ready to face what awaited her outside: her father's intractable problems, her husband's silent disapproval.

Entering her daughter's room, she took in Amy's small body snug in her sleep suit, her lips slightly parted, and her half-moon cheeks still with repose. She felt the draw of milk in her chest as her body automatically responded to the sight of her baby. As if on cue, Amy stirred, emitting a small wail. Glad of the excuse, Kate scooped her up and settled in the nursing chair, raising her daughter's half-asleep face to her breast. Amy suckled instantly, for once accepting her without reluctance. Feeling the milk drain from her, Amy calm and moulded to her body, Kate felt herself relax, the dormant muscle memory from her days of nursing Archie resurfacing. The feeling of peaceful purpose, of her body knowing its place in the world.

Kate grazed her finger gently along the soft down of her daughter's forehead. It occurred to her suddenly how much her feelings of displacement were linked to Amy's fractious feeding; her seeming rejection of her body, the one thing that was entirely hers to give. A side effect of how Amy had entered the world: pre-term and not yet ready to tackle the intricacies of feeding. Amy's developmental difficulties were just another stone of guilt to add to her heaving pile. In her weaker moments, Kate had caught herself pushing away from her daughter, taking refuge in her son's company, whose ledger she had yet to discernibly taint.

Her daughter lay heavy in her arms, lulled into deep sleep by her feed. Kate remained seated, stretching the moment for as long as she could, enjoying the feel of Amy tucked into her side. Careful not to wake her, she gently burped and placed her daughter back in the cot. Leaving the room, Kate allowed herself a moment of lightness, uninfected by shame, willing the feeling not to fade.

Stepping outside onto the deck, the cool evening, sharp like a blade and spiked with tension, sucked at her quiet contentment. Geoff sat stone-faced on one of the wicker chairs, nursing a glass of red, and didn't look up at her entrance. When she had called him hours ago, she had relayed only the briefest rundown of the day's events, downplaying the risks to her own safety. No doubt he had made up his own mind from the TV news reports. About her demotion, she had said not a word, prevented by an overwhelming feeling of shame. But also, the dogged conviction that she could somehow claw it all back.

Her father sat several metres away on the timber steps entertaining Archie, pretending to conjure up coins from her son's ear. Four cans of VB lined the timber floor beside him. Her heart sank. How long had he been here? She wasn't up for a combined lecture from the two of them.

'Mummy,' cried Archie, spotting her. 'Grandpa's doing magic. Come and see.'

'Kit! We weren't sure if you'd gotten in or not.' Her father's pleasantries felt forced; she could hear the jagged strain beneath. 'Big day, I hear.'

'I was with Amy,' she said, choosing to ignore his last comment. Geoff looked up but said nothing. He didn't need to. He knew her too well. Could read her moods and intuit her motives. He had already formed an opinion about her detour into her daughter's room; that it was driven more by the need to avoid their company rather than any urgent maternal impulse. She flushed with shame at the version of herself she saw reflected in his eyes. At how close he came to the truth.

'Grandpa, do it again. Come and see, Mummy!' Archie was insistent. Kate could hear the hyped, overtired edge in his voice that could tip over at any moment into tears and tantrum. He should be in bed, though she knew there was little chance of that while his grandfather was around, egging him on.

She forced a smile as Gray pulled another couple of dollars from behind Archie's ear and her son squealed in delight. 'Did you see? Did you see?'

'I did, matey. That was amazing. Hey, how about Grandpa does a couple more tricks and then it's time for bed?' Lately, all her interactions with Archie seemed to involve putting an end to his fun.

Archie pretended not to hear her, concentrating on trying to prise the coins from his grandfather's hand. Gray winked and opened his palm, presenting Archie with the money. Laughing, he slurped from his beer can, a thin trail of brown liquid escaping and cutting a path down his stubbled chin. He wiped it off and started to tickle Archie, who screamed with delight.

Kate stared at her father, trying to catch his eyes, but he didn't look her way. Watching him interact with Archie, she knew it was a cover. An avoidance strategy so he wouldn't have to talk to her. He had made it all this way but had lost his courage.

While their attention was trained on Archie, they could hold up the pretence that this was a normal family gathering. For his part, Archie seemed to sense the tension pinging off the adults, the silence yawning large in the darkened evening. He seemed to realise his role as the peacekeeper, his laughter deliberately louder and more enthusiastic than Gray's half-hearted tickling warranted.

Gray knocked back the last of his beer and burped loudly. Archie giggled. 'I'll take it to the recycling, Grandpa.' He grasped at the empty beer cans, inserting his fingers into the metal rings to collect them all in one hit.

'Owww.' The beer cans clattered as Archie grabbed his finger in pain. The metal edge of one of the can openings had sliced into his finger.

Before Kate could react, Gray had Archie in hand. 'It's okay, bud. Just suck on your finger and it'll feel better. It's only a little cut.'

Archie's eyes welled, but he held back the tears, determined not to cry. Kate felt a sudden pang, wondering when that had happened; Archie growing out of crying. She moved towards him, but he shook away her attention. He sucked on his finger, his face serious as he concentrated on the task.

Watching Gray's face, his features softened with emotion as he attended to Archie, Kate felt a memory surface within her like a wraith. Another face, another cut finger. Kate as a young girl no older than Archie walking in on her father and Martin Jackson in the Jacksons' kitchen. Martin gently sucking her father's finger and licking the trickle of blood.

Kate blinked and turned abruptly away. 'I'm going to get a Band-Aid.'

Inside, she stumbled into the kitchen. Her mobile, which she had placed on charge on the counter, winked to life, the familiar ring tone playing as she entered. She grabbed it out of habit. An unknown number, but she answered anyway.

'Is this Detective… Miles?'

'Yes, that's right.'

'I'm calling from Esserton Central Hospital, Detective. I thought you should know that Ms Chalmers discharged herself about an hour ago. I would have called earlier, but it's been a bit of a madhouse tonight.'

Red flags sprang to attention. The hospital had been informed of Lena's DV risk status, and briefed about Veliu. Kate had specifically left her own details with the duty nurse to be contacted in case Lena needed anything. 'Was she well enough to leave? Had she been cleared for discharge?'

'It was made clear to her that she should remain overnight for observation, but there's no telling some people,' the nurse sniffed. 'The minute her boyfriend came in, all she wanted to do was leave—'

'She left with her boyfriend? He was the one who put her in hospital.' She tried to control the frustration in her voice. 'That should be on file. You were meant to call the police if Jason Veliu turned up at the ward. She's petrified of him.'

'Well, what do you think I'm doing right now? I'm calling you, aren't I?' The nurse's defences were up. 'I told you, we've been run off our feet. This is the first time I've had a moment to think since my shift began…'

Kate closed her eyes. Of course, the changeover of shifts and a whole new set of nurses on duty. It didn't surprise her that the specifics of Lena's situation hadn't been picked up.

'…And I don't know about being petrified… They were all over each other in her bed, as far as I could see,' the nurse muttered.

'What time did they leave?' Kate forced herself to be civil. Taking out her anger on this nurse, overworked and understaffed, would make little difference now.

'According to the discharge papers, they left at 6.15 pm.' Kate's eyes took in the clock digits on the kitchen microwave. It was now close to 7.30. Anything could have happened to Lena in that time. Panic swarmed her brain like a cloud of insects.

Kate thanked the nurse and hung up. She tried Lena's mobile first. It went straight to voicemail. Unsurprising. No doubt Veliu had switched it off. She tried Lena's parents' next, confirming that they had not heard from their daughter. The kids at least were safe. After updating Lena's mother on what had occurred at the hospital and stressing the need to be alert for any sign of Veliu, Kate rang off. She called the station next and dispatched a patrol to get a hold of the hospital's security tapes. If there was footage from the carparks, they could at least get a handle on the vehicle Veliu was driving.

She took a deep breath, every nerve pulsing with apprehension. She needed to call Josh and explain what was happening. Each minute of delay meant further risk to Lena, assuming she was still alive.

'Thought you were getting a Band-Aid.' Geoff had followed her into the kitchen. He watched her warily, taking in the phone in her hand, the expression on her face.

'Something's come up. I'll need to head back in. Sorry.'

'Kate, haven't you put in enough hours today? Your dad's been waiting all evening. You can't just leave. What am I supposed to tell him?'

'Just tell him I was called away. He'll understand.' She controlled her irritation. She didn't have time for this. Her father, a career police officer, was the last person who required an explanation.

Geoff glared at her and turned his back. For a second she hesitated, knowing she should do something, say something to make things less fractious between them. But everything that came to mind felt inadequate, a pat platitude that wouldn't change anything. He wanted her home and she needed to go.

She grabbed her keys, deciding she would call Josh from the car. She left Geoff rummaging inside the medicine cabinet.

27

'It looks to me like she went with him voluntarily. She clearly wants to be with him. For all we know, she's in on it with him.' Josh cleared his throat and sucked on a can of Red Bull. 'Not that I'm pegging Veliu for Sienna's abduction, mind. Ricci's still my bet.' He marked Kate with a look. 'But at the very least, it's suspicious that she would just walk out of the hospital ward with him, don't you think?'

Kate exhaled, trying to contain her frustration. Josh did this sometimes. Played devil's advocate. She could never quite tell if he meant what spilled out of his mouth or whether it was just a ploy to get under her skin. It infuriated her that he was choosing this moment to thrash out Lena's involvement in the Ricci case, when her life was in danger and every minute was of the essence.

Lena had been in hospital at the time of Sienna's abduction, courtesy of Veliu. If she had had any involvement, which Kate seriously doubted, it was after the fact and would have been at the behest of her controlling and violent partner. None of Kate's conversations with Lena had made her suspect the woman of lying, only of trying to survive. She had come to Kate with information on Veliu at considerable risk to herself. And now it seemed her fears had eventuated.

'It's interesting that she made no protest at all, don't you think?' Josh downed the rest of his drink and clunked the empty can into the nearest bin.

She ignored him, not trusting herself to speak.

Against the dark blank of night, the station window reflected their dishevelled forms in an empty, partially lit office. The station was deserted apart from a duty officer manning reception and a couple of patrol cars covering the night shift. With the discovery of Sienna's body, they were back to straight shifts. No overtime. Josh was clearly unhappy that he had been dragged into the office after-hours and was doing his utmost to rile her up.

They had just viewed the CCTV forwarded on from hospital security. It showed Veliu, unperturbed and calm, complete with a small bouquet of flowers, gaining entry into the secure ward by slipping in behind a large family party during visiting hours. He had simply waited while the family had spoken into the speaker to identify who they were coming to see, and brought up the rear once the doors had swung open to admit the group. Less than twenty minutes later, the footage showed him walking out of the ward with Lena in tow, his arms wrapped around her, holding her close. CCTV from the hospital grounds showed the couple exiting by foot via the hospital's southern entrance. If there was a vehicle waiting for them in the residential streets beyond, they didn't have footage of it.

Veliu's utter brazenness astounded her. From the patrol she had dispatched to the hospital, Kate had learned that the ward had been dealing with a convulsing patient in bed eight when Veliu had duped his way in. The senior staff had been distracted and Veliu had managed to talk his way around the harried duty nurse, the woman Kate had spoken to over the phone, without raising any alarm bells. Lena had discharged herself and they had walked out together.

'If they don't want to be helped...' He shrugged eyeing her meaningfully.

'Lena is terrified of him,' she snapped. 'She went with him because she felt she had no other choice. Everything she does, any physical affection she shows, it's all about appeasing him and avoiding escalation. Who knows what he threatened her with? He probably told her he had the kids in the car with him.'

Josh raised his hands and stepped back in mock defence at her tone. He was ridiculing her and she could feel her hackles rising. She willed herself to speak calmly. 'When she's with him, she does whatever he says without question. It doesn't matter if she's in a hospital or a police station. That's how much control he has over her. That's the point.'

Kate tried to put into words what she knew in her gut to be true from everything she had observed in her interactions with Lena and Veliu. 'She defied him this afternoon. When she got away, she humiliated him. Don't you see? Veliu came for her because even at the risk of getting caught, he had to show her who's boss. He's going to punish her for what she did. She is in danger. If we don't do something, he's going to kill her.'

He did not respond. She needed her words to fight their way through his antipathy towards her, to get past his desire to always be in the right when it came to the two of them.

'Josh, I know it's been difficult at the station with me coming back. I know you think I've got too much going on to concentrate on the job properly. And maybe you're right. But I'm telling you, this is real. I'm not your enemy on this.'

He rolled his eyes, but the challenge in them had abated. He would yield to her, for the moment at least.

'Fine, whatever,' he said. 'So, what now?'

She stopped. The enormity of the task stretched before her. How would they find Lena? They had no vehicle details and Veliu would have switched off both of their mobiles. Narrowing down their location through ATM and credit card transactions was a non-starter until the banks opened in the morning, and by that time she feared it would be too late anyway. Lena's parents had been confused and apathetic. Kate had not been able to glean any useful details about where Veliu could have taken Lena.

'He must be taking her to a location he knows. A place where he has privacy and time, and where no one would think to look.' She met Josh's eyes. 'The lawyer. What's his name... Arnot. He's some sort of cousin of Veliu's. Call him and see if he'll talk. Also, try Rayna Gardiner,' she added. 'She remembers things from when Elissa was with Veliu.'

Josh made no comment on how thin it all sounded and for that, at least, she was grateful. He turned to his desk without a word. She hoped Rayna would speak to Josh given that she was still refusing to return Kate's calls. She doubted they would get anything from Veliu's lawyer.

The time that had passed since Lena had been abducted thrashed in her mind like a caged animal. She had let down so many people already, the thought of failing Lena felt unbearable. Veliu could be anywhere. She brought to mind Lena's DV history. The police being called to multiple addresses up and down the north coast to whatever cheap rental the family had managed to secure before the bills proved too large and they moved on. She retrieved the records on her laptop and scrutinised the locations.

Josh swivelled around in his chair to face her.

'Anything?' she asked.

'Arnot's not answering. But Rayna was happy to talk. No names of any friends that she can recall. It was always just the two of them, she says. But she reckons she does remember Jason taking Elissa to live somewhere near Kyogle way when they were first together, renting off one of his relatives. Apparently, Elissa hated it because it was nothing more than a bush shack with an outhouse and tank water. But they stayed because it was so cheap and only left when part of the roof sheeting blew away in a storm and Jason's uncle or whoever refused to fix it. She doesn't remember the address, but she thinks Elissa might know.'

Kyogle. Something pinged inside her mind. Not Lena's DV records, but Elissa's. One of the very few times Elissa had ever called the police in, towards the beginning of her relationship with Veliu, before he had pummelled all sense of autonomy and confidence from her.

'Hang on. Near Kyogle, you said? There's a DV record here for Elissa from around that time. I'm sure it was an address down that way.' Kate scrolled furiously through the information on her screen. 'There' – she pointed – 'number twenty-one Stoneville Road, Boorabee Park.' She turned to Josh, triumph lighting up her face. 'Call Elissa, check if that's the house.'

'Kate… Even if it is the same place, it's a bit of a leap, don't you think, to assume he's taken her to Kyogle? We don't even know if he's got a vehicle.'

'If it belongs to his family, it'll be a safe place for him to go. And he'll have a car. Trust me, Jason Veliu will not have a problem organising transport. Let's just check with Elissa. If it's the same address we can ask one of the Kyogle officers to do a drive-by. If they're not there then so be it.'

Josh swallowed a retort and reached for the phone to make the call.

Kate focused on her screen and located the property on Google Maps, zooming in on the satellite view to find the house. It was no more than an isolated speck, a shack hemmed in by tracks of bushland and grey-green paddocks. She felt fear harden into certainty. Veliu's words when she had first interviewed him about Sienna's abduction came back to her. *They don't leave until I say so.*

—

Asphalt stretched before her, the headlights of her vehicle cutting through the night. The road snaked across the landscape heading south west, following the twisting curves of the Tweed River, past sleeping villages and black streaks of pasture into increasingly wooded land. White reflector posts with their glinting red eyes separated the bitumen from the darkened countryside beyond. Kate kept her eyes trained on the road, concentrating on the winding turns.

The digits on the console ticked over to 10 pm. She had been on the road for just on an hour. Before leaving the station, she had promised Josh that she would leave the matter with Kyogle. The constable she had spoken to from Kyogle Station had assured her that a patrol would be dispatched to the property directly. She had emailed photos of Lena and Veliu and left her number with the officer with instructions to call her if anyone was found.

She didn't need to be doing this. Except for the fact that the officer she had spoken to had sounded half awake and just as interested. His voice had told her that she was being humoured and placated. That, and the fact that she couldn't get Lena's frightened and desperate face out of her mind. She glanced at her silent mobile. Still nothing. *Had they even bothered to send anyone out?*

Past the township of Kyogle, she followed the backroads moving from open dairy country into the wooded hinterland of Boorabee Park, her GPS informing her that the turnoff was getting closer. The familiar peal of an emergency vehicle rang through the air and her heart thudded in response. She slowed and moved to the verge, allowing a Rural Fire Services truck to scream past her. She followed the crimson tail-lights of the truck, her nerves on high alert.

In 200 metres, turn left into Stoneville Road. The computerised voice of the GPS made its pronouncement as ahead of her the fire truck shuddered and decelerated to take the turnoff that she was being directed towards. Kate swung left, following after the truck into the narrow slip of track that was hardly wide enough to qualify as a road, pressed in on both sides by thick bushland. Rutted gravel crunched underneath her wheels and soon enough the illusion of bitumen gave way in earnest to dirt road. A few hundred metres in and she could smell the smoke entering through the car vents, prickling at her nostrils.

The trail wound to the right and widened, opening up into a clearing carved into the bush. The RFS vehicle lumbered to a stop, a couple of fireys springing out even before it had come to a full halt. Ahead of them, amidst a junkyard of out buildings in various states of disrepair, a timber homestead lay ablaze, flames shooting up into the night sky. As Kate killed the engine, she heard the tear of splintering timber and watched the front verandah of the building collapse.

Smoke stung her eyes as she exited the car, the heat and roar of the flames evident even from a distance. There were shouts and hurried instructions as the RFS volunteers got to work. Practised and disciplined, they moved in on the perimeter of the blaze, training hoses from the on-truck tanker to the flames, which were starting to lick the scrub at the edges of the property. The RFS had clearly deemed the building unsalvageable and were directing their efforts to ensuring that the fire didn't escape into surrounding bushland. The wind was picking up and avoiding a larger-scale disaster had become the priority.

'Is anyone in there? Do you know?'

'Ma'am, you shouldn't be here. This area is for emergency services only.' A painfully young-looking volunteer, his slim build disguised by the bulky protective gear he had on, stood in her way.

Kate held out her ID and waved off his protest. 'Police. Do you know if anyone's in there? Has the building been cleared?'

'There's no one there. We were told it's abandoned.' He pointed to a parked patrol car at the far end of the clearing upwind of the fire. An officer was pacing next to his vehicle on the phone. *Kyogle.*

'Wonder how the fire started, then?' Kate retorted, already moving away towards the police vehicle, not waiting for an answer.

'Detective Kate Miles, Esserton Station,' she introduced herself. The officer turned at the sound of her voice, regarding her for a few seconds before putting his phone away. 'Detective.' His voice was deliberate and unhurried. 'I'm Constable Stoltz. I was just calling the station to give them an update. No one said anything about a detective being called.' There was an edge to his words, though his tone remained friendly enough. A large man with a gut to match his height. His paunch straining underneath a non-police-issue dark-grey anorak.

'What's happened here?' she pressed.

He turned in the direction of the burning house to watch the firefighters. 'Got a request earlier to undertake a drive-by of the property, from your lot, I believe?' He briefly glanced her way for confirmation and went on.

'I got here about quarter to ten. Could smell the smoke as I was coming in, so I rang Derek from the car.' He motioned towards the burly RFS captain who was directing operations. 'We had some bad fires right through summer. Didn't want to take any chances. Luckily, the crew are local, only a few minutes out. They got here fast.'

'And what about the house? Was there anybody in there?'

'Couldn't tell.' He shrugged. 'It was already on fire when I got here. Well and truly. Couldn't get in, even if I wanted to. Not that there'd be anything in there worth saving. The place is a dump. Been abandoned for years.' He caught the expression on her face and continued defensively. 'There was no sign of anyone when I got here. No vehicles or anything like that.'

Kate gritted her teeth, not wanting to think about what Constable Stoltz may have found if he had bothered driving out here earlier, when she had first put in the request.

'And the fire? Who do you think caused that?'

'Local kids, probably,' Stoltz replied, looking unconcerned. 'Abandoned buildings are good places for kids to do whatever they're not meant to be doing. Smoking and what not. My bet is it was a stray cigarette. We had a case like that a couple of years back. A house fire, where the bloke fell asleep on the couch and his cigarette burned through the material and smouldered for hours before catching alight. He was lucky to live.' He motioned to the burning house. 'Who knows what junk's been accumulating in there over the years? I'm surprised it hasn't gone up in flames before now.'

Kate turned away. The officer's pat answers and easy assumptions were infuriating, partly because they had the ring of plausibility. Had she been wrong? Had she driven all this way for nothing, convincing herself of a danger that didn't exist? She pulled out her phone to try Lena's number again. But before she had the chance to pull up the number, the screen lit up, indicating an incoming call.

She answered it.

'Detective Miles. It's Darryl Murchison here...' Kate felt a twist in her belly at the unexpected voice, her thoughts suddenly scattering like a flock of startled birds.

'I thought you'd want to be contacted directly...' A beat of silence that felt strangely familiar. She'd had this conversation before, except that she had always been on the other side.

'Sarge, I'm sorry, but there's been a single-vehicle accident along Eltham Road. It's... The person at the wheel's been identified as ex-Chief Inspector Grayling.'

She shuddered, feeling her world closing in.

A scream went up from one of the firefighters. It was the young volunteer she had spoken to when she had first arrived at the scene. He sounded panicked and terrified.

'Help! I need help here. There's a body... We need to call an ambulance!'

28

Sunlight flickering on her face. The world outside whizzing past. The rear window wound down slightly, even though she knew it would annoy her father to have the wind whistling unevenly inside the vehicle. Cheese-and-vegemite sandwiches, a packet of tiny teddies and a juice box.

Happiness swelling. A pure, firm ball of contentment that fit snugly under her ribs and expanded with each breath. She had him all to herself. No annoying little brother to hog the attention. No mother to dampen the day with her pinched face and the weight of her unknow-able worries, an invisible swaddle of sadness that coiled the entire family in its grip.

A smile and a wink from the rear-view mirror.

'You right there, Kit?'

'Uh-huh.' She nodded, basking in his smile. He seemed just as elated as she was. Happy to have a rare day out, just the two of them. Or maybe it was just the thought of the bass biting at Clarrie Hall Dam, his favourite fishing haunt. Hours of contented silence paddling the kayaks in mirror-still, lily-pad-strewn waters. His excitement was palpable. She could almost see the sparks bouncing off his skin.

The ute bumped along and her eyes followed the clouds, meringue-white beyond the tree line; the landscape outside languid under the humid breath of summer.

She felt the vehicle slow. Had they arrived already?

No, her father was pulling into a rough layaway carved into the bush on the side of the road, parking behind a Land Cruiser. She spied the familiar figure, tall and tanned with a shock of biscuit-brown hair and laughing eyes. He waved at them, grinning widely, and she felt something shift within her, seeing the reflected happiness in her father's face.

'Is Martin coming too?'

'Yes, I thought it would be nice to invite him along.' No explanation. No hint of apology. Just a statement of fact.

As her father stepped out of the vehicle to greet his friend, she recognised the sting of jealousy, her tight ball of comfort unravelling and dissipating.

Her mood clouded over, resentment and disappointment invading her previous good humour. For the rest of the day, she tried to convey her hurt by withdrawing into herself to make him notice. The same tactic that had been used unsuccessfully by her mother for years. It didn't work. Her father was oblivious, absorbed in his friend and the rhythms of the water and the lure of unseen bass. It was Martin who noticed, who tried his best to draw her out and engage with her as she sat silent and mulish in the kayak.

Later, driving back to Martin's car in the afternoon, her head heavy with tiredness, a headache biting after hours in the sun, she watched her father and Martin converse softly in the front, their hands resting beside each other on the centre console. Occasionally, their fingers would graze each other, curling together for the briefest of moments before letting go. As her eyes succumbed to sleep, it struck her that she couldn't recall when her father had last clasped her mother's hand in the car.

—

Kate ripped her mind from the unexpected shard of memory. She drove on, cursing the distance and following the GPS instructions by rote with little consciousness of the routes she was navigating. She was only aware of the rope-holds of guilt that bound her, pulling ever tighter.

She should have spoken to her father. Given him five minutes of her time. He had clearly driven to the house and waited all those hours because he had wanted to speak to her, but she had walked away. Used the excuse of the job, like she had seen him doing countless times in her own childhood. Behaviours she had absorbed. He had trained her up without her even realising.

Let him be okay. Let him be okay. Let him be okay.

She wondered who else knew. Was the news already spreading through the ranks via the police rumour mill, nudged along by Murchison? Her mind flitted to Geoff, to the heavy judgement in his eyes as she had left the house that evening. She had yet to call him. Another task she was running from. Putting it into words would make it real and she wasn't ready for that yet. She shivered, thinking of her brother unaware in Sydney. And Archie. Oh God, what about Archie? How could she possibly break the news to her son, who only hours ago had been playing with his grandfather. *How? What would she say?*

Stop! She needed to stop her thoughts from spiralling. All she knew was that her father had been taken to hospital. Murchison had promised to call if his condition changed.

She drove on, mile after mile of grey bitumen falling away under her tyres, the edges of the road disappearing into hazy shadow. A blur of grey-brown fur swam in her headlights and she swerved, instinctively slamming the brakes. A sickening second of anticipation as the wheels screamed and she waited for the moment of impact. To her left, a wallaby bounded away unhurt, deciding not to cross the road, after all. She exhaled, her breath coming out in ragged gasps, relief spinning through her.

She regained speed, her scattered thoughts trying to find purchase and settling on Lena. How she had been found – her charred clothes and burn injuries. God knew how she had managed to escape the building before it had caught fully alight, but she had done it. The fire crews had discovered her on the ground in the scrub bordering the rear of the house, stinking of petrol and with second-degree burns covering the length of her back and legs. She had been right there when Constable Stoltz had apparently done a circuit of the property.

Kate had been correct in her assumptions, though it gave her no comfort. Veliu had brought Lena to the ramshackle homestead with the intent of killing her in the most painful manner possible. He had viciously beaten her before dousing the building in petrol and driving off, leaving her inside, broken and semi-conscious, to die of smoke inhalation, burns, or both.

Lena had been incredibly lucky to survive. Based on what Kate had gleaned from the RFS captain about the ferocity of the fire, it appeared that Veliu had used up the majority of accelerant on the front half of the house, leaving Lena a small window of escape before the back of the building had become engulfed. Kate could only imagine Lena's terror as she had dragged her broken body out of the burning building, unsure if Veliu was waiting just outside. No wonder she had hidden rather than calling out for help when she had spied Stoltz's silhouette, tall and bulky. With his uniform disguised beneath his jacket and his patrol car hidden from view at the front of the property, Lena had no doubt assumed it was Veliu returning to finish the job.

Despite her injuries, Lena had been determined to speak, providing a description of the vehicle Veliu had been driving, a silver Subaru Impreza sedan, and a partial licence plate. Kate had updated Josh, ploughing through his annoyance that she had travelled to Kyogle without informing him. Their conversation had been brief and confined to logistics. Josh would issue the necessary alerts for Veliu and his vehicle while she coordinated with Kyogle to secure the scene ahead of the fire investigators getting to the property the following morning.

Kate had remained by Lena's side, providing what solace she could until the rescue chopper had arrived in a storm of thrashing wind and noise. Lena had been airlifted onboard and the helicopter had thundered north. Its destination, the Royal Brisbane and Women's Hospital – the nearest burns unit. Every minute's delay with Lena had meant time away from her father, but there had been no alternative.

The outline of a lone police patrol banked up on the verge jolted Kate back to the present. Pulling up behind the car, she killed the engine, suddenly hesitant. She should have driven straight to the hospital. What was wrong with her? This ridiculous need to inspect the scene. What did it matter, anyway?

The officer was heading towards her and she made herself get out and meet him. A uniform from Tweed Station tasked with waiting for the tow truck to arrive and remove the wreckage. She explained her presence and told him to wait there.

This road. It was just south of Terranora, fifteen minutes from Tweed Heads. *What was her father doing here?* It was nowhere near his cottage, which was west of Esserton, half an hour in the opposite direction. She took in the scene, her eyes seeking out the crumpled shell of her father's ute carved into the side of a huge tallowwood. A horrific sculpture of metal melded into timber. Unnervingly similar to the kaleidoscope of vehicle accidents she had attended as a newly minted police officer, but at the same time, appallingly different.

She knew this section of road, with its ancient tree that sat just a step too close to the bitumen. It caught out motorists who were unfamiliar with this particular stretch and not accustomed to rounding the bend with care, not expecting the tallowwood that would loom quick and hard in their windscreen if they were stupid enough to disregard the posted speed limit. But her father would have known. Even with a few drinks under his belt, he should have known.

The smell of peaty alcohol hit her like a slap as she drew closer to the wreckage. The smashed remains of a bottle of whisky lay scattered on the passenger side, the amber liquid soaking into the seat and pooling on to the rubber floor mat. Her eyes moved to the driver's seat, empty apart from broken glass and spilled blood. The telltale signs of where the jaws of life had been used to slice through metal. Her father's favourite cap, the faded maroon of the

Broncos leagues club, lay useless on the floor, felled from its owner.

She heard the shudder of an engine behind her. The tow truck had arrived. She reached for Gray's cap from amongst the confetti of glass on the car floor and moved away.

$10,000 OR SHE DIES.
TELL ANYONE AND SHE DIES.
CALL THE POLICE AND SHE DIES.

I KNOW YOU HAVE IT. OR HE DOES.

TICK, TOCK. YOU KNOW HOW TO
CONTACT ME.

I look at the words. The words that I hadn't acted on. The words that had felt like a bad joke, at the time. Just a stupid scene from a B-grade movie. Not real life.

The words that had dissolved into gibberish the more I had stared at them. A jumble of shapes on a page. The pills I had taken cutting off my exhausted brain. My body shutting down. And then, it had been too late.

Slowly I crumple the single sheet of paper. Changing my mind, I tear it into tiny pieces, walk to the bathroom and flush it down the toilet.

No one needs to know.

29

Tuesday

Kate was startled awake, the tendrils of a dream in which her father lay helpless and punctured by tubes in a hospital bed trailing her into wakefulness. Sunlight streamed into the bedroom through the open blinds, harsh and over-bright.

She felt sluggish and spent, her brain dunked in a viscous sludge. *What time was it?* She reached for her mobile on the bedside table, her fingers fumbling and knocking it to the floor. *Fuck!* Exhaustion crashed over her. She had fallen into bed without getting changed and could smell the sour, crumpled staleness of her day-old clothes. She lay still, eyes scratchy and heavy, unable to summon the energy to begin the day. To face the seemingly intractable series of crises that stretched before her, each more paralysing than the last. She wanted to lie here forever, cocooned in a nest of blankets.

It felt like only minutes since she had crawled into bed, after driving home from Tweed Hospital, where her father had been transported, and where she had sat alone in the ward, waiting to speak to the doctor on call.

He's alive. He's stable. You can see him again in the morning.

The door opened, revealing her husband shaved and dressed with the gift of coffee. He sat with her while she gratefully swallowed the bitter liquid, calmed for a moment by its reassuring warmth.

'Did you get any sleep?'

Geoff's voice was gentle, tentative. She could feel his eyes probing her, watching for fissures. Trying to gauge how close she was to breaking point. He had switched into protective mode. She had no doubt that a call had already been made to Pip Hutton. That he had sought advice on what to say and how much to push.

'A little,' she said, placing her half-finished mug on the bedside table.

He smiled, tenderness smoothing out the tired lines of his face. His fingers traced the tendrils of veins fanning out across her hand. She couldn't recall the last time he had reached for her. She felt a sudden yearning for the version she and Geoff had been, before. *Before Amy.*

'I called preschool. They're happy to take Archie in for a few hours today. I thought we could go and see Gray together with Amy.'

'I can't. There's a mountain of paperwork after last night.' She concentrated on her hands, avoiding his eyes.

'You're still going in?' Disbelief and shock hardened his expression, his fingers drawing away from her.

'I sat with him all last night...' she replied, immediately on the defensive. 'I told you what the doctor said. It's a broken collarbone, whiplash and bruising. He got lucky. He's conscious and he'll just need to be in a sling for a few weeks. They're just keeping him in as a precaution, for observation.' She caught his eyes and stumbled, tripping on her explanation. 'I was going to visit him this afternoon after work.'

The inadequacy of her words sank like a stone between them. How could she explain that she wasn't ready yet? To speak to her father. To watch him try to explain away what he had almost done. She had scarcely made it through last night, marooned with him inside the curtain divider that separated his bed from the patient next to him. The antiseptic, hospital smell. Her father slack and sedated, a plum-coloured wave of bruising fanning his face. Regret and anger had fought for space, expanding inside her ribcage until she could hardly breathe. She had left to wait for the doctor outside.

'Mummy! You're awake.' Archie scrambled into bed and crashed into her body.

Grateful for the interruption, she pulled him in for a hug and nuzzled his little body, still encased in pyjamas and smelling of Milo and Weet-Bix.

He cupped her face in his small hands and exhaled into it with an open mouth. 'Smell my breath. I haven't brushed my teeth.'

'Phooey. Smells like old socks and garbage.'

He cackled with laughter. 'Again,' he demanded, blowing air over her face.

'Ughhh. Smelly cheese and rotting fish.'

Her son rolled onto his back, helpless with laughter, and she took the opportunity to tickle him. His hysterical giggles expanded in her ear. When she looked up, her husband had already left the room.

'C'mon, matey, let's see what your sister's up to.'

–

Kate suppressed a yawn in the car as she waited for Josh to arrive. She sipped her takeaway coffee. Scalding liquid. Burnt coffee beans. She glanced at the house a few metres ahead on the opposite side of the narrow suburban street. An address in Currumbin, Queensland. Only the gleaming metal roofline of number fifty-six was visible, while the house itself was tucked below the elevation of the road.

Josh had texted her the address. The offer for her to accompany him to the interview was a favour. She knew that. It had been clear in his tone. She noticed that he hadn't suggested they drive here together.

She rested her head against the car window, a speckle of dried bird shit partially obscuring her eyeline. A man strode past with a staffy on a lead and his eyes on his phone screen, scrolling with one hand. His gait and height made her think of Murchison. The constable had waited for her at the hospital, despite the time it had taken her to arrive. He had been sympathetic, which had made it worse, somehow.

She had stressed to him the importance of details about her father not getting out to the press, wincing at the pleading note that had crept into her voice. Hating herself for seeking this favour. Flinching away from the pity she thought she could discern in his eyes. *Not from him. Never from him.* He had mentioned something about his mother, his own struggles with having to care for an elderly parent who was slowly disappearing into dementia. It had been a gesture of solidarity, but she hadn't listened. She couldn't wait until he had finally left.

A sharp rap on the passenger window.

'You weren't having a kip, were you?' Josh looked rested and pressed. He clearly had made an effort for the media update that morning, the reason he had been held up. Kate exited the car and joined him. He smelled of aftershave and coffee. No doubt he had managed to find a takeaway that didn't incinerate the beans.

'Any news on Lena?' she asked.

'She had surgery last night. She seems stable for the moment. The parents have been informed, and I think the mother's planning on heading to the hospital today. Nothing yet on Veliu.'

Kate nodded, sending a silent prayer for Lena and her family.

They had reached number fifty-six. A steep driveway and landscaped front yard that featured river pebbles, succulents and lush grass leading down to a sleek, modernist cube. Cement-rendered walls and a black, brushed-metal door. Josh raised an eyebrow.

The response to their ringing was quick, like she had been waiting. She barely glanced at their IDs, leaving the door open and expecting them to follow.

They trailed her. Kate felt Josh's eyes devour the skin of expensive spandex that adorned the woman, taking great pleasure in each curve and bounce as she moved ahead.

A light-filled space opened up in front of them. A deceptively small room designed to look bigger through high ceilings, an expanse of glass, sparse furnishings and a white palette. Monochrome artwork clung from the walls and luxurious throws in pastel colours lay across spotless furniture.

Behind a sleek countertop of natural stone, Allison Garrett busied herself with a plunger, adding generous scoops of ground beans and placing out three cups. The smell of fresh coffee filled the kitchen.

'Nice place you've got here, Ms Garrett.' Josh spun around, slowly taking in the room. 'I must say, most people don't have access to such luxurious hideouts.'

'It's a friend's place. She's on holiday in Cambodia. She's letting me stay until she gets back next week.'

'And you arrived here when?' Josh had started already, not interested in niceties or waiting until Allison Garrett had set the scene with coffee and biscuits.

'Saturday night.' Her voice was subdued – an edge of sullenness audible.

'Have you been watching the news, Ms Garrett? We've been trying to reach you since Sunday.'

'Look, I called you, didn't I? I know I should have called you earlier or whatever. But I didn't know, all right? I turned off my phone and dumped it in a drawer the minute I got here. I just needed to escape for a while. All I've done the last couple of days is lie in bed and watch Netflix.'

'You weren't interested in finding out what was happening with Aaron's daughter? You're in a relationship with him, aren't you? Don't you care?'

'Of course I care!' Her calm demeanour had cracked, the anguished words ringing across the space. She closed her eyes and breathed deeply, trying to regain control, the plunger abandoned.

'Sienna's all I've been thinking about. Every day. All the time.' She pressed a hand to her chest, as if to still a physical pain. 'That's why I had to leave. It's the only way I can deal with things sometimes. I just need to be away from everything. From my place and Aaron. Everything that reminds me of him. To block it all out. You may not believe me, but it's how I cope.' She clenched her fists. 'I only turned on the news this morning. I didn't even know she was dead.' A strangled sound escaped her.

Allison tore a wad of tissue from a box and blew her nose. Kate exchanged glances with Josh. It seemed like a lot of emotion to expend on a child that wasn't her own.

'Sorry. I'm okay now.' She pulled open a pantry door and dropped the crumpled tissues into a pedestal bin inside. Kate caught a glimpse of a recycling tub stacked with empty wine bottles before the door closed shut. Clearly, the woman had been doing more than just watching Netflix. A two-day bender carefully masked under expertly applied make-up.

Allison Garrett folded her arms across her body as if to comfort herself. 'It's just the thought of anyone hurting that little baby, you know,' she sniffed.

'We understand, Allison. It must be a shock.' Kate's words were mild. 'We do need to ask you a few questions, though. About your whereabouts when Sienna went missing.'

'I know you think I was involved. I mean, why else would you be searching my house?' A bitter laugh escaped her lips. 'Shit! How the hell am I going to go back there now? They all think I'm some sort of baby killer.' She shook her head, her eyes wide and glittering coal-black. 'But I would never hurt that child. And neither would Aaron. He loved that baby. He loves his whole family.'

Her eyes flashed at Josh, sensing his incredulity. 'You won't find anything at my place. Search my car. My devices.' She motioned to a laptop and a mobile charging on the kitchen counter. 'Look all you like. You won't find a thing.'

Josh returned Allison's stare, a challenge in his eyes. 'Ms Garrett, we know Aaron didn't call you from his personal mobile. He used a second mobile whenever he contacted you. What about you? Do you also have a second set of devices that hide your secrets?'

She glared at him and wrenched open a kitchen drawer. She pulled out a flip-top Nokia and slid it across the kitchen island to him. He caught it before it fell to the floor.

'That's Aaron's. His stupid bloody *burner* phone that he used to call me with. He forgot to take it when he left my place on Friday. And, no. I don't have a second set of anything. I don't have a family that I need to hide my vices from.' She waved her hands. 'As you can see, it's just me.'

In the silence that followed, Allison poured out the brewed coffee, fussing with the milk and sugar, which both Kate and Josh declined. Kate sipped her drink – mellow, smooth and perfect.

'Can you take us through your movements on Thursday and Friday, Allison?' she asked. 'You mentioned being with Aaron. Can you talk us through that?'

Allison nodded into her mug. 'I was working from home all Thursday, back-to-back video-conferences. We had planned for Aaron to stay over at my place on Thursday night. We wanted to have the whole of Friday together. He was attending a conference in Broadbeach for the two days and Elissa was only expecting him home late on the Friday. So, we thought he could skip Friday and we could spend it together. There's never enough time, usually. Just a couple of hours here and there.' She paused, taking a moment. The spiel sounded rehearsed, which no doubt it had been in the hours before they had arrived at her doorstep.

'I... I know a person at the conference venue and she agreed to add Aaron to the Friday attendance sheets so it looked like he had been there the whole day.' She sipped at her coffee and set it down carefully before continuing. 'He drove to my place after the last session on Thursday. Got in after eight. We hadn't seen each other in a while, so it was… nice.' She glanced at Kate, her eyes alight with the memory.

'We ordered takeaway and Aaron went and picked it up. We had it in bed and watched a movie.' She was quiet for a moment. 'Aaron had left his mobile in the car and we only realised about Sienna when we turned on the TV news the next day. It must have been around eleven-thirty. He left straight after.'

'You said Aaron went out for takeaway on Thursday night. Can you remember how long he was away for?' Kate probed, testing how much of Allison's story tallied with the version provided by Aaron.

She shrugged. 'I don't know. Thirty minutes, maybe. There was some kind of a holdup on Leeson Road. A van breakdown, I think. We were late ordering. It was probably around nine-thirtyish when he got home with the food?'

'And apart from that, Aaron was with you the whole time? Did you leave the house either together or separately for any other reason? Particularly on Friday morning?'

'We had better things to do, didn't we?' A hint of self-satisfaction. 'Why do you think he always came back to me? There were certain things his good little wife wouldn't let him do. So yeah, we were definitely home all that time.'

'Are you sure about that, Ms Garrett?' Josh interjected. He held up Aaron's Nokia. 'We have the call records from this phone and there are two calls made from this mobile to your number at approximately 9.07 am and 9.09 am on Friday morning. Why would Aaron need to call you when he was at the house with you?'

She frowned, her face showing puzzlement more than fear. And then her brow cleared. 'I couldn't find my mobile. I rang my number from his phone to try to find it. I think Aaron was in the shower at the time. I found mine under the couch.'

Josh exchanged the barest of glances with Kate. It was plain to her that he didn't believe Allison Garrett.

'Have you had any contact with Aaron since Friday, Allison?'

Her face changed. A spark of anger. 'No. I haven't called him and he hasn't called me. He's gone back to his family.'

For a second, Kate spied the ocean of hurt that lay beneath her facade, a knot snagging the silky-smooth surface.

'Allison, I understand you've been seeing Aaron for some months now?'

'Coming on seven and a half months,' Allison mumbled.

'That's a long time. He must really care about you. Did you have plans to make things more permanent?'

Allison laughed. 'Ha! You don't need to be so polite, Detective. What you see before you is the cliché of clichés. To answer your question, no, that was never an option. And to his credit, he never lied to me. He always said he would never leave her. I went in knowing the rules.'

'Shame. You, Aaron and Sienna would have made such a cute family. A new start for all three of you.' Josh's words were like barbs on flesh. Allison's face paled. 'It was a good plan, too. Nice and easy access to Elliot Pass through the bush reserve behind your property, then a quick getaway with the baby across the border.'

'Shut up. That's not true.' Kate saw the glimmer in her eyes. If nothing else, she had thought about it.

'So, what went wrong on the day, Allison? I assume it was Aaron who actually went inside the house to steal the baby? It would be easier to explain his presence in the house than yours.'

'I said shut up. None of that happened.'

'A quick couple of phone calls from Aaron to confirm it had all gone to plan? And then what? Was there a third person whom you handed the child to? Someone you were meant to meet up with later? Did they stuff up? Or was it you? Did you kill Sienna, Ms Garrett? Was it you who caused the baby to die?'

'Shut up! Shut up! Shut up!' Allison screamed and collapsed into a ball on the floor, hands pressed to her ears.

Kate rose, motioning Josh out of the room. She kneeled beside Allison, but the woman was having none of it.

'Get away from me. Get out the both of you.'

Outside, Kate rounded on Josh. 'Jesus, you couldn't have taken it easier in there?'

'The woman's lying. It's clear as day. She obviously has a connection to the child. You can't tell me that someone who isn't involved would get that upset about Sienna.' Josh glared at Kate, his face scornful.

'That may be, but you don't need to bloody steamroll her. She called us. She was willing to talk. Now she's just going to lawyer up and we've lost our chance.'

'Thanks for the interview tips, Sarge. I'll be sure to use them next time I let a suspect smash my car and get away.'

Anger reared, white-hot. 'That's it. You're done. You're off this interview. Get back to the car and cool off.'

'I'm the case lead. I'll decide who fucking conducts the interview.'

'Josh, you need to step away. She is not going to talk to you after that. Just let me handle it.'

He flung her a look of pure fury and stalked off.

She glanced towards the house, wondering if Allison was behind one of the shaded panes and had seen her confrontation with Josh. Maybe it was a good thing. Maybe it would make her trust Kate. Allison had wanted to speak. Kate was sure of it. The woman was carrying something that she wanted to unburden; she just needed to be given the chance.

She took a deep breath and headed back to the house.

30

Josh's car was nowhere in sight when Kate left Allison Garrett's for the second time. He had driven away rather than waiting to see if she would succeed with Allison. Bloody sook.

Her phone buzzed as she climbed into the car. Geoff. Her eyes caught the time on the console: 3.14 pm.

'Hey, I'm heading to the hospital now.' Kate spoke into the handsfree as she pulled away from the kerb.

'That's why I'm calling. Gray's discharged himself.'

'What? When?'

'A couple of hours ago.'

'How's he getting home?'

'A taxi, I assume.'

'Had the doctor seen him?'

'No idea.'

'Fuck. Okay, I'll call him.'

Her husband hung up. No goodbye. No asking when he should expect her home.

Kate dialled her father's number, her fingers drumming impatiently on the steering wheel as it rang out. Of course, he wasn't answering. *Jesus!* Her family.

–

She ended up at the beach. She knew it was a cop-out. She should be driving back to the station to update Josh, to accept her share of the task load. The team would be busy chasing up Veliu's contacts and his old rentals, trying to run him to ground.

Or she could get home early for once. Smooth things over with Geoff.

Or she could just sit on a lone beach running her fingers and feet aimlessly through the wet sand. She could feel the damp seeping into the arse of her suit pants. Her boots lay beside her. The only soul along a windswept expanse. Just her, the ocean and the sand dunes under winter bright skies.

She recalled her mother's frequent escapes to the beach, alone. As a child, Kate had resented her mum's time away. For not being allowed to accompany her with Luke to play in the sand. But now, she could understand her mother's need for truancy. A few stolen hours away from the needs of others.

Her thoughts returned to Allison. Her statement provided Ricci with an alibi, and if they both stuck to their stories, it would come down to the physical evidence. So far at least, the preliminary forensics were firing blanks and nothing obvious from Ricci's car or Allison's townhouse had been uncovered to link either party to Sienna's abduction. Aaron had frequented Allison's townhouse, and any lawyer worth their salt would argue cross-contamination of any fibres found at Allison's place that matched the Ricci home. And yet, there was something about the woman that made Kate uneasy.

It had taken some work to make Allison speak with her again. She had been emotional and fragile. It had taken a new brew of coffee and a half-eaten packet of double-choc biscuits Kate had found at the back of the pantry. The cheat meal of a dedicated exerciser; someone who very likely substituted liquid calories for food on a routine basis, because wine didn't count. Kate recognised comfort food when she saw it. Slowly, she had managed to edge Allison towards Aaron and his family, the crux of her discontent.

'I used to go by their house and watch them sometimes.' Her voice had been quiet. Wistful. 'Mostly when I was out jogging, but sometimes in the car, too.'

She had glanced at Kate then, watching for her reaction. Wary of her judgement. Kate had remained neutral, not wanting to spook her, sensing that Allison had waited a long time to get this off her chest.

'Once I found out how close we lived to each other, it was too much of a temptation. Aaron never knew, but I used to follow them to the shops. To Bunnings. Even to Daniel's school. There are so many women at pick-up time, you can just walk inside the school and no one questions you. They just think you're one of the parents.' Kate caught the faint flare of shame in her eyes. But also, the gleam of self-satisfaction. She was proud of what she had done. Of inserting herself into Aaron's life without getting caught.

'I saw her on Thursday afternoon, you know, at pick-up. She had Sienna all bundled up in one of those body-wrap things. They look so unsafe, don't you think? If I had a baby, I would strap her in a proper carrier with a harness.' Allison made a face before continuing. 'She pretends to be all *earth mother*, but you should have seen her go off at Daniel just because he tried to look under the cover sheet at Sienna. I mean, I know the baby was sleeping, but still. I honestly don't know what Aaron sees in her.'

Kate recalled the prowler who Elissa had heard in the early hours of Thursday morning in her backyard. Could it have been Allison? A woman who got a kick out of being a voyeur into her lover's life. How many times had she ventured inside their house without Elissa noticing? Would the baby have proved too much of a temptation?

'In all the times you've seen the family, Allison, did you happen to notice anyone else hanging around the house, particularly when Aaron was not around? Any friends dropping by? Male or female?'

Allison had shrugged, uninterested. 'It's only Elissa's mother who visits the place.'

'Did you happen to run past the house on Thursday morning? Early?'

Allison had looked at her, curious. 'I run after work in the evenings. I like my morning sleep-in.'

'And what about the house itself, Allison. Ever been tempted to step inside?'

She had been ready for the question.

'I've never been inside. Not even once.'

Kate scooped a shell from between her feet, brushing sand grains off its delicate scallops. She knew Allison was lying, but about what? Had her voyeurism stopped at stalking, or had it gone further than that?

Her phone beeped, pulling her back to the present. She glanced down, clocking an email from her bank. A dip in her stomach. The mortgage broker had replied to her loan enquiry.

—

In the supermarket, she picked things at random and returned them to their shelves, undecided. Her plan was to speak to Geoff over dinner. She would cook something. Something special. And they would talk. Really talk. She needed to unburden herself of this poison. To share some of the load with Geoff.

She picked up a dressed lamb rack and then replaced it in favour of a tray of mince. No need to overestimate her abilities.

In the parking lot, she waited for a man to return his trolley to the bay before rolling in her own.

'Detective Miles, hello.' A hesitant voice.

Kate looked up to find the sun-creased face of Richard Markham, the reporter from the *North Coast Leader*. Jeans, scuffed steel caps and a plain blue work shirt, like he was auditioning for *Farmer Wants a Wife*. Jesus, the man seemed to have the worst possible timing.

'Richard, how are you?' She pasted on a smile, aware that she owed him for choosing not to run a story highlighting her shortcomings.

'I didn't see you at the press briefing this morning.' A question disguised as a statement.

'Yeah. Had a couple of things I needed to chase up.' Like sleep.

'Listen, Detective. I know you're busy, but I was wondering if we could make some time to speak this week. I believe you have a history with Constable Darryl Murchison from Tweed Heads. I would be interested in getting your take on a couple of things.'

He held out his card and Kate accepted it without thinking. He nodded goodbye and moved away.

What was he asking her? What had he meant about Murchison? Had Murchison spoken to the reporter about her father's accident? Or was it something worse?

31

The kitchen smelled of tomato and herbs. A thick bolognese sauce sat bubbling away on the stove. She had stuck to what she knew. A recipe learned and perfected during her younger days as a single copper in Grafton. Ideal for freezing in batches to reheat after a twelve-hour shift. She lifted a spoon to her mouth. Eating it fresh worked too.

Geoff walked into the kitchen and leaned against the counter, taking her in.

'What?'

'Nothing.' A half smile. Part teasing and part watchful.

Kate knew he was assessing her, wondering at her earlier than expected appearance at home, groceries in hand. Wanting to take comfort in her presence but also unwilling to let go of the months of petty resentment that had built up between them, like some sort of calcified plaque.

'Wine?'

She nodded. He reached for the wineglasses on the shelf, brushing against her and not moving away. His hand grazed her shoulder. The warmth lingered. He placed a generous glass of red by her side.

'Amy can have formula tonight.' He smiled, clinking her glass and taking a sip.

'Dad, did you see the shells Mum got me?' Archie looked up from the dinner table, where he sat surrounded by materials from his craft box, busy incorporating the shells into an elaborate artwork.

'I did, mate. Mummy seems to have had a very busy day.' His eyes twinkled at her from above his wineglass and she grinned back. Amy babbled from her mat on the floor next to Archie, swatting at the toys hanging from her activity mat. Kate breathed it in. The calm before the storm.

Later, when the kids were in bed, Kate sat facing Geoff on the couch, the TV on low in the background. Something about recreational fishing licences and river water quality on the local news. Geoff looked relaxed, lazily swirling the last of the wine in his glass. It was a shame to break his mood, but she knew she had to.

'Geoff, I need to talk to you.'

'Sounds serious.' He met her tight-lipped smile with a curious glance.

'Do you remember when we bought the house, the deposit Dad gave us?'

He nodded.

'I... I think it's caught up in Martin Jackson's property deals. I reckon that's maybe how Dad made that money.' Saying it out loud had made it much worse than the soundbite trapped in her head.

'The press is onto the story. They know about Martin and Dad. If his name crops up when they start unpicking the financial trail, they're not going to have any issues about publishing it. And with the money he gave us, I'm connected too. We'll both get dragged into this.' She felt the bile rise as she said the words.

'Have you spoken to him about it?' Geoff had placed his wineglass on the floor, his eyes intent, awake, assessing the implications.

'I'm going to take a day-in-lieu tomorrow and go to the cottage.' It was time she stopped running and faced up to him. She had only managed to speak briefly to her father that afternoon, after he had finally answered his mobile following multiple calls. Their conversation had been short. He had clearly been in pain and not in the mood to speak. He had stayed on the phone just long enough to reassure her that 'he was fine', 'completely capable of looking after himself', and that 'she needed to stop fussing'. He had hung up before she had got anywhere near broaching any other subjects.

'And what do you suggest we do about the money?' Geoff urged, breaking into her thoughts.

'I emailed the broker about remortgaging options.'

'Remortgaging the house? You're not serious? We're barely scraping by with just your salary. We can't add to the loan.'

'What other choice have we got? We need to give back the money.'

'Do we? It was a gift, wasn't it? How is this our fault.'

'I can't keep it, Geoff. You know that. It could get really messy if they decide to make an example of him, and of me. It'll depend on how bent the property deals were, but worst case, they could pursue *proceeds of crime* charges. Even if it never gets that far, you know the stench will follow me around for the rest of my career.'

'What? Why would they charge you? You didn't know where he got the money from.'

'But I should have. That's the point, isn't it? I'm a police officer. I should have known to ask those kinds of questions. If I had stopped to think about it even for a second, it was obvious that the sum was well outside his means. That's exactly the sort of thing this type of case relies on. Whether I had reasonable grounds to suspect something wasn't right. Given the amount involved. Given his salary.'

'Kate, you can't know any of this for sure, until you talk to him.'

She spoke through gritted teeth. 'I've been such an idiot. All these years, I just thought it was his savings and maybe something left over from selling Nan and Pop's place in Uki after they passed. But that money got sunk straight into Mum and Dad's mortgage. So, where did he get this cash from?'

'If we need to give it back, can we ask Luke for help?' Geoff's mind was already on options for salvaging the situation. 'He's got money, hasn't he? Can't he help us out?'

'Maybe, I don't know.' Kate baulked at having to ask her little brother for a favour. She had never directly enquired into Luke's financial status, though the casual motorbike purchases and overseas holidays gave her some inkling. Maybe she would have to swallow her pride.

'Shit! I don't believe this.' Geoff dragged a frustrated hand through his hair, his wine-softened evening shattered.

'Hang on,' Kate shushed her husband, her attention caught by the TV. The news anchor was speaking to camera, an image of the Riccis – Elissa, Aaron, Daniel and baby Sienna – a family photo from happier times, framing the background.

'...*Today Ms Rayna Gardiner, the grandmother of deceased baby Sienna, came out in criticism of the police's handling of* the case, strongly condemning the investigation's focus to date on her son-in-law, Aaron Ricci. In a statement released earlier this afternoon, Ms Gardiner described her son-in-law as a loving father who lived for his family, characterising the police enquiry as chaotic and lacking direction and not in the best interest of her family. She has called on the police to focus their efforts on Ms Ricci's ex-partner, who is currently on the run following several violent incidents, including an altercation with police on Monday and an alleged attack near Kyogle overnight involving his current partner, who is understood to be recovering at the Royal Brisbane Hospital burns unit. Ms Gardiner has appealed to police to do the right thing and focus on the real killer of her granddaughter.

'A few minutes ago, Inspector Skinner of the Esserton police addressed the media to respond to Ms Gardiner's concerns...'

The screen switched to footage of Skinner standing tall and commanding, facing an impromptu press conference at the front of the station. Josh stood crisp and tailored by his side. Two calm and confident men. Officers in whom the public could place their trust.

Kate felt herself go cold. She had dropped into the station on her way home to file her report on Allison Garrett, and she had spoken to Josh. He had been distant and aloof and she had put it down to their earlier argument. He had made no mention of either Rayna Gardiner's complaint or any planned media conference, the second of the day. Kate had been lanced neatly and cleanly out of the loop.

On screen, Skinner was speaking.

'...Thank you, ladies and gentlemen. I'm here to provide you with an update on the status of the investigation into the abduction and death of Sienna Ricci. Firstly, I want to address the comments made by Ms Rayna Gardiner earlier today. We understand that this has been an extremely stressful time for *the family. I want to reassure the public and the family in particular that our officers have been working tirelessly and are doing everything in our power to find the person or persons responsible for the death of baby Sienna. In saying that, I note that there is always room for improvement in any investigation, which is why I'm very pleased to be announcing a new task force led by Detective Josh Ellis, who will be reviewing all the evidence collected to date and directing the investigation moving forward. I want to emphasise that Ms Ricci's ex-partner remains a key person of interest in the case and the team will be redoubling our efforts to ensure that he is found and taken into custody. We have reached out to the Ricci family to ensure that their concerns are being heard and that they are being adequately supported...'*

So, she was being thrown under a bus and Skinner was going to take credit for all her efforts in ensuring that Veliu was kept in the picture. She switched off the TV, unable to take any more.

She felt Geoff's hand reach for hers, warm and solid. To catch her as the floor fell away beneath her.

32

Wednesday

'Sarge... Hi... Hello.' Constable Roby's voice sounded nervous and young through the handsfree.

'Roby, I'm not in today. I wanted to ask you a favour, though. Could you give me a heads-up if there's any change to Lena Chalmers' condition, or if you bring Jason in?'

'Of course, Sarge, not a problem.'

'Anything come in on Veliu?'

'The usual, Sarge. Dozens of sightings up and down the coast. Some in Queensland. We're checking them all.'

'Can you send me the list?'

There was a beat of silence before Roby agreed, probably relieved that she wasn't asking anything more difficult of him. She didn't want to put the young constable in an awkward position, but she needed someone she could trust in there. She had expected to feel worse, having this conversation, but it was less mortifying than she had imagined. She said her goodbyes and hung up.

Ahead of her, the traffic was slowing down. Road works. A detour. The usual flare of irritation didn't materialise. She had nowhere important to be, so it didn't matter if she was delayed. She turned up the volume on the radio, something bland and boppy, her mind reliving her morning with her family. Sleeping in. Legs tangled, Geoff's bristles tickling her neck. Her ears. Her shoulder. Making love slowly, leisurely, as the sky bled from shadow to dawn. Falling back to sleep and waking up to the sounds of Archie. Feeding Amy cocooned in bed, like she had done years ago with Archie. Cereal. Toast. Coffee. Dropping her son at preschool. It had been nice, having time.

Nodding to the traffic controller, a bored-looking woman with half an eye on her mobile, Kate followed the detour around. At the lights, a billboard advertising *Independent Living at Scottsdale House* rose into view. A group of trim-looking seniors grinning amiably at their carers. The lights changed to green and she made a quick decision, slipping abruptly into the right-hand-turn lane. A horn bleated its displeasure and she raised a hand in apology. The traffic surged ahead and she followed the line of vehicles turning north into Murwillumbah.

–

Walking into the residents' lounge, her eyes searched the overheated room. Paisley carpet and floral lounge chairs arranged to catch the sun and views of the gardens outside. Potpourri heavy and dominant to mask the ingrained scents of other less palatable things – sour, overboiled food and loneliness. A handful of occupants sat in an arranged half-circle. Woollen blankets encasing thin bodies. Slippers and walkers. An attendant bustled, depositing cheery greetings with a side of tea and biscuits from a trolley. The elderly, finally old enough to be treated like infants again, sat uncomplaining, compliant.

Kate turned, heading for the corridor that led to the care units. She stopped, doubled back, and stepped out into the terrace. A tiny, wizened figure sat in a wicker chair, bundled in knitted wool and blankets. Spectacles perched on ebony skin, thin like parchment paper and creased with fine lines. She had forgotten Aunty Iris's favourite spot, out on the verandah, where she could breathe in the sky and watch the birds, whatever the weather. The care nurses had long given up trying to hustle her into the climate-controlled confines of the home.

Kate crossed the floor for all the world like a truant being called in to face the principal, feeling the weight of her prolonged absence. She pulled up a chair and sat beside her surrogate grandmother. Had it been three months, or four, since she'd last visited? Minutes ticked by without any acknowledgement. It was only when Iris had finished her chapter, calmly denoting her place with a bookmark, that she deigned to look up at Kate.

'Well, to what do I owe the pleasure? Must be something big, if it warranted a personal visit.'

'Sorry, Aunty. I should have come by earlier. It's just work and the kids…' she trailed off, suddenly shamefully conscious that Iris hadn't seen Amy since Geoff had driven her over to the hospital when her daughter was born.

'Thought I'd have to call the undertakers just so you'd make an appearance,' she harrumphed, though Kate thought she detected a touch of mirth underneath the ire. Aunty Iris was enjoying herself.

'Do you want to see some pictures of the kids?' Kate held out her phone.

'No need. I see the real thing every couple of weeks. Your husband brings the bub to see me, and Archie, too, sometimes, after preschool.'

Kate lowered her phone. She hadn't realised that Geoff was doing that.

'You've got a good one there. Make sure you don't stuff it up.'

Kate nodded. It was a work in progress. She reached for the novel on Iris's lap. 'What are you reading?' she asked, flipping the book to clock its dark, moody cover.

'Hmm? Don't know. Load of rubbish about a cop solving a murder in a week. It's a good read, though.' She looked hard at Kate. 'And how are you doing? You look like shit.'

Kate smiled. Iris had never been one to shy away from a serve.

'Things have been a bit full on at work.'

'Hmm. Well, just don't forget your own family while trying to solve everyone else's problems.'

God. She sounded just like Geoff sometimes. Kate wondered exactly how much Geoff confided in Iris in their regular chats.

'How's your brother. Have you spoken lately?'

'Sort of.'

Iris rolled her eyes at Kate's guilty smile. 'And your father? You know he gets lonely up there all by himself in that bloody cottage. He needs to find himself a man, that one.'

'I'm going to see him, straight after here.' Kate stopped short of mentioning her father's accident. It wasn't her news to tell.

'What? It's *visit your old people day*, is it?'

Kate laughed. 'Something like that.'

She left an hour later, stopping on the way to exchange a few words with the nurse. The conversation with Iris had done her good. Her mind was still as sharp as a knife, though her body was slowly giving way. It had felt good to spar with her again. To reminisce and recount old family memories. Of the past. Of her mother. Memories long dormant that had come alive with Iris's retelling and embellishments. Kate felt lighter as she stepped through the sliding doors into the weak August sunshine.

'Detective. I thought it was you in there.'

Kate smelled the cigarette smoke before she noticed the presence of Darryl Murchison. She felt the sense of ease drain from her limbs, her world closing in that tiniest bit. She stepped back, an automatic animal reaction to his proximity, her body creating space between them. As always, dread and something else more primal collided against her chest. Why did he still have this effect on her?

Because it was his actions as much as hers that had led to her being shot while pregnant with Amy.

Because his presence was a constant reminder of what she could have lost.

Because she'd had the chance to report his behaviour, the threats and intimidation that had proceeded the incident, but had chosen to keep it to herself.

Because it had been his hands that had stemmed the blood, that had called the ambulance, that had saved her life and Amy's.

'Constable, what are you doing here?'

He detached himself from the wall, snuffing out the lit butt under his heel and unfurling his body to its full height. 'Just had a tour of the place. I'm looking at places for Mum. It's getting too hard for her at home. She'll need to move to one of these places soon.'

Kate nodded, recalling that he had mentioned his mother's struggles with dementia when they had met in hospital for Gray. *Please let him not have chosen Scottsdale.* She didn't need this place infected by his presence. Having

236

to plan for a possible run-in with Murchison every time she visited Aunty Iris was too awful a scenario to contemplate.

'And what did you think of the place?'

'Bit pricey for the room sizes. Mum'll probably prefer being near Tweed Heads anyway.'

Kate breathed a sigh of relief.

'How's the chief inspector going? I heard he discharged himself.'

'He's fine. He'll live.'

'He's a lucky man. What with coming in under the limit and all.'

'He knows when to stop,' she retorted a little too quickly. She had been as surprised as Murchison that her father's blood alcohol levels hadn't tested over the legal limit, given how much whisky she had smelled in the smashed vehicle.

She glanced at him, wanting to leave, but the reporter's words nagged at her. She forced herself to speak. 'Have you been talking to the press, Darryl? About what happened.'

He met her eyes. 'Not me, Sarge. His secret's safe with me.'

'There's no secret, Constable. My father was in a car accident. That's all.'

He nodded, not replying. Letting it go.

She felt her hackles rise. 'I had a reporter approach me from the *North Coast Leader*. He asked me about you. Do you happen to know what that's about?'

He regarded her, his face suddenly blank, wiped of emotion. 'You know me, Sarge. Clean as a whistle.' He waited a beat, a challenge in his eyes before adding, 'Unlike some others I could mention.'

'What the fuck's that supposed to mean, Constable? If you've got something to say, why don't you just say it.'

He shrugged, the hint of amusement clear in his eyes. Teasing her. 'I would be happy to speak to your reporter friend, Sarge. Tell him some home truths about my time at Esserton Station. I'm sure he'd find it incredibly illuminating.'

Heat flushed her face. What did this man have on her father? 'What do you mean?' Her voice was unsteady, fear constricting her throat.

'Do you really think I'm going to tell you? So you can run straight to him.' He spat at her feet and turned away, the change in his demeanour swift and disconcerting.

'Constable, wait!' She made herself go after him. He couldn't just leave, not like this. She needed to get ahead of the situation. To work out what knowledge he had over her father. 'Darryl, listen to me. I need to know what you're talking about.'

He dismissed her with a wave and continued down to the visitor carpark. She jogged by his side.

'Constable, I covered your arse once. Remember that. You owe me. Professional Standards are just a phone call away. I'm happy to open it all up again. Is that what you want?'

He stopped, glaring at her. 'Oh, that's right. Let's resort to blackmail.' He shook his head. 'I'll tell you what, he's taught you well.'

She recoiled like she'd been slapped. A young aged care worker heading to her car eyed them with curiosity.

'This is why I fucking left Esserton! Favours and dodgy money. There's no end to this shit. No fucking chance of promotion. Always under obligation.' He stabbed a finger inches from her face. 'I'm not telling you anything. You and Skinner can just fuck right off.'

The world tilted, and she felt herself slip, confusion and doubt storming her brain.

'Wait. Hang on.' She stumbled after him as he strode away. 'Darryl, just wait. What do you mean, Skinner?' She had been expecting a revelation about her father, gearing herself up for it. The fuel that would finally set ablaze the stacked kindling of her suspicions. Instead, Skinner. A discordant note, off-tune and jarring. She grabbed at his jacket sleeve. 'You can't just leave. We need to talk.'

He jerked her hand away and whirled around to face her, his voice shaking with fury. 'I put all this shit behind me. For years, I looked away. I kept all his fucking secrets, all right? What more does he want?'

She stepped back. 'Constable, believe me. I don't know what you're talking about. I am in the dark about all of this. Please help me understand.'

He exhaled in frustration. 'You're honestly telling me that *you* don't know? And, what? I'm meant to just buy that?'

'It's the truth, Constable. Whatever history you have with Skinner, I am the *last* person he's going to confide in. You can take that as a fact.' He must have heard the bitterness in her voice, because something shifted in his expression. The smallest hint of hesitation.

'I just want to know what's going on, Constable. Look, maybe I don't have a right to know. But I'm asking you to trust me.'

His eyes bored into hers. She could feel him waver, self-preservation wrestling with the urge to disclose. Years of frustration fighting for release. For a second, she thought he wouldn't break after all. He was silent for so long. And then, finally, he nodded and began to speak.

-

He felt a headache coming on as he navigated the narrow, bushland-fringed road. Deep shadow alternated with shards of light from the overhanging trees as the car swept past, the setting sun flooding his eyes depending on the direction of the vehicle. He knew he was going too fast, but the momentum of the car felt good. Like he could escape the screams.

His sergeant sat silent in the passenger seat, engrossed in his own thoughts. Murchison glanced over at Andrew Skinner and back onto the road. He couldn't get a handle on the man. One second he was the life of the party, and the next minute a surly, moody prick. You never knew where you stood with him. And he was a calculating bastard. You didn't want to cross the man.

Skinner had been in his element at the farmhouse. Talking down the hysterical woman and driving some sense into the bloke. Making him understand what it would mean if they were forced to drive down to the property again. He was good at that. Cajoling and manipulating until the situation was under control with the minimum of paperwork. Murchison's job had been to take care of the screaming kid. Red-faced, grubby and inconsolable, snot greasing his puffy face and a half-eaten rusk crusting his hands. Finally, the mother had been calm enough to take hold of the child.

'Community policing, Constable.' Skinner had winked as they had climbed into the patrol to drive back to Esserton.

He slowed around a curve and put his foot down as the road straightened. They passed a vehicle parked on the side of the road, partially tucked into the surrounding scrub. A gleam of silver amongst the verdant green.

'Hang on, stop the car.'

'What?'

'You heard me. Stop the car and park up here.'

Murchison pulled over at a makeshift layaway along the side of a horse paddock and waited for further instructions.

'Well, come on, then.'

Killing the engine, Murchison followed Skinner on foot back up the road they had just driven down. It took them a few minutes of tramping in silence to reach the spot where they had seen the parked vehicle. A new model BMW.

'I knew it,' Skinner said softly. Murchison could hear the contained glee in his voice.

'What is it?'

Skinner shushed him with a raised hand. He stole quietly to the side of the door and rapped hard on the passenger window. Murchison saw the man in the driver's seat startle in surprise, his hands thrusting aside the face of his young passenger, which only moments ago had been trained on his groin. The older man fumbled for his trouser zip as the young man beside him jerked upright.

Jesus Christ. Murchison looked away, embarrassed and sickened, but not before the driver's face had implanted in his brain. His shock of brown hair and square footballer's jaw was impossible to mistake. His broad, smiling face had been bearing down from state election posters for weeks on end. Murchison had been stationed at one of his rallies less than a month ago, at the local town hall. He had watched him step onto the stage with his family – his elegant and charming wife and their two grown daughters. Martin Jackson, their local MP and the newly minted State Planning Minister.

Murchison saw Skinner motioning for the car window to be wound down.

'Evening, Minister. Out for a nice drive, I see.'

'What do you want, Officer? We're not doing anything.' The flustered voice of a man wrong-footed and looking for an out.

'Well, that's for us to determine, isn't it, Minister? Can I see some identification, please, mate?'

The boy, sullen and withdrawn, had wiped his mouth on his shirtsleeve and pulled out an ID from his wallet, handing it over. For a second, the young man reminded Murchison of his nephew, his sister's son, all of fourteen and full of bravado — gangly-limbed and thin-chested, nursing an unknown grudge against the world. But as the boy turned, the similarity melted away, replaced by a face marked by experience, already world-weary.

Skinner had taken his time examining the card. 'You sure this is you, mate? You haven't swiped it from an older brother or a cousin?'

'I'm sure. It's my ID.' The boy's voice was defiant and hostile.

Skinner pulled out his phone and took a series of quick photos of the ID, the car and its occupants, before returning the card.

'Well, it looks like everything here is in order.' He reached for his notepad and scribbled something down. Tearing the single sheet of paper, he reached in and placed it on the dashboard. 'My number, Minister. Next time you need anything, don't hesitate to give me a call. We're here to help.' Skinner tipped his forefinger at them. 'Have a good evening, gentlemen. I look forward to the next time we meet, Minister.'

He nodded at Murchison and they walked to the patrol car in silence.

'That, Constable, is what you call leverage.'

33

Kate sped west, her hands on the wheel instinctively navigating the familiar turns to her father's property, oblivious to the swathes of green pasture and bushland hugging the road. Her mind swam with Murchison's words, one revelation tripping behind the other. Once begun, he had been like a bath overflowing. The memories, etched with frustration and vitriol, had poured out without any filter. Conversations and scenes that had clearly been playing out for years in his brain had finally found an outlet.

What pained her the most was his disclosure regarding the power Skinner had held over Martin Jackson. Martin had carried that weight all those years, doing what he needed to keep his private turmoil from touching his family. But in the end, it had all been for naught. Her thoughts flashed to the newspaper articles tearing open Martin's life. Except it was Gray, rather than Martin, left to deal with the fallout.

Dodgy money and favours. The press allegations of insider deals involving a senior police officer in the Northern Region Command – it had been Skinner all along, not her father. Could she really have got it that wrong? All this time, conflating Gray and Martin's relationship woes with something bigger. She flushed with shame at the ease with which she had gone there. Skinner had always been a political player. His eyes always trained skywards towards the next arse he had to lick to get ahead, at all times seeking how to spin a situation to his advantage. Did it really surprise her that he had found a way to insert himself into Martin Jackson's life and bend it to his benefit?

Had her father known or guessed of Skinner's hold on Martin? Is that where his long-standing antipathy of Skinner stemmed from? Surely, Gray would have reported him, Kate mused. Unless, her father too had benefited from Martin's deals? She tried to recall the media articles she had read. None of them had actually named her father in any financial impropriety. But then, what of his wedding gift? How could he have access to such a large sum? Her mind picked through Gray's erratic behaviour since the media storm on Martin Jackson had broken: his unavailability, his drinking, his accident. The possibility that her father's collision reflected a deliberate decision on his part, a moment when he felt that was his only choice, terrified her.

Beyond her windscreen, thin ribbons of cloud streaked across a brittle indigo sky. Views of the ancient volcanic mountain, Wollumbin, sacred to the local Bundjalung people, rose on the horizon, the breadth of Bundjalung Country spread before it in a patchwork of vivid jades and browns. In front of her, an aging ute trundled along a good twenty k's slower than the speed limit, coughing diesel fumes in its wake, a sleek chocolate-brown kelpie keeping watch in the back tray. Kate waited for an opportunity, and overtook the vehicle, accelerating once she got clear, her impatience to see her father growing with every kilometre.

She thought back to Murchison's tirade. Until she had disabused him of the notion, he had assumed Kate to be one of Skinner's acolytes, and she understood how it could appear that way. Only a few months earlier, she had been charged by Skinner to review a case in which Murchison had been the lead officer. The events of that case had landed both Kate and Murchison in front of Professional Standards, not to mention her firearm injury, a permanent reminder of decisions they had both made. From the outside, at least, it would appear that her career hadn't suffered from any of it. She was back from maternity leave and in the front seat of one of the highest-profile cases in the region.

No wonder Murchison saw her as one of Skinner's inner circle, presumably privy to much more. If only he knew the reality. She wondered if Murchison's long dislike of her had ultimately stemmed from this one misconception? He clearly blamed Skinner for the woeful state of his career. Was it true? Had Skinner stymied Murchison's efforts to get ahead all these years, perhaps because the constable had, at some point, stood up to his senior officer? His transfer to Tweed Heads suddenly took on a very different light.

Kate's thoughts shifted to her own battles with Skinner. Was that what was happening to her? Was she in the process of being sidelined because her usefulness to Skinner had started to wane, just like Murchison's had? Since moving to Esserton some three years ago, she had mostly found Skinner supportive of her work. Now she had to wonder. Had it been because she had never made waves, complying without rancour to his obvious and clumsy manoeuvrings to use her as a diversity cover? In the last handful of months, even before she had gone on maternity leave, she had begun to reveal a vein of intractability, a propensity to ask inconvenient questions and follow her own mind. Had she already been marked by Skinner as a potential problem, to be edged out if possible? Her mind raked across the last few days, all the instances where she had felt Skinner's obstruction, undermining her and making her doubt herself at every turn. Anger curled within her.

The heavy bougainvillea boughs marking the entrance to her father's property swam into view. The plant looked overgrown and unkempt, long lines of leafy tendrils reaching out every which way and bending against her vehicle as she turned into the dirt driveway that led to Gray's cottage.

Her thoughts were a seething mess. She needed to speak to her father, to sort it out once and for all.

In the informal layaway next to her father's property, she pulled up beside an unfamiliar car, her wheels crunching on the loose gravel. An immaculate white Toyota sedan was parked underneath the wide expanse of a lemon myrtle tree, her usual spot. A sudden memory bobbed to the surface, her mother's ancient and dented maroon Toyota Corolla hatch. A car she had refused to give up on, even after it had clocked over 200,000 k's, so attached was she to its perfectly compact size and reliability. The only car she had been confident enough to parallel park, something she would never consider attempting in Gray's oversized ute.

Kate made her way to the front door, through the ornate latch gate that linked together the picture-perfect picket fence surrounding her father's cottage. The rose gardens and ornamental house were an ode to Martin's tastes. Her father's more prosaic inclinations, the chicken coop and vegetable garden, lay out of sight around the back.

At the front verandah, the door was closed but unlocked. She walked in, calling out for her father.

The lived-in interior looked the same as always, although possibly in slightly better condition than usual. Gray's well-worn couch and matching armchairs retained their same positions around the wood burner, though she observed that the usual stack of old newspapers that lived on the coffee table seemed to have been tidied away, and the weary-looking cushions plumped to attention. The wall unit along one side of the room remained packed two-deep with books and CDs and family photos – mainly of her own kids. She placed the Broncos cap that she had retrieved from her father's car on the sideboard. The house was silent but didn't feel empty.

At a rustle by her feet, she looked down to find Bunty, her father's well-indulged and oversized tabby. She kneeled and picked him up, taking comfort in his heft and burrowing her head into his fur.

'Where's your Dad, Bunty? Do you know?'

The cat meowed pitifully. She knew that cry. Bunty was the best-fed cat in the world, though it never stopped him from pleading his case. She carried him to the kitchen, noticing its spotless state. Not a crumb in sight and no sign of the multiple cups of half-drunk tea that usually littered the countertops. A couple of dishes lay washed and neatly stacked on the drying rack. A clean, folded tea-towel hung off the oven handle. She opened the pantry and pulled out a can of cat food, emptying the glistening meat into Bunty's waiting bowl. She watched as he wolfed it down in less than a minute.

'That cat will need to join Weight Watchers soon. That's the second can he's had in less than an hour.'

A man she had never met had entered the kitchen. Barrel-chested and stocky, he was barefoot and dressed in boardshorts and a hoodie. With shoulder-length salt-and-pepper hair and a jawline speckled with silver bristles, he had the look of an aging surfer. Cheerful, green-flecked eyes were set into a deeply weather-worn face.

'I'm Caleb, by the way. Caleb Harte. You must be Kate. It's good to finally meet you.' At the sound of his voice, Bunty had sauntered over and begun running figures of eight round his feet. It appeared that the cat was well ahead of her. The man clearly knew who she was, and had expected his name to ring a bell for her.

'Hi. It's good to meet you.' She blinked and made for the sink to rinse the cat food residue from her fingers and to hide her confusion. Although Kate was sure she didn't know the man, there was something familiar about him that she couldn't place.

'I was actually hoping you'd drop by today, so I could take you through Art's medication. You know how he is. Not the best at following orders.' He made an exaggerated eye roll.

Art. She had never heard that nickname for her father before. It had always been 'Arthur' or 'Gray'. Art was a new one. Kate smiled at the man, who was still speaking.

'I mean can you believe he checked himself out of the hospital? Ridiculous. He never even told me he was in there until last night. I would have been only too happy to drive him home. But oh no. Mr Independent. Has to do it all on his lonesome. Calling a taxi and clumping around here all by himself.' He waved his hands in an expression of mock despair. 'But look who I'm talking to. You know how your dad is.'

She grinned. 'Yeah, I do. He's a stubborn bastard, that's for damn sure.'

Caleb chuckled. 'That he is.' He glanced at her, his expression suddenly knowing. 'Your dad's never spoken about me, has he?'

The look on her face must have given it away because he threw his head back and laughed, a deep, booming cackle that shook the room. And abruptly, it came to her. The shape of Caleb's face, something about the turn of his jawline and how the creases across the bridge of his nose bunched together when he smiled. It all reminded her of Martin. It was only a passing resemblance, but it was there. Her heart dipped.

'Let's start again. I'm Caleb Harte, your father's boyfriend. We've been together for the best part of two months. Met at Bunnings of all places.' He winked. 'Who knew that the timber aisle of Bunnings could be so conducive to romance.'

She grinned and held out her hand. 'Kate Miles, daughter of the said boyfriend. Absolute pleasure to meet you.'

He caught her hand and pulled her into a hug. He smelled of cologne and salt spray.

'He promised me he would tell you, but he has been quite nervous about it, the poor pet.'

Kate reflected on her father's jitteriness on Tuesday night. Had this been the source of his discomposure? Not the media reports of Martin Jackson or all the other sinister machinations she had imagined, just her famously taciturn father's inability to articulate the start of a new relationship to his daughter. She felt her limbs turn to jelly as relief took hold.

Caleb was still speaking, and she concentrated on his words.

'He was on his way to surprise me, the silly thing, when he took that turn too fast and wrapped himself around that tree. Obviously, couldn't wait to see me.' He managed a watery smile. Both of their thoughts, she knew, were on how differently the night could have ended up for Gray. 'Smashed a perfectly good bottle of Glenfiddich in the process, too. My bloody favourite.' Caleb hiccupped a laugh.

'You live near Terranora, do you?' Kate asked, trying to divert the conversation away from the distressing incident.

'Yeah. I run a landscaping company. I'd prefer to be closer to the beach, but hey, beggars, choosers, et cetera, et cetera.' He motioned around him. 'But this place is cute. An ode to the *one before*, I understand,' he murmured sotto voce. 'Don't worry, I've been briefed on the great Martin Jackson. Been making sure I check out the news each day. It's like we're starring in our own soap opera. So dramatic.'

A giggle escaped her, the tension of the last week diffusing into nothing in an instant. Caleb was exactly what her father needed.

'Where is he, by the way?' she asked.

'When I left him, he was in the shower. Insisting that he can do it all by himself. Just waiting to hear the thump of when he falls over.'

'Who's going to fall over?' They turned to find Gray, his hair still dripping and patches of water staining his inexpertly buttoned shirt. His right arm was bundled in a sling and he stepped forward gingerly, favouring his left side, his upper body held rigid and straight. His face and neck bloomed bluish-purple, tracking the bruising from the air bag. Kate had no doubt that underneath his shirt, a diagonal bruise line would be slicing his chest, marking where the seatbelt had saved his life. In his free hand, he carried a cushioned neck brace.

He stopped short as he entered the room, his eyes swinging between Kate and Caleb. Cottoning on that they had already moved past introductions, he held the neck brace out to Caleb. 'Help me with this, would you?'

Kate watched as Caleb gently attached the brace around Gray's neck, his hand lightly grazing her father's cheek, before pulling out one of the chairs from the kitchen table for her father to sink into.

'How're you feeling, Dad?' she asked, hugging Gray carefully, mindful of his injuries.

'I've been better.' His voice was a growl, but Kate could tell there was no heat in his words. She got the impression that he was enjoying the unexpected domesticity that had descended on him. Bunty stalked Gray's chair, purring loudly, and he leaned down stiffly to rub the cat under his chin.

'Cup of tea?' Caleb sang out from near the kettle.

'I had one out before. Just need to heat it up in the microwave.'

Caleb turned to Kate and shuddered. 'I'll get you a new one. Tea for everyone, I think,' he pronounced.

The kettle boiled and Caleb placed two steaming mugs in front of them. Next to Gray's mug, Caleb added a couple of painkillers from a blister pack. He held the packet out for Kate to see. 'Two tablets every four to six hours for the pain.'

Gray pressed his hand to Caleb's in a silent thank you and swallowed his pills. 'I saw the media conference on the news last night.' He turned to Kate, his voice carefully neutral. 'Josh is stepping up, I see.'

Kate grimaced. 'Ha, you could call it that.' That was certainly one way of putting it. Or one could say her career was being flushed down the toilet. *To-may-toes. To-mah-toes.* She caught the concern in her father's eyes.

'It's fine, Dad. I've got it under control.'

He nodded and concentrated on his tea.

'How are you going with all the news articles?' she asked, risking a glance at Caleb, who was busy in the pantry rummaging for something.

'Back in a tick,' Caleb called out. 'No paper towels. I think I saw some rolls in the laundry.' He was clearly giving them space to speak.

Gray sighed, his gaze following Caleb out. 'I feel for Lindsay and the kids, but there's nothing new in there that I can't handle. And Caleb knows everything, by the way. Thought if I was going to start afresh, I might as well do it right. Have everything out in the open.' He cleared his throat, reaching once more for his tea.

Kate blew at her mug, a smile forming. She was happy for her father. 'Yeah, he mentioned.' She risked a sip of the tea. It was strong and scalding, made to her father's specifications. She placed the cup back down. Not meeting his eyes, she forced herself to say the words. 'What about all the coastal development deals they're talking about? Do you know anything about that?'

Gray looked at her and away again. 'We tried not to talk shop when we were together, Kit. He had his life in Sydney. He was a politician. Business deals and favours, that all went with the territory. I never asked and he never enlightened me. But if you're asking me if I'm surprised, then the answer, unfortunately, is no.'

Kate bit her lip. This was it. She had to ask. She couldn't chicken out of it. 'Dad, the money you gave me before the wedding. Was that...? Did... Were you in on any deals with Martin?'

'Sorry? What do you mean?' He sounded confused more than anything.

'The money...' her voice faltered as she took in his expression. Surprise slowly curdling into hurt.

'Shit, Kate.' He placed the mug down on the table harder than he had intended. Tea the colour of teak sloshed out and ran across the timber grain. 'What kind of question is that?' His voice held more pain than anger. 'That money was your mother's inheritance from her parents, your *achchi* and *seeya*. That was the money that came through after their land in England was sold off after the fire. We saved it for you and Luke.' His voice rose, the bitterness building. 'The other half is still sitting there, waiting for Luke to get married, whenever that's going to happen. That's what your mother wanted. I can show you my bloody bank account statements if you want to check. It was always from the both of us, for fuck's sake. How could you even doubt that?'

The silence that followed his words was absolute.

'I'm sorry, Dad. I got my wires crossed. A reporter's been sniffing around and I just...' she trailed off, not knowing how to finish.

Even to her own ears, the words sounded pathetically inadequate. All these years, and she had never given her mother the credit she deserved. Never thanked her while she had had the chance. So enamoured had she been of her father, she hadn't even considered the possibility that the money hadn't originated from him. Her mind scrambled over her memories of that day. Had Gray mentioned her mother when gifting Kate with the cheque? She couldn't remember. Not that it mattered. So eager had she been to believe, it hadn't occurred to her to ask.

She started again. 'It doesn't matter. It was just something Luke and I read online and we—'

'Of course!' Her father's fury cut through her. 'Of course, what else could you possibly think but the worst. Both my children.' He shook his head, hurt and disbelief fighting for control.

'Dad—'

'Enough, Kate. All right? That's enough now.' His chair scraped back as he heaved himself up.

'Everything okay in here?' Caleb had joined them again in the kitchen, a roll of paper towel in his hand. He glanced from Kate to Gray with concern.

'Need a rest, I think,' Gray mumbled, moving towards Caleb.

Kate could only watch as her father shuffled out, leaning on Caleb for support.

34

Kate stumbled out of the house to her car. The momentary relief she had felt, realising that her misgivings over Gray were nothing but the fevered imaginings of a bewildered child, that her financial worries were baseless, had disappeared in the face of her father's distress. Over the last year or so, it had felt like her relationship with Gray had matured, shrugging off the bonds of complicated hero worship into something more akin to an equal footing. But she feared this last encounter had unstitched a lot of that work.

She noticed a new notification on her phone as she scrambled into the driver's seat; an email from Constable Roby with the information line sightings of Veliu, yet to be verified. Her eyes scanned the list without really taking any of it in. She should call her brother. Inform him about Caleb. Maybe persuade him to call Gray. She almost laughed out loud at the thought. If she ever managed that feat, then she would deserve her father's forgiveness. Luke and Gray had barely spoken in over six years.

Throwing her phone into the passenger seat, she slammed the door shut. Gravel sprayed as she reversed and sped away from the house. When she reached the road she continued west, away from town, not yet ready to face the inevitable questions from Geoff. She needed time to decompress. A dull gloom had settled into the afternoon as she followed the road, keeping pace with the Oxley River, a brown coil of water glimpsed in places through breaks in the vegetation.

Her chest prickled, reminding her that she hadn't used her breast pump as she had intended to at her father's. A competing signal rose from her stomach, the aborted cup of tea at Gray's being the only thing she had consumed since breakfast.

Nearing the village of Tyalgum, the scenery changed again, returning to grazing country dotted with bushland. Stopping at an eatery, Kate ventured inside, navigating the tables peppered with tourists to a counter laden with homemade pies and pastries. Ordering a chicken-and-leak pastie and a latte, she retired to the covered landing at the front to await her takeaway coffee. The pie was warm and filling, all she needed it to be.

The eatery was one of a small cluster of shops set amongst picturesque cottages with views of the surrounding Border Ranges. A vivid green playing field, the colour of a child's drawing, stretched the length of the street verge opposite. Parking spaces marked its tree-lined frontage, empty except for a handful of cars.

Kate studied the back silhouette of a man, all in black, a hoodie, tracksuit pants and beanie. He ambled towards one of the cars at the far end, an olive-hued, older-model sedan. He pressed himself against the driver's side door. Swallowing the last of her pie, she felt something stir within her, a butterfly flutter of unease.

The door behind her swung open with a clatter, and one of the café staff emerged in a flurry of tinkling bangles and beads, holding an extra-large coffee cup and a takeaway bag. Harried eyes peered above spectacles and flyaway hair escaped multiple hairpins. She paused at the door as someone called out to her from inside.

'What? I've got the burger with the lot and a long black.' She ducked her head inside and then out again. 'Oops, sorry, love. Wrong order. You're the latte, aren't you? Back in a tick.'

When Kate turned to the playing fields, the man was inside the vehicle, his body bent over the steering wheel and ignition. The scratch of foreboding at the base of her skull flared into a scream. *Fuck!*

'Here's your coffee, love.' The woman had returned.

'Sorry, don't need it anymore. Changed my mind.'

'What?' The woman stared after her in surprise.

Without bothering to explain, Kate took the landing stairs two at a time, her chest tender and protesting every pounding step. As she charged down the street, the man looked up and their eyes met.

Jason Veliu: his hooded face frozen in a snarl of angry surprise.

'Stop right there, Jason.'

For a split second he sat still, waiting for her to draw her gun. But it didn't come. It was her day off and the Glock was stored securely away in her safe at home. Seconds ticked past and she saw Veliu's reach for the screwdriver which he had forced into the ignition to break the steering lock and start the engine. As Kate gained on the sedan, she heard the ignition catch and roar into life.

Veliu put the vehicle into gear, and with a squeal of exhaust drove headlong towards her, his face above the steering wheel alive with menace. She flung herself to the right, rolling onto her side and falling heavily on the footpath, only just escaping being side-swiped by the accelerating car. Kate looked up, expecting to see Veliu speeding away. Instead, the nineties model Commodore had screeched to a halt. A second too late, she realised that the fucker was going to reverse over her.

She stumbled to her feet and scrambled away, leaping behind another of the parked cars, a bulky Land Cruiser. There was a screech of metal and the Land Cruiser convulsed and shifted as Veliu's stolen Commodore slammed into its front carriage. Kate felt the shudder of the impact vibrate through her body, but the robust frame of the Land Cruiser held. It had absorbed most of impact and had been shunted sideways only a metre or so. Still, Kate had suffered a glancing blow to her hip and left side. She rose unsteadily in time to see Veliu speed through the intersection, heading north.

A growing crowd of shocked onlookers were gathering. Dazed tourists streaming out of the cafes. A red-faced man in cargo pants and a lilac shirt with his sleeves rolled up, obviously on holiday, was storming towards her, his family watching on from the kerb. It was clearly his Land Cruiser that had been damaged by Veliu's ramming session. Kate waved him away, jogging to her car, ignoring the pain radiating from her bruised body.

She peeled away in the direction she had seen Veliu driving off. Struggling with her seatbelt one-handed, she waited for the Bluetooth to connect, praying that her phone, its casing cracked from being in her jeans pocket when she had fallen, was still working. Neither Josh nor Skinner were answering. She swore and tried the station number, getting on to Constable Grant at reception. She explained the situation, rattling off the vehicle details and licence number. 'I'm in pursuit, heading north along Limpinwood Road.'

As she spoke, the road curved around a corner and she caught the gleam of ash-green bodywork a hundred or so metres ahead, before it disappeared around the bend. She hung up on Grant, gunning the accelerator and willing the car forward. She needed to catch up to Veliu before he disappeared again. God only knew where he had been holed up the past twenty-four hours. The hinterland around this region was littered with rural properties that Veliu could melt into; the road dotted with hidden driveways that led off into isolated pockets of land tucked into bushland. Today's chance encounter had been pure bad timing for him and a stroke of luck for her. She had no intention of wasting it.

She followed the winding bitumen road, feathering the throttle and navigating the turns at speed. A deep, premature dusk had set in, her headlights cutting tracks into the dark clumps of vegetation that lined the road. She almost drove past it: a rough track cut into the surrounding bush on the opposite side of the road. She slammed the brakes crossing the carriageway and skidded along rutted gravel before shuddering to a halt.

She had come to a stop at what looked like the start of a disused fire trail or an old construction access track used for road works. It had mostly regenerated and been reclaimed by surrounding bushland, and she would have missed it entirely if not for the clear mark of fresh disturbance. In the glare of her headlights, she could see that the younger saplings looked bent and torn, as if something had recently crashed through them. Something like a vehicle.

Exiting her car, Kate examined the area. If she was wrong, Veliu could be getting further and further ahead by the second. The smell of petrol fumes lingered in the cold air. Was that from her own car or a vehicle that had come before? Something glittered on the ground and she saw the fragment of a broken brake light. Flecks of olive green duco glinted at her.

She reached for her mobile. A text and a couple of missed calls from Josh. So, Grant had been able to pass on the message. Mobile reception was patchy in the area, and his calls apparently hadn't connected while she had been driving.

She opened the message. *About 20 min out with Darnley. Where are you?*

She messaged back: *Bush track approx. 7km north of Tyalgum on Limpinwood Rd. Look out for my car at layaway. Heavy bushland. Likely to need search team and canine support.*

A message pinged in response almost immediately: *Stay put. Will assess when we get there.*

Her eyes grazed the text. Josh was now the case lead. If she defied him, she would be disobeying a direct order. She was unarmed and evening was steadily closing in. It would be a monumentally stupid decision to try to take on Veliu alone under these circumstances.

And yet. Waiting for Josh meant that Veliu would almost certainly get away. Right now, he had a few minutes' head start on her, at most. If she could catch sight of him at least, they'd have a chance. By the time Josh got here and a coordinated search team was deployed, Veliu would be long gone.

Something of Josh and Skinner's press conference from the previous evening swelled in her mind. The injustice of it. Once more, she was being asked to step aside. To wait for the cavalry so that someone else could take the credit. *Fuck that shit.*

Grabbing a torch from the boot, she locked the vehicle and started out. She would be slower on foot, but there was less chance that Veliu would hear her coming. Plus, she needed to leave her car so Josh and the team would know where to find her.

She ran lightly up the trail, pressing through the vegetation, the bruising from her earlier encounter with Veliu now a pulsating ache down her left side. Tangled greenery and vines brushed her shoulder and face as she pushed past. The bush creaked and rustled, settling in for the evening. Something stirred in the branches of a nearby tree. She heard the distinctive *oom oom* of a tawny frog-mouth in the distance. The nocturnal creatures of the bush were waking up.

She could clearly make out the path that Veliu's Commodore had cut through the undergrowth. She padded along the edge of the disturbed trail, using the bush for cover, as far as possible. At some point, the original track would peter out and Veliu would be forced to continue on foot.

Another few metres and the track seemed to be widening. She switched off the torch as a precaution, allowing her eyes to adjust to the fading light. A clearing of sorts had opened up, peppered by thinned-out scrub and low saplings. Her first guess had been correct. The site had the look of an old construction laydown area. The abandoned remains of a gravel stockpile slumped under the base of a straggly grevillea – frayed sections of sediment lining still visible around its base. Parked haphazardly in the centre of the clearing stood the stolen car, its back carriage a mess of crumpled metal.

She scanned the site but could see no sign of Veliu. She surveyed the shadowy mass of trees encircling the car, trying to discern any movement. Was he standing there right now, watching her? The fear that she had been containing suddenly flared. She exhaled, allowing the wave of panic to wash over her. *No!* Jason would be long gone. His overwhelming impulse would be to put as much distance as possible between himself and the authorities, not hang around, pissing in the wind.

She steeled herself and walked to the car. As expected, it was empty, the driver's door left ajar. The bonnet still felt warm to the touch, so it hadn't been long since he had left. She heard a faint scratching in the undergrowth like footsteps and she whirled around, adrenaline soaring, her fingers holding tight to the torch, her only weapon. Nothing. Just the strange, secret sounds of the bush. *Stop it*, she told herself. *There's no one there. It's just some creature in the scrub.* There was a loud screech and a bird shot out of one of the trees. She jumped, blood pounding in her ears.

And then she felt it. Movement, more of a change in the breeze. The unmistakable sense that she wasn't alone. Someone was approaching her. She turned, ice flooding her veins, her eyes scouring the black void of the trees beyond.

'Sarge, you're here.' A shadow rippled and separated from the vegetation, coming into view.

She took in Constable Anthony Roby, his face pinging with nervous excitement. He looked around. 'Any sign of him?'

'Nothing, but I only just found the car.' Her relief was sharp like pain. 'What are you doing here?'

'I was in the area. Following up on a sighting of Veliu down Brays Creek way. I was driving back near Tyalgum, when the call came through from Detective Ellis, sending me here.'

As he spoke, a vague memory of seeing Brays Creek in the list of locations Roby had emailed her earlier came to mind. In the state she had been in, the sightings had not registered.

'When I pulled up, I recognised your car but couldn't see anyone. You didn't answer your phone, so I thought I should... you know... come and see if everything was okay.'

She pulled out her mobile, which was turned to silent in her pocket. She had done so deliberately to avoid giving away her position to Veliu, if Josh or the station were to call.

'Thanks, Roby. I think it's safe to say he's taken off. But you did the right thing. I appreciate it.'

He nodded, a hint of pink flushing his ears.

She rang Josh to update him. 'I've found the car. It's in a clearing about fifty metres in from the road. Roby's with me. But there's no sign of Veliu.'

'You sure it's the same vehicle?'

Kate controlled her annoyance as she replied, 'Yes, Josh. The bloody thing is right in front of me. It's a green Commodore, the same as the one he tried to run me over with earlier, and it has a smashed rear end to prove it.'

'Yeah, okay, just checking. How bad is the terrain?'

'Probably a good few kilometres of bushland and rural properties. I'd say he's probably after another car. Have you called the search team?'

'Yeah, they're on their way. Not far behind us.'

She turned at the sound of a scuffle and froze. *Veliu*. His face gleaming with sweat, and chemical-induced agitation. He had materialised out of nowhere and taken Roby unawares from behind. His left arm held Roby in a stranglehold while his right hand pressed a knife to his neck. The constable had paled to a bleached-flour white, his hand frozen in the act of reaching for his Glock.

'Don't even think about it, fuckhead.' Veliu's voice was harsh, right in Roby's ear, his eyes jittery, pupils dilated to enormous orbs, pinging back and forth between Kate and Roby. This was not a man who was in any state to be negotiated with.

'Kate, you there?' Josh was still speaking to her on the phone.

'Yeah, yep, I'm here.' Her mind raced, trying to think of a way to communicate the situation to Josh.

'I said, we're about ten minutes out.'

'Okay, sounds good—' The call ended. Josh had hung up.

She lowered the phone, her eyes not leaving Veliu. She could feel her heart pounding, panic starting to scrabble up her chest. She would not lose control. Not now. Not in this moment.

'Jason, this is pointless. That was Detective Ellis on the phone. He's going to be here in a few minutes with backup. You're going to be surrounded. There's no getting away, Jason.'

'Shut up, bitch. Just need your car keys, then me and Constable Piss-face here are gonna go for a ride.'

'Jason, that's not a good idea.' She could feel Roby's eyes drilling into hers, but she focused on Veliu.

'I said fucking shut it!' he screamed at her. His eyes skidded from Kate to Roby, leaning wet lips directly into Roby's ear. 'You. Stay fucking still or I'm gonna cut your face.'

In a quick movement, Veliu swapped the knife to his left hand – the arm that held tight around Roby's neck –

while his free hand reached into the constable's hip holster for his pistol.

Kate met Roby's eyes and he took his chance, elbowing Veliu hard in his ribs. Veliu howled in anger more than pain, his fingers failing to grasp Roby's gun. The constable pulled at Veliu's arm, swift and hard, jerking away, but not before the knife had torn at his flesh. Kate saw a spurt of red bloom across Roby's collar as he rolled to the ground.

'Go,' he yelled, pointing at Jason.

Veliu was running and Kate was pounding after him. He stumbled in the dark and she was on him, tackling him to the ground. They rolled across branches and damp leaf litter, her torch flung out of her grasp. He had the knife in his hands, still wet with Roby's blood. He was on top of her now, his hot, fetid breath on her face, the weight of his body pinning her down.

'You never fucking learn, do you? Stupid cow.'

Pain seared across her milk-engorged chest as his elbows found purchase on her torso, his hands pressing down hard on the knife. The blade was inches from her face. Her hands fighting against the force of his wrists, she bucked and contorted, the knife landing on the ground centimetres from her ear. She heaved him off her and tried to scramble away.

'Not so fast,' he growled, grabbing a fistful of her hair and wrenching her back. She screamed, her scalp aflame with pain. She turned and bit his arm, her tongue tasting salt mixed with dirt and blood, her teeth sinking into his flesh. He let go of her hair, hollering and swearing. She rolled away, her hands scrabbling in the ground for the knife. She clasped at the handle and pulled, but it was stuck. The force with which Veliu had struck had buried the metal deep into a tree root. She could hear

Jason getting up and stumbling towards her, furious and vengeful.

She heaved again and the blade broke away, jagged at the end, the tip still buried in the ground. He was beside her now, one foot raised to kick her. *Do it. Do it now!* She sat up and stuck the jagged end of the knife into his raised thigh, pushing and twisting. Blood spurted and Veliu shrieked, falling to the ground, his hands on the blade hanging from his flesh.

'Fuck! Fuck! You stupid bitch. What have you done?'

'Stay on the ground. Don't move. Hands where I can see them.'

It was Roby, a deep-red gash running along the side of his jaw, the front of his uniform soaked with blood. He cuffed Veliu, and moved to attend to his wound. Removing his jumper, he wrapped it firmly around Veliu's leg to stem the blood flow, careful not to remove the blade to avoid exacerbating the injury.

'Stop moving. You're only making it worse.'

'The bitch could have taken out my artery. I could have bled to death.'

'Everyone's got problems, mate.'

Kate rose unsteadily to her feet to join the constable. 'You all right, Roby?' She nodded to his face. 'That's going to be some scar.'

He grinned. 'Always did have a soft spot for The Joker.'

35

Thursday

'You can't keep doing this, Kate. We can't keep doing this.'

'Geoff, he's a suspect in an abduction and suspicious death. He was right in front of me. What would you have me do? I had to go after him. It's the job. You can't just pick and choose the bits you want to do.'

'Don't fucking give me that. There are ways of managing the situation. You could have called it in. Let someone else be in the firing line. You don't have to do everything, Kate. No one will think any less of you. Skinner would support you.'

She had laughed then. A deep-throated, hysterical cackle that she hadn't been able to stop. Geoff had glared at her in disgust.

'And what about us, Kate. What about your family? Are we a joke to you, too? What about the kids? Have you included us in any of your calculations? What if you'd died out there today? You barely survived last time—'

'I'm fine—'

'You're not fine. I'm not fine. Every time you leave the bloody house, I don't know if you'll return. You're never at home. Archie misses you. You only interact with Amy when you're feeding her. And now you can't even do that. Wake up, Kate. Something has to change. Otherwise, none of us are going to survive your fucking career.'

Kate blinked away the memory. The long argument that had ensued with her husband after she had finally got home last night. After a debriefing on scene with Josh, she and Roby had been driven to hospital, to document their injuries and be subjected to bloodwork to check for transmittable diseases including HIV & hepatitis, given that they had both come into contact with Veliu's blood. The nurses had allowed her to pump her breasts, the milk discarded. Until the test results came back negative over the next week, she wouldn't be able to breastfeed Amy. After all her fretting regarding feeding, the decision to wean her daughter had, in the end, been made for her.

Once she'd been cleared by medical staff, Josh had been waiting to take her statement, separate to Roby, before she had finally been allowed to leave. She had arrived home close to ten o'clock. Someone from the station had already informed Geoff and he had been waiting up. All she had wanted to do was have a shower and crawl into bed. Instead, they had argued, furious whispered sniping that had ended with Geoff collecting his pillows and stalking out to sleep on the couch.

'Mummy, look at me. Look at me.' She smiled and waved at Archie as he navigated the jungle gym in the playground. From the picnic blanket, Amy showed off her newly acquired skill of rolling from her back to her tummy, grinning up at Kate, inordinately pleased with herself. Kate chuckled. 'Clever bub.'

She had driven the kids to the park in town, which flanked the wide flat banks of the Tweed River, so they were out of Geoff's hair. To let him cool off and recalibrate. His anger towards her had yet to diminish, not helped by a night on their old and lumpy couch. She had called the station and taken another day off, since yesterday hadn't really worked out as a personal day. There was no longer any urgency. Veliu was in custody and Skinner was happy.

Amy reached for a rattle toy and Kate bent down to kiss her and breathe in her milky, powdery scent. Amy returned a wet, gummy smile and Kate felt a lightness in her heart. Geoff's words last night about her not bonding with Amy, thrown at her at the height of his fury, had hit home hard. Her worst fears about herself confirmed and verbalised. Geoff was right. She had to do better with the kids. Guilt and shame over the past weren't good enough excuses to lose sight of what she had right now. She adjusted her weight away from the bruised side of her body. The winter sun was warm on her back and a light breeze rose from the banks of the river, ruffling the feathery boughs of the palm trees dotting the esplanade. She tickled Amy's tummy, and laughed as her daughter squealed with delight. Archie rushed to her side and rustled through his snack pack for food. She handed him a box of sultanas and a rice cracker and he was off again.

A shadow fell over them and she turned to find Rayna Gardiner, Elissa's mother, straight-backed and impassive, her eyes hidden behind sunglasses.

'You're a very lucky woman.'

Kate didn't respond, knowing there was little she could say. The presence of her two children, healthy, happy, alive, lay sharp and painful between them. Rayna's eyes were trained on Archie as he ran around the play equipment with another little boy, their excited whoops loud and uncontained. Not once did her eyes slide down to Amy, sucking enthusiastically on her rattle.

'One of your officers called Elissa last night. Told her what you did. How you found him…' she hesitated, stopping short of saying Veliu's name. 'I wanted to come by the station to thank you. They said you weren't in. But here you are.' Her words were delivered like an accusation, though Kate knew that's not how she had intended them. Rayna had never struck her as someone who put much stock on social pleasantries, and the last few days seemed to have entirely stripped her patience for niceties.

'I'm glad we found him, Rayna. I know it must be a huge relief for you.'

'It's finally over,' Rayna said, speaking almost to herself. 'He's in custody. I thought I would feel differently, but nothing's the same. Aaron's moved out, you know.' This time, the words did feel like an accusation. 'He's in a motel up near the caravan park.' Her lips curled. She clearly categorised Aaron's behaviour as a desertion of her daughter.

'I'm sorry, Rayna. I didn't realise. He probably just needs some time.' It was a platitude and they both knew it. Aaron and Elissa's relationship was already scoured by cracks and betrayals. Add to that the death of a child, and the intense police and media scrutiny that had followed, it was no surprise that their marriage was at breaking point. Couples fractured under much less pressure. A shiver went through Kate at the thought of her own marriage.

'Let's hope he turns up to the funeral. He hasn't lifted a finger so far to help with the arrangements.'

Kate studied Rayna's hardened features. Aaron was dealing with his grief differently to his family, but that didn't mean he didn't care.

'The service is on Sunday. A closed casket. Elissa and I agreed. She wanted to visit Sienna at the morgue. But

I told her it's better this way. No good can come from seeing her now. We can remember Sienna the way she was.' Rayna pursed her lips.

Kate didn't argue. It was a personal choice that each family had to make, whether or not to view the body following an autopsy. Though she recalled Elissa's clear distress when they had informed the family of Sienna's discovery; her repeated requests to see her child one last time. She wondered at the power Rayna seemed to exert over her daughter.

Rayna nodded and turned abruptly. 'I need to get home to Elissa.' She walked away without saying goodbye.

–

Kate could hear her mobile beeping from the bedroom but ignored it, concentrating on holding Amy upright in the bath, while Archie splashed in the suds.

'Gentle, Arch. Watch out for your sister,' she said as Archie spun in the water, creating waves. Amy giggled and babbled in response, splashing her hands in the bubbles.

It was evening and she was organising the kids' baths while Geoff cleared away after dinner and did the dishes. Things between Geoff and her weren't fully resolved, but her efforts with the kids today had helped. He had thawed over the course of the day, a couple of hours to himself at the driving range with a bucket of balls having done its part. The atmosphere had been civil, almost pleasant during their meal. If she hadn't known Geoff for close to a decade, she could have fooled herself into thinking that everything was back to normal between them. But she knew better. The hurt ran deep, and it would take more than a day of no arguments to heal the breach.

After PJs and stories with Archie, and nursing Amy to sleep with a bottle, she finally checked her messages. It was after eight and there were multiple missed calls from a private number, left over an hour ago and a single voicemail.

She played the message, a lick of disquiet stirring within her.

'*Detective… You need to know. She's got everyone fooled… I saw the car…*'

Kate recognised the slurred voice of Aaron Ricci. Drunk, on edge and teary. She heard the sound of loud music and voices in the background, followed by canned laughter. He had the TV on.

Ricci mumbled something away from the phone, which Kate didn't catch. '*…wanted children. It wouldn't have worked.*' There was a pause as Ricci seemed to lose his train of thought. He sniffed hard and came back on the line, his voice full of emotion already in the middle of a sentence '*…Thai food and… the driver had a heart attack…*' Kate held the phone closer to her ear, trying to understand his garbled words. There was the sound of a thud and loud swearing followed by dead air, before the message ended with a beep. She tried the number she had for Ricci, but it went straight to voicemail. Leaving a brief message, she hung up.

She sat on the edge of her bed, the mobile in her hand. What the hell had that been about? Had Ricci been referring to Allison Garrett in his message? So was she somehow involved, after all and he was now finally ready to give her up? That line about wanting kids felt like it was directed at Allison. But the rest of the message was confused and all over the place. Ricci was clearly plastered. Had she just heard the ramblings of an alcohol-soaked mind, or was there something more in there? Something he said had struck a chord within her, pinging a note somewhere deep in her memory banks that she couldn't yet place. But she knew it would come.

She could feel her brain humming, that special hit of energy that she only got from an investigation as her mind puzzled through a problem. This was what she couldn't explain to Geoff. This buzz. The feeling of being close to something, even though she didn't know what. It was what made her go back to the job, again and again.

She would drive around and visit Ricci tomorrow, to see if she could get more sense out of him sober. In the meantime, it was worth getting a patrol to check on him to make sure he wasn't so drunk as to be a danger to himself. No doubt Elissa would know which motel he was staying at. She called it in, leaving instructions that she be notified once Ricci had been seen to.

Close to forty minutes later, longer than she had expected, the call came in.

'Sarge, we're at the motel. Reception says Ricci's checked in and paid up for the week. His car is parked out the front and his room's a mess, so he's been in here. But there's no sign of him. And, Sarge... there's blood all through the room.'

36

Friday

Kate had deliberately got into the station early. The first fingerlings of dawn were just breaking across the sky when she had woken to Amy's faint whimpers in the adjoining room. Getting up, she had fed her a bottle, changed her nappy and settled her next to Geoff in their bed.

'I want to get a head start and finish off a few things,' she said, concentrating on Amy and not looking at her husband, the rest of the unspoken sentence sitting heavy between them – *so I won't be late home again.* 'I've got the breakfast things out.'

His fingers had reached for her hand and she had felt a brief squeeze of pressure. Meeting his eyes, she had seen the softening of his expression. An acknowledgment that she was trying. Kissing her daughter's forehead, and brushing her lips against Geoff's, she had left the room.

Now at the station, she paged through the report filed by the officers who had attended Ricci's motel room the previous night. Josh had been on call and had directed the incident. From the photos, the room looked to be littered with empty beer bottles, including at least one longneck shattered on the tiled floor. The photos showed a fist-sized bloodstain near the base of the bed, and droplets trailing from the smashed glass to the en suite. A smear of red was

274

visible on the edge of the sink, along with wads of bloody toilet paper in the bin.

The motel wasn't fully occupied and the rooms on either side of Ricci were vacant. None of the nearby guests had reported hearing any sounds of disturbance. Aaron wasn't answering his mobile, and he hadn't turned up at any hospital or back at Elissa's.

Josh's view of the incident was plain from his notes on file: Ricci had clearly been on a bender and was letting off steam. He would show up in due course. Patrols had been instructed to be on the lookout. In the meantime, Josh had recommended that Allison Garrett be brought in for another chat. In his view, Ricci's voice message had raised enough questions to warrant another push in Allison's direction.

Kate didn't disagree with Josh's assessment regarding Allison. However, it was something else about Ricci's message that had stuck with her, nagging at her through the night. When she had woken up this morning, it had been there waiting, her unconscious mind working free the burrowed splinter of memory onto the surface.

The driver had a heart attack. She remembered now why it had sounded familiar. She had heard the patrols talking about it around the station. The delivery driver who had suffered acute chest pains and had clipped the kerb, taking out a parking sign in town. Police and ambulance had attended the scene. With everything going on with the investigation, she hadn't immediately made the connection. But of course, it had occurred on Thursday night, on Leeson Road, a block away from Cromer Street, where Ricci had been on his way to pick up his takeaway Thai. Allison Garrett had mentioned a traffic delay when Ricci had gone to collect their food. A report of the accident had subsequently been in the paper, likely explaining how Ricci had picked up on the detail about the heart attack. She had absolutely no idea how the traffic incident could link to the case, but there would be footage from the patrols who had attended.

On her laptop, she clicked onto the server, bringing up the video captured by the first patrol car on scene. The footage from the onboard camera showed the vehicle approaching the rear of the stationary van, which had slammed headlong into a no-parking sign, the metal pole askew and bent backwards. Per his training, the officer had parked his vehicle slightly offset from the van, creating a barrier between himself and any through traffic as he approached the driver's side. The angle provided the in-car camera with a direct line of sight of the officer as well as part of the opposite road carriage.

She watched as the patrol assessed the situation, pulling the van door open to check on the driver and radioing in for help. Kate had already run some brief checks on the man. Con Adritti, a 53-year-old delivery driver from Lismore, currently recovering from bypass surgery at Tweed Hospital. She could not make out how he fit into the story. She ran through the footage, watching the arrival of an ambulance and Mr Adritti being attended to by paramedics.

And there it was. Just as the ambulance had been about to drive off, the footage had captured vision of a dark-coloured Mitsubishi station wagon on the opposite side of the road. She snipped the two seconds' worth of footage and zoomed in, her mind racing as she clocked the licence plate and the figure at the front wheel. *What the fuck?*

This had to be it. In his message, Ricci had mentioned seeing a car. This had to be what he had been referring to.

She played the rest of the footage, and her suspicions were confirmed. Within minutes of the ambulance driving off, the patrol officer on scene had started to clear the traffic backed up behind the accident, and she saw the flash of a dark-blue Mazda 6 sedan – Ricci's vehicle – driving off.

She flicked through the file notes, searching through Ricci's and Allison Garrett's statements. They had both stated that they had ordered takeaway food late on Thursday, getting up to the store's closing time. The restaurant records had confirmed their statements; the takeaway food had been picked up at 9.17 pm that night. The patrol-vehicle footage had captured the Mitsubishi travelling west on Leeson Road at 9.09 pm and Ricci's Mondeo travelling east soon afterwards at 9.11 pm. The times tallied. Ricci had been stuck in traffic behind the accident and would have seen the station wagon travel past on the opposite side of the road.

But what did it mean? How was it significant?

She leaned back in her chair, trying to sort through the information flooding her mind. So, the car had been caught on camera on Thursday night. Why did Ricci care? There was no connection to Sienna's abduction. Or was there?

She stared up at the map of Esserton splayed across the side wall of the office. Walking up to it, she found Leeson Road. The turnoff to Layton Reserve ran off it to the east three intersections down. She stared at the map, her mind suddenly alight with questions.

Returning to her desk, she opened her email and hurried through the dozens of unopened correspondence awaiting her attention. There it was, the preliminary autopsy report they had been waiting on from Barlow, which he had finally emailed through overnight. Her

277

eyes flew over the words, searching for the window of death. *At least twenty-four hours from when the body was found, likely upwards of sixty hours.* Her blood ran cold. That stretched the timeframe of Sienna's death somewhere between Thursday afternoon and Friday night.

Thursday. Her mind did the calculations, running and rerunning the scenarios. Was it possible?

She turned to Barlow's report and scanned the text for the cause of death. *Awaiting toxicology results. However, no indications of external or internal trauma or pathology have been uncovered. At this stage, the cause of death is undetermined.*

Kate checked the time: not even 8 am. Too bad. She rang Barlow's mobile.

A hoarse cough answered the phone after multiple rings.

'Dr Barlow, it's Detective Miles. I'm sorry to call you so early, but I was hoping you wouldn't mind taking me through Sienna Ricci's autopsy results.'

He hacked another phlegm-filled cough before answering. 'It's all in the report, Detective. I trust you're not asking me to repeat myself.'

Kate controlled her impatience. 'I've been going through your notes this morning and I would appreciate it if you could run me through your thinking around the cause of death. You say it remains undetermined?'

'Well, as explained in the report,' he said in a tone that implied he was doing her a massive favour, 'there's nothing obvious to determine how she died. If it wasn't for all the postmortem injuries, I would have put this down to positional or mechanical asphyxiation—'

'Hang on, you mean like in a cot death?' Kate asked.

'As you say,' Barlow replied, sounding annoyed at being interrupted. 'In infants, there are often very few post-mortem signs, if any, with incidents of that nature.'

Despite his stated objection to speaking, Kate could sense Barlow hitting his stride. His voice falling into the rhythm of a university instructor. 'As you well know, Detective, the manner of death in such cases, is determined almost entirely based on environmental factors. The bedding, the position that the child is found, any obstructions found near the face, indications of lividity pointing to the sleeping position, and so on.'

Kate thought back to the one SIDS investigation she had been involved in during her career. Barlow was right, the case had relied primarily on the conditions in which the baby had been found at home.

'In this instance,' Barlow continued, 'the child was moved postmortem, causing lividity to shift, so the limited signs of lateral and posterior lividity recorded at autopsy, in my opinion, can't be relied on to indicate position of death.' He stopped abruptly as another coughing fit seemed to overtake him. Kate moved the mobile from her ear and waited him out, wincing at the sounds of Barlow hocking up a lung.

He was finally back on the line, clearing his throat loudly. 'As I was saying, if I had to guess, I would put her death down to wedging by another person, adult or child from co-sleeping or the overlay of bedding material leading to the lethal rebreathing of carbon dioxide. Deliberate mechanical suffocation using a soft material like a pillow is also a possibility. Given that Sienna also showed signs of nasal congestion at the time of death, it's very likely that it contributed to her difficulties in breathing, leading to asphyxiation. But as I say, this is all pure conjecture, with no external evidence to support it. I would need other forms of corroboration before I can put any such opinion in my report.'

'I understand, Dr Barlow. Thank you. And the time of death. You've indicated a window upwards of sixty hours?'

'Despite the cold weather, which preserved her remains, there are signs of insect activity and the beginnings of bloat, which to my mind places her at the upper end of the time limit rather than the lower estimate. I've already spelled this all out.'

'Thank you, Dr Barlow. I really appreciate you going through it again with me.' She said her goodbyes and hung up, her saccharine approach having achieved her aim.

The new information hummed through her mind. Suddenly, a number of disconnected incidents seemed to fall into place: the prowler at Elissa's property, the soft toy that had been discovered up the road after Sienna's disappearance, what Allison Garrett had witnessed when Elissa had picked up Daniel from school, and Sienna being discovered at Veliu's favourite fishing spot.

Had she been looking at the case backwards all this time? It all came down to a single person. Her mind spun back to the patrol-car footage. Ricci had noticed the Mitsubishi. Did that mean he had been spotted in return?

37

Kate followed the river and headed in the direction of Esserton's tourist parks and motels, which were clustered along the bend in the river on the south-west end of town. The sun beat down and reflected off her windscreen as alternating beats of green, bushland and pasture, drifted past her window.

Her mind thrummed with contained energy, her thoughts thrashing about like fish caught in a net. She had not been able to catch Josh that morning, to unload what she had uncovered. He had messaged to say that Allison Garrett had agreed to be reinterviewed at home with a lawyer and he was heading there now. Harris would be joining them. Kate had been excluded from the interview and it had hardly given her pause. None of that mattered now, given what she knew.

She tried to rein in her thoughts. It was all still conjecture, she reminded herself. She needed corroboration on the timeline before bringing things to a head. She had been part of investigations before where they had moved too quickly, spooking a suspect into lawyering up. Allowing them to hide within the loose ends of a case and start compiling the grounds for reasonable doubt. Maybe it was for the best that she hadn't yet spoken to Josh or confided her theories.

Regardless, it was a relief to be out of the office. She'd had several of the team stop by her desk this morning, to congratulate her on bringing Veliu in. It was gratifying but exhausting, her survival being more a matter of luck and instinct than any heroics on her part. Another close encounter to bear the weight of, rather than crow over. Roby, who was at home recovering, also seemed to have advanced in the station's hierarchy of notoriety as a result of almost getting killed. It was a side of the police force that Kate least enjoyed, the hyper-masculine glorification of strength and toughness.

Skinner had been one of the many to drop by. Sucking on what appeared to be a green smoothie, he had smiled serenely at her through sage-tinged lips. 'You did well, Miles. Both you and Roby.'

'Thank you, sir.' Kate's reply was automatic, the compliment sitting unabsorbed like oil on water. She trusted his sincerity about as much as she would enjoy tasting his vile-looking drink.

'Make sure to use the counselling service if you need to,' he had added, his eyes not leaving her face. 'And don't forget the link-up with Sydney has been confirmed for Monday.'

'Sir.' She watched him stride back to his office. That was more like it. A sting to every compliment.

His comment had been alluding to her interview by videoconference with Professional Standards, scheduled for Monday to go over Veliu's arrest. Veliu had put in a complaint regarding the circumstances of his apprehension, which had landed him with serious lacerations to his upper thigh. Allegations of excessive force, which she would need to explain away, like why she hadn't stopped to retrieve Roby's gun to apprehend Veliu rather than rushing headlong into the fray. Instinctive decisions taken in the heat of the moment that she would need to defend in the cold light of day. This would be her second appearance with Professional Standards in less than six months. She was earning herself a reputation.

She shook away the thought and concentrated on the present. Up ahead, she could see the sign for the motel: Palm Grove Motor Lodge. She pulled up in front of the building, a modest, brown-brick affair, with rooms stacked above each other over two storeys, accessed by a covered walkway with metal railings. A small single-storey amenities block and reception jutted out, creating an L-shape, and a parking lot took up the remainder of the space. Across the road from the motel the Tweed River glinted, tea-bag-brown behind a sagging farm fence, swathed between green pasture and clumps of tea tree scrub.

As she exited the car, the motel reception door swung open and a man stepped out; polo shirt, slacks and carefully brushed hair.

'Can I help you there?' He smiled a set of perfectly formed teeth.

'Police.' Kate held out her ID. 'Are you the owner of the property?'

'Yes, that's right. Steve Lee is my name. My wife, Una, and I run the place. Going on nine years now.'

When Kate didn't reply, the man rushed to fill the silence. 'We've never had any trouble with the police. Last night was a bit of a shock, I must say, seeing the room in that state. We told the officers all we knew, which wasn't much, to be honest.'

He was clearly one of those people who prattled on when nervous. All Kate had to do was let him talk.

'Has Mr Ricci been back to his room, do you know?'

'We haven't seen any sign of him this morning, and his car hasn't moved.' He pointed to a blue Mazda 6, parked neatly in its allocated spot in the carpark.

Kate nodded. 'Do you mind if I have a quick look around where he's staying?'

'You can, but I don't think there's anything much to see. Room service has been through this morning. Mr Ricci is still our guest, after all,' he twittered. Perhaps expecting a rebuke, he continued hurriedly, 'We did ask if we could clean up. The other detective gave us permission.'

Kate nodded. 'That's fine, Mr Lee. If you can just point me in the right direction?'

'Yes, of course. Just follow me.' He practically jumped in his eagerness to help. After ducking into reception to retrieve a spare key, he led Kate through the guest carpark to a concrete stairwell covered in pebblecrete. 'Mr Ricci is just up these stairs, the third room to your right. Number twenty-seven.'

'Thanks, Mr Lee. You've been a great help. I can take it from here.'

He stopped in the act of climbing the steps and smiled. 'Of course. Not a problem.' He handed over the key to Kate and turned away.

'Mr Lee,' she called after him. 'I'm sure Detective Ellis already mentioned this, but I just want to reiterate the need for discretion, including on the part of your cleaning staff. We wouldn't want any details of last night or of Mr Ricci's room appearing in the paper, for instance, or on social media.'

'Yes, of course, Detective. I completely understand. Our staff are entirely trustworthy. I guarantee it.'

Kate nodded and waited for the motel owner to walk away before starting up the stairs, her eyes automatically scanning her surrounds, an ingrained habit.

On the third step from the bottom, she stopped to observe a small rust-coloured stain like a drop of paint, difficult to discern against the pebblecrete but visible. She photographed it and continued on. At the top of the stairwell, she photographed a dull-maroon smudge on the underside of the railing, no larger than a ten-cent piece. Nodding to a middle-aged couple who had emerged from a room at the far end of the corridor, she moved towards Ricci's door. They walked past, sending curious glances her way.

As far as she could tell, there were no other signs of blood. But from the marks down the stairwell, Ricci had clearly still been bleeding when he had ventured out last night. Whether he had sustained his injuries as a result of an accident or following an altercation with someone, she couldn't be certain, though from the incident notes she knew Josh's views on the matter.

Using the key Mr Lee had provided her, she unlocked the door. Just as the motel owner had predicted, there was little to see. The room had been cleaned back to an anonymous blankness, complete with the overpowering scent of lemon cleaning product. The bed remade and floors vacuumed. She scanned the room, clocking Ricci's phone and car keys on top of the bar fridge next to a tray of complimentary tea and coffee sachets. An open carry-all revealed a jumble of hastily packed clothes. Walking into the en suite, Kate noticed that all signs of the mess and blood, documented in the scene photos, had been washed and disinfected away. New towels and soap products adorned the railings and vanity. The motel's promise of a 'Spotless Budget Experience' appeared to be justified.

She heard heavy, stumbling footsteps out in the corridor before the room door swung open, pinging against the wall.

'What the hell? What are you doing in here? How'd you get into my room?'

'Mr Ricci, I'm glad to see you're safe. We've been looking for you.'

'What? What are you talking about? I'm fine.'

Aaron Ricci looked exactly the opposite of fine: washed-out and fidgety, his eyes bloodshot, and his clothes creased and crumpled and smelling faintly of wood smoke. A discoloured bandage covered his right palm and the dull sheen of dried blood stained his skin and the front of his sweatshirt. Kate wondered what other substances apart from alcohol he had consumed last night. Had his temporary disappearance merely been the result of Aaron chasing a fix? A short-term escape from his problems? If so, Josh's instincts had been spot on.

'Aaron, you called me last night. You left a message on my phone, sounding really upset. And then you disappeared. There was blood all through your room and we've been trying to find you, to make sure you were okay.'

'What? I'm fine. I just dropped a beer bottle and cut my hand.'

'Well, I'm glad it wasn't anything serious. You didn't sound fine last night.'

Ricci sighed and slumped on the bed. 'I just needed to get away. Didn't feel like being alone... I just can't get the images of her out of my mind you know? How she looked at the morgue. So small and just fucking wrong. My little girl,' his voice broke.

'You viewed Sienna's body?'

'On Tuesday. I drove up with Elissa.'

So Elissa had managed to say goodbye to her daughter after all, despite Rayna's views on the matter.

'It's all been so messed up with Elissa, since…' Aaron shook his head unable or unwilling to complete his train of thought.

'Last night, I messaged a friend and he came and got me…' he mumbled, circling back to his original point. 'He had the fire pit going and let me crash at his place.' Aaron turned fiercely to her. 'You know, after everything with Sienna, no one wants to know me. Even Todd. He only let me stay because his missus is out of town. He couldn't wait to get me out of his car this morning. It's like I'm a leper or something.' He buried his head in his hands. 'This is never going to end, is it? This is going to follow me around for the rest of my life.'

Kate joined Ricci, sitting beside him on the bed. 'Aaron, that's why we need to get to the bottom of what really happened. I listened to your voicemail message. I checked out what you said about the delivery driver. There's patrol footage of the incident. It shows the car you spotted, the Mitsubishi station wagon. I think I understand what happened. But I need you to tell me what you know.'

He turned to her, emotion overwhelming his face.

'It means you'll have to testify against her. It's time to end this, Aaron.'

He met her eyes and nodded.

Two police cars have turned up.

Will today be the day? Every time they come around, I assume my time is up. I've dreamed of this moment. Seen myself handcuffed, imagined the cold steel against my wrists. Heard the satisfying clink of metal securing into place. I've seen myself being led away across the front garden, past the stupid bloody gnomes, phones flashing, cameras recording every detail of my face, the media baying for blood. The same scene I've witnessed multiple times in movies and documentaries. And finally, it's my turn.

I always thought it would be the male detective. He seemed to fit the role with his gelled hair, designer stubble and blank, expressionless face. The hard-nosed, handsome policeman sent to secure the heartless baby killer. But it's the woman who has arrived. I've never been able to get a handle on her, with her worn clothes and worried expression. Her eyes always watching and calculating, like she was peeling layers off me. And then a shard of uncanny knowledge in her eyes, like she understood and grasped exactly how I was feeling. Like she could see inside me. It was unbearable.

Did she know? Has she guessed all the details? Will she understand if I tell her the truth? All of it. All the horrible details of the kind of mother I have been. How I'd sometimes looked upon my mewling, squalling daughter with something close to hatred. The constant need. The constant crying. The constant demands on my body. The never-ending exhaustion. Had the woman detective ever felt this way? And then finding Sienna that day, blue and lifeless. Her tiny, pudgy face no longer able to wail and whimper, her plump limbs like the stuffed appendages of a doll. I had done that. I killed Sienna. I had willed it into being with every breath of impatience, every ugly thought and shameful feeling.

Part of me is glad that the detective is here. Glad that it might finally be over. I'm so tired of pretending. If it wasn't for Daniel, I would have ended it already. Daniel with his solemn, wet eyes, who seems to see right through me. All my lies. Will he understand? Will he ever forgive me? I told the truth and look where that got me.

I can feel the pain in my heart, like the muscle is actually tearing and shrivelling. I've made a mess of it all. But I have to stay strong, to see it through for Daniel. Maybe I can still protect him.

The detective is inside the house now, moving towards me, a young copper in uniform following behind. Why is she looking at me like that? With compassion rather than revulsion. It's too much. I hear her voice, reaching me through the fog in my brain.

'Elissa, I need to find your mother. Do you know where she is?'

'What?'

'Your mother, Elissa. Where is she? She's not at her house.'

'She… she said she was taking Daniel for a picnic. Have a day off school as a treat.'

'Do you know where they've gone, Elissa?'

'By the creek. She said it would be peaceful down there.'

38

The reserve sign indicated two main trails: *Layton Creek Track (140 m)* and *Layton Ridge Loop Circuit (2.4 km)*.

The last time Kate had been here, she, along with the first responders, had scrambled up the first section of the Layton Ridge Circuit, approximately fifty metres or so of trail that had gradually wound its way uphill until it reached a low ridgeline. Sienna had been discovered there, dragged and deposited by a feral animal. There had been no need to venture any further up the trail, which continued on to Layton Ridge Lookout and eventually looped back down to the reserve carpark.

The surrounds felt familiar but also entirely different. On her last visit, the area had been shrouded by night, the vegetation a dense, claustrophobic mass that she had to press through, the path an obstacle course of hidden ruts, stones and branches. In the daylight, the landscape felt recognisable and benign, settled into the familiar shapes of shrubs and trees. She could appreciate the beauty of the place.

According to Elissa Ricci, her mother had been planning on taking Daniel for a picnic by Layton Creek. 'So Daniel can be close to Sienna,' Elissa had said, her eyes wide and fervent.

More like traumatising Daniel, Kate had thought but not said aloud. On her way from Aaron's motel, she had instructed a patrol to meet her at Elissa's. She had left the constable in charge of Elissa and driven on to Layton Reserve. She turned now in the direction of the creek trail.

The walking track was flat and laid with decking for easy access. She jogged ahead, reaching the end of the path at a small timber landing. A visitor information sign perched alongside detailed the once-abundant flora that had characterised the area, lowland subtropical rainforest, less than one per cent of which remained today. The trail gave way to a tangle of ferns, palms, vines and fig trees, a small, remanent pocket.

The ground felt damp underfoot, heavy with leaf litter as Kate pressed forward. She headed for the creek, which flowed deep jade and brown. It snaked between boulders smoothed over by years of running water and banks buttressed by tangled tree roots. She caught sight of Rayna perched on a sunny rock ledge, next to a huge fallen tree trunk, wedged against the bank and part of the landscape. Daniel appeared to be resting, his body curled into Rayna.

Some metres back from where they sat, Kate could see the vegetated embankment inclining gently up to the ridgeline, where Sienna had been found, the flank of the cave wall visible as an overhang. The ground still showed faint signs of disturbance where forensic officers had searched and found the location of Sienna's original burial site near the waterway, close to where Mrs Gardiner now sat with her grandson.

She made her way towards Rayna and the boy, the sound of rushing water becoming louder as she got closer. She saw that the flat ledge on which Rayna and Daniel were perched gave way to a deep, wide pool, which the creek flowed into via a small, foot-high waterfall. Beyond the rock pool, the creek appeared to continue downhill, curving around rocky intrusions into the bush.

'It's a beautiful spot, isn't it? I can see why Jason liked it here.' Rayna had barely looked up at her approach. Her eyes were trained on the water, one hand stroking Daniel's hair. The boy seemed to have fallen asleep on his grandmother's lap.

Kate lowered herself onto an adjoining rock, smooth and warmed by the sun.

'Is that why you chose this spot for Sienna? So you could connect her death to Jason?'

'Men like Jason get away with things every day. So much suffering that no one cares about. No one gave a shit about what he was doing to Elissa. It's only because it's a child that people are taking notice.'

'That's not true, Rayna. Veliu's been arrested for what he did to his ex-partner. But he's not going to be found responsible for Sienna's death because he didn't do it.'

Rayna pursed her mouth. 'You don't know what that man's capable of.'

'Oh, I've no doubt at all what he's capable of. Doesn't change the fact that he was at the station on Thursday, the day Sienna died, being interviewed by me, in fact. So, it couldn't have been him.'

'Sienna was alive on Thursday.'

'I have an autopsy report that says differently, Rayna. I have an autopsy report that says the signs of decay on Sienna's body don't match the timeframe you and Elissa gave us. It says Sienna most likely died much earlier than what we've been working off, maybe even as early as Thursday afternoon, two o'clock, three o'clock, maybe? Does that ring any bells for you, Rayna?'

When Rayna didn't respond, Kate went on. 'You know that puts Aaron and his girlfriend right out of the picture, too, don't you? He was at his conference and she was in video calls all afternoon for work.'

Something crossed Rayna's face at the mention of her son-in-law. 'You can't narrow it down to specific times. Don't take me for a fool. I'm not an idiot.' Her voice rose, yet Daniel didn't stir, apparently deep in sleep.

'Rayna, I already know what happened.' Kate's voice was mild. 'Aaron told me. Elissa confessed everything to him after she and Aaron visited the morgue to view Sienna's body. You didn't realise she had done that, did you? Turns out you can't control everything Elissa does. She wanted to see her daughter, and she was sick of holding onto everything. What you did. What you both did.'

Annoyance sparked in Rayna's eyes as she shook away Kate's words. 'He's as weak as a dog.' Her lips curled in derision. 'Elissa swapped a sick bastard for a weak one. If I had known he was cheating on her with that woman—' A harsh bark of laughter escaped her. 'Well, it's too late now.'

'Is that why you went through all this? To keep Aaron from finding out?'

'I could see they were struggling. Elissa wasn't coping. She just didn't take to the baby. It was obvious even to Aaron. And the medication that damn fool doctor of hers prescribed, did nothing at all. It just made her drowsy. That day, with Sienna... I knew there was no way their marriage would survive that. If Aaron had come home to find Sienna dead, that would have been the end. And I was right. Look what happened the minute she told him. He checked out. Couldn't wait to get away.' Her lips tightened, a swift cloud of emotion passing across her face. 'I had to do something.'

Daniel gave a soft moan and Rayna bent her head over him, gently rocking and shushing him as if he were a baby. Something shifted within Kate as she watched the scene.

'The cover-up was your idea.' It wasn't a question. Kate already knew the answer.

'You know, Detective, I sat through all of Elissa's relationship with Jason without doing anything.' She eyed Kate and returned to comforting Daniel's immobile body. 'I didn't get involved. I stayed out of their business and he almost killed her. Elissa loves Aaron. She needs him. I wasn't going to stand by and do nothing again. The baby was already dead. What mattered was what happened afterwards to make sure Aaron stood by Elissa.'

Kate flinched at Rayna's apparent indifference when she spoke of Sienna. Would she speak this way if she realised what her actions had led to? If she had seen the state of her granddaughter's body when it had been uncovered, mauled and desecrated by feral animals?

'You chose Veliu as the fall guy.'

'It's no more than he deserved.' Rayna's voice was uninterested. 'If you're going to do something, you might as well do it right.' She glanced at Kate, holding her gaze. 'The abduction story wouldn't have worked by itself. When a kid dies, the family is always the first place you lot focus on. I needed something to make you take it seriously. So you'd look away from Elissa. That's where the report of the prowler came in. Elissa didn't want to, but she went through with it in the end. And it worked perfectly. The young copper who came to the house on Thursday, he fell for it hook, line and sinker. It created sympathy around Elissa. You all felt guilty the next day, when Sienna was reported missing, that you hadn't taken our earlier report seriously.'

'Did Elissa know where you chose to bury Sienna?'

'Of course not. She wouldn't have been able to hold her nerve. Her reactions needed to be genuine so you'd all believe her. She had no idea where Sienna was.'

Kate nodded. Rayna had worked it all out, played them like pawns. Keeping Elissa in the dark and running interference at each turn, always leading them towards Veliu and away from Aaron. Sweet revenge orchestrated against the reviled ex-partner of her daughter. It had been Rayna who had shared Elissa's relationship history with the police, even though Elissa, fearful of what Veliu was capable of, had clearly been uncomfortable with bringing her ex-partner into the equation. It was Rayna who had buried Sienna in a spot linked to Veliu, his favourite fishing spot, and then nudged the investigation along by passing on that piece of information. One of Sienna's toys planted along the roadside for good measure, to give further credence to the abduction theory.

Had Rayna been working on other strategies, too? Perhaps convincing Elissa to lie about Jason threatening Sienna? A fabricated demand for money, tucked inside the Ricci's house? Who knew? The woman had been desperate.

She had been lucky, as well. The coincidence of Veliu supplying meth to a customer near Elliot Pass on the morning of the supposed kidnapping had been a gift to Rayna, shoring up the breadcrumbs she had laid out earlier. Kate's thoughts flew to Lena Chalmers recovering in the hospital burns unit; collateral damage of their pursuit of Veliu.

Only one thing had gone wrong for Rayna: a traffic accident on Leeson Road that had led to her Mitsubishi being captured on camera and spotted by her son-in-law as she travelled back from Layton Reserve on Thursday night after burying Sienna's body. By the time she had realised the extent of Aaron Ricci's perfidy, it had been too late. Rayna was in too deep and committed, even though the marriage she had been trying to save had already ruptured beyond repair.

Rayna shifted her position, causing Daniel's body to slip. She scooped him back, tucking him against her.

Kate eyed the boy, foreboding erupting in her belly. Did his lips look blue? 'Is he all right?' she asked.

'He's fine. Just a deep sleeper.'

'Rayna, I need you to move away from Daniel.'

'He's fine.'

'Move away from the child, Rayna.' Kate stood up taking a step towards her. Rayna glanced at Daniel and towards the water. The boy looked barely conscious. If he was submerged in his condition, he wouldn't last long. Was that what Rayna had been planning?

'It's for his own good. He's not going to have anyone, after all this. Aaron's not going to look after Veliu's bastard child. Did Saint Aaron happen to mention that? What he said to Elissa before he ran off to the motel. That he won't be looking after his stepson?'

'Don't even think about it, Rayna. Do not move.'

Kate lurched forward, just as in one swift movement Rayna tipped Daniel into the water.

'Fuck!'

She didn't hesitate. Kate jumped after the boy, the shock of the icy water seizing her and knocking the breath from her lungs. Gulping in air, she reached for

Daniel's limp body, clutching at his clothes and pulling him towards her. She found purchase around his torso. Treading water, she made for the rock ledge, holding his head up. Her fingers felt for the edge of the outcrop. Latching on, she heaved the boy over.

There was a shadow of movement blocking the sunlight. Something hard and heavy smashed into her temple. Kate fell back, stunned, swallowing water, pain flaring across her forehead and her hand losing grip of the boy. She emerged gasping for breath, liquid thicker than water filming her eyelids. She saw the boy slip once more into the water with hardly a splash, just as Rayna came at her again. She was on her knees at the rock ledge, one hand wedged against the fallen tree trunk to steady herself, and the other swinging a rock down at Kate's head. Kate ducked as Rayna's arm cleaved the air next to her face. Still treading water, she grabbed the woman's arm, twisting it under the rough flank of the rock ledge. Rayna gasped and the rock shook free of her hand, falling into the water with a soft plop. She stumbled but held onto the log to stop herself from being pulled in.

'That's enough, Rayna. You need to stop this.'

She met Rayna's feverish eyes, Kate's grip still pinning her arm against the ledge. There was a sickening snap. Rayna shrieked and Kate let go. Rayna fell onto the rocky bank, panting and moaning, her mouth a howl of pain, clutching at her broken arm.

Kate whirled around in the water, searching for Daniel. The commotion had caused his body to drift a couple of metres. He was floating facedown. She swam for him, her wet clothes dragging her down, and her body rapidly draining of energy. She held onto him, clutching his weight to her, and made for the ledge.

The boy was unresponsive when she finally hauled him out and joined him on the rock shelf, dripping and exhausted. She turned him on his side, the recovery position, opening his mouth to allow excess fluid to escape, and began resuscitation.

'Come on, Daniel. Come on, matey. Don't you fucking die on me.' She screamed at Rayna between compressions, 'Call the ambulance, Rayna. Use your phone and call the ambulance.' Kate knew that her own mobile, cracked and waterlogged in her pocket, would be less than useless.

The woman shrank away from her but obeyed.

Kate's arms strained, and despite the sun she could feel herself shivering, a combination of her drenched clothing and the adrenaline pulsing through her. The boy moaned and she felt the soft pressure of his chest rise, his lungs taking in a shallow breath.

Relief stormed and she rolled him onto his side, allowing him to cough up the water he had ingested. Daniel was alive and that was all that mattered.

39

Three weeks later, Saturday

'So, she was carrying a dead baby around with her?' Caleb tickled Amy's cheek as she sat on Gray's lap, babbling and gurgling, chewing on a teething ring. 'That's messed up.'

'She probably went into shock. You never know how people are going to react in situations like that.' Gray bent down to kiss Amy. 'I reckon waking up from an afternoon nap to find you'd accidentally smothered your baby would mess anyone up.'

'Still, turning up at school pick-up with a dead baby strapped to your chest. That's pretty extreme.' Caleb shuddered as he picked the last piece of cinnamon scroll from his plate and popped it in his mouth.

Kate met her husband's eyes as he sipped his coffee beside her. She felt his hand reach for hers under the table and give it a quick squeeze. Geoff understood her mixed feelings over Elissa's actions. Kate had made an effort to talk through the events of the past few weeks with her husband, difficult though it was to rehash the details, working on healing the fractures between them.

Elissa's interview was one of the hardest she had ever had to run. Everything she had recounted about that day had sent shivers through Kate. How many times had Kate herself fallen asleep while feeding her children?

Nights lying exhausted and sleep-deprived on the couch or hunched upright in bed. It could so easily have been her waking up to find the lifeless body of her baby – her ordered life slammed sideways in an instant. In Elissa's case, the antidepressants she had been prescribed had had the side effect of making her drowsy, a thick, woolly-headed stupor that had clouded her days. She had even booked herself in the following week to see her doctor to review her medication. Just a few agonising days too late.

Kate understood why Elissa had shut down in that moment. Her brain not ready to accept the reality of the situation, needing time to process the horror. She had resumed her day without conscious thought. It was two-thirty on a Thursday, half an hour till the school day ended. That meant it was time to strap Sienna to her body and walk up to Daniel's primary school in time for pick-up. So, that's what she had done.

And yet, a part of Elissa must have known. She had covered Sienna with a muslin cloth to avoid prying eyes, allowing people to assume the baby was asleep. Kate recalled Allison Garrett's account of Elissa flying off the handle at Daniel when he had tried to peek under the sheet. She had not wanted Daniel to find out. And then there had been Daniel's assertion that his mother had not let him inside Sienna's room that afternoon. Kate shuddered at the memory. The baby Daniel had wanted to play with was already gone. Only a puny, inert body had remained in the cot behind the closed door. Elissa must have been terrified when the police had visited the house, the start of Rayna's misinformation campaign. To have to answer Constable Roby's questions when her daughter lay immobile in the back room. She remembered how Roby had described her as being jumpy and nervous the entire time.

'How is everything today? Anything else I can get you?'

They murmured their thanks as the waiter fussed around the table, refilling waters and removing empty coffee cups. Kate and her family had met her father and Caleb for brunch at a café

at Terranora, walking distance from Caleb's place, a brick bungalow tucked within a riotous profusion of tropical foliage, and the exact opposite of Gray's sculpted garden at home. Her father, she noticed, had taken to staying over at Caleb's quite often these days.

'Dad, can we play now?'

Archie had been itching to try out the playground that abutted the café, ever since polishing off his breakfast pancakes. He had been eyeing his father's plate, waiting for Geoff to swallow the last of his bacon and eggs before jumping on his case.

Geoff drained his cup and stood up, ruffling Archie's hair. 'All done, matey. Let's have a go at these monkey bars, shall we?'

Kate mouthed a thank you as Geoff followed Archie to the play equipment.

The catch-up had been Caleb's idea, another slow step towards mending the breach between father and daughter, and she was grateful to Geoff for entertaining Archie, so that they didn't have to rush their meals.

There had been a number of these impromptu meetings since her disastrous encounter with Gray some three weeks ago. Her father looked good; he had lost his neck brace and the bruising across his face had faded. Only a slight stiffening of his shoulder and wincing when he moved indicated that his collarbone was yet to fully heal, though Gray had started removing his sling for short periods. She too had a new scar to add to her collection, a faint mark along her hairline from her clash with Rayna. The details of the case were still making the local news, and their conversation had inevitably turned to shop, a safe haven for them both.

'Is the boy all right?' Gray asked, referring to Daniel Ricci.

Kate nodded. 'Physically, anyway.'

Rayna, it turned out, had crushed and fed the boy sleeping tablets in a drink, accounting for his extreme lethargy and drowsiness. Her intention had been to immobilise the boy so he wouldn't be in a position to save himself when she tipped him into the water at Layton Reserve. Without Kate's intervention, she almost certainly would have succeeded in her plan. Since her arrest, she had persisted in her assertion that Daniel would have been better off. Her reasoning being that she had known Elissa was close to cracking. She could see it in her face. If Elissa and Rayna went down for their actions surrounding Sienna, there would be no one to look after Daniel. After Aaron had renounced responsibility for the boy, Rayna had once more taken matters into her own hands.

'Who's looking after him now?'

'He's in care. Elissa's got visitation rights until the trial, and afterwards... we'll have to wait and see, I guess.'

'Okay, enough of this doom and gloom,' Caleb broke in. 'Kate, your father has some news.' He rose and stared meaningfully at Gray. 'I'm going to get the bill and let you two talk.' He stepped away quickly before Gray had a chance to object.

Kate eyed her father. 'News, you say?'

Gray glanced at her, a trace of embarrassment in his expression. 'I'm thinking of selling the cottage and moving into town again. I'll be able to help out more with the kids and… you know… be a bit closer to Caleb.'

'Wow, okay. Things are moving fast.'

'Yeah well, I think I've wasted enough time in my life.' He avoided her eyes, concentrating on Amy.

'Dad.' She reached for his hand. 'I think it's great. Caleb's lovely. Both Geoff and I are really happy for you.'

Gray smiled, his eyes creasing with happiness. 'Thanks, Kit. I appreciate it.'

'Also, I really am sorry about what I said before… at your place about the money and Martin and everything.'

'Forget it, Kit. Honestly, I'm over it. I'm just enjoying the show.' Gray smirked.

Kate grinned. 'I know, it's chaos at the station. Skinner's taken an indefinite leave of absence.'

Three days ago, the *North Coast Leader* had run a special investigation, detailing allegations of corruption and blackmail against the chief inspector of Esserton Station spanning over ten years, stretching back to when Skinner was a senior sergeant at the station. The allegations included accusations of using Minister Jackson's sexuality to extort money as well as inside information on property deals and other favours. It was like a bomb had gone off at the station. Rumours were flying everywhere and the force was in full damage-control mode. She had heard that Skinner had been called down to Sydney to meet with Professional Standards. A review was underway and there was talk of an acting chief inspector being appointed to Esserton, brought in from a different Police Area Command to oversee things until a decision was made regarding Skinner's future. It would take some months for the station to regroup after the fallout. Josh's loyalties to Skinner were being tested, and the cracks between Josh and her remained. She was unsure if his resentment of her was now too far ingrained to erase.

Her father's voice broke into her thoughts. 'Martin used to ask me about Skinner, you know. Just every now and then. I never knew why. I wish he'd let me know so I could have helped. Fucking slimeball. I would have decked the bastard.'

'That's probably exactly why Martin never told you. He didn't want to compromise you or risk you doing anything stupid.'

'I would never do anything stupid. That doesn't sound like me at all.'

Kate grinned. 'No, me either.'

Gray studied her, the laughter in his eyes dimming for a second. Amy started to grizzle and Kate reached for her daughter. She knew that just like Geoff, her father worried constantly for her safety. It was an inner conflict that both men were learning to manage.

Gray cleared his throat. 'You know what I'd like to know? Who the journo's source is. I'd be first in line to buy them a slab of beer.'

'No idea,' said Kate, burying her face in Amy's neck.

Two weeks ago, she had contacted Richard Markham and passed on Murchison's details. The reporter, it seemed, had managed to convince Murchison to speak his mind. The article had clearly settled a number of scores. If her role in the tip-off ever came to light, she had no illusions that there would be consequences. Skinner still had access to powerful friends, including loyalties within the station and beyond. For the moment, all she could do was keep her head down and ride it out.

'All done?' Caleb was back and looking from one to the other, smiling.

'Yes, I got the full lowdown. I think it's great, Caleb.' She hugged him tightly.

Amy squirmed and arched, and Kate let the two men walk ahead of her as she strapped her daughter into the pram. Amy was clearly tired, having been petted and cuddled and handed from person to person over the last hour. She was going to fall asleep the minute she was in the car. Kate bent down to blow a soft raspberry on her daughter's tummy. She was rewarded with a wide smile, Amy's little wrist swatting at Kate's face. Swift contentment swelled in her chest, solid and reassuring.

The case had dislodged something. Elissa's situation had provided perspective. She couldn't change how Amy had arrived into the world, but unlike Elissa's, Kate's daughter was still alive – her whole family was intact. The shame and guilt that had stalked her for months felt less oppressive, its chokehold over her emotions more manageable. The simple act of enjoying her daughter felt possible.

Her anxiety and feelings of remorse hadn't abated entirely, but they felt within her control, at least for the moment. She couldn't deny that rescuing Daniel and holding her own against Veliu had played their part, restoring a semblance of her confidence. A week ago, she had called the office of Pip Hutton to reinstate her counselling appointments. She could do this, but not alone.

Geoff and Archie had joined her father and Caleb, waiting for her at the café door. She smiled and wheeled the pram to join them.

Author's Note

The events and characters in this novel are fictional. Whilst some real-life localities are referred to, the people and places that live on these pages exist only in the author's imagination. The township of Esserton, set in the Northern Rivers, New South Wales on Bundjalung Country, is a fictional place that does not appear on Google Maps. (Thank you to the readers who have gone looking!) All errors, liberties and failures of description, are my own. This novel was written on Dharawal Country.

Acknowledgements

To Alex Adsett, super-agent and friend, for always (always!) having my back.

To my brilliant, supportive and very funny publisher, Anna Valdinger, for continuing to believe in Kate, and for acquiring this manuscript despite berating me to this day for *that* plot decision. Sorry, Anna!

To the wonderful folk at HarperCollins Australia for bringing this book to life and cheering it on, especially to the editorial team of Alexandra Nahlous, Lachlan McLaine and Abigail Nathan, my incredible publicist, Lucy Inglis, and the sales and marketing teams. Thank you all for weaving your magic. A very special thanks and shout out to Louisa Maggio for this stunning cover. I could not love it more!

As always, I relied heavily on the generous advice and feedback of barrister Les Nicholls for police procedural matters, Rexson Tse for autopsy and pathology procedure, and Rajeev Wijesekera on matters relating to mobile tech. All errors and bending of facts to fit the story are entirely my own.

The character of Pip Hutton was named after the winning bidder of the Lismore Flood Appeal auction to name a character in this novel. Thank you, Pip, for your generous donation to the appeal and for keeping Kate on the straight and narrow.

To the very many writing friends who make the Australian writing community such a pleasure to be a part of, thank you! Especially to Alayne Campbell and Christine Jackman, for your fearless advice, support and the best zoom chats. And to the one and only #debut-bookgang, for being the best cheerleaders, and behind-the-scenes therapists, a newbie writer could ever wish for. (Someone please invite us all to a festival so we can all finally be in the same city at the same time!)

To all the readers, booksellers, podcasters and reviewers who have embraced *The Torrent* and Kate Miles into your reading lives, I will forever be in your debt. Thank you.

To the McKenzie, Vitelli and Wijesekera/Wickramas-inghe clans for all your love and support. And to Scott, Harvey and Edie, without whom all of this would be nothing.